THE CALDECOTTE CONUNDRUM

Book One of The MK Murders

Rosie Neale

Copyright © 2024 Rosie Neale

All rights reserved

The characters and events portrayed in this book are fictitious. Any similarity to real persons, living or dead, is coincidental and not intended by the author.

No part of this book may be reproduced, or stored in a retrieval system, or transmitted in any form or by any means, electronic, mechanical, photocopying, recording, or otherwise, without express written permission of the publisher.

Cover design by: Rosie Neale

CONTENTS

Title Page
Copyright
Chapter One — 3
Chapter Two — 10
Chapter Three — 21
Chapter Four — 31
Chapter Five — 40
Chapter Six — 55
Chapter Seven — 65
Chapter Eight — 75
Chapter Nine — 82
Chapter Ten — 99
Chapter Eleven — 111
Chapter Twelve — 121
Chapter Thirteen — 134
Chapter Fourteen — 145
Chapter Fifteen — 151
Chapter Sixteen — 172
Chapter Seventeen — 183
Chapter Eighteen — 191
Chapter Nineteen — 199

Chapter Twenty	207
Chapter Twenty-one	213
Chapter Twenty-two	228
Chapter Twenty-three	239
Chapter Twenty-four	246
The MK Murders	251
Books By This Author	253

The Caldecotte Conundrum
By
Rosie Neale
Book One of The MK Murders

CHAPTER ONE

Drop-Off

At first glance, she appeared to be a very normal passenger. Just like thousands of others. There was nothing obvious to make her stand out from a crowd. Nothing to warn me that meeting her would change my life. Forever.

Mid-forties, perhaps. Pleasant features, a genuine, engaging smile, which lit up her eyes. Unmemorable clothes, paired with flat black shoes, for comfort rather than style. No shopping, although I picked her up outside the centre. No sign of a handbag to express her personal tastes. An ordinary voice, with no particular accent. Even her name was almost too plain and simple. Smith.

She was a little hesitant approaching the vehicle, even when I had called her name. Smiled shyly and slid into the back seat, fastening her seatbelt swiftly, without a reminder.

I confirmed our destination with her.

"That's right, Caldecotte Lake, please."

I nodded, wove my way carefully through the queues of impatient traffic to leave the car park, and set off down the V7.

"Are you in a hurry?" I asked. "I can use the A5, if you like, but it costs a bit more, because of the distance."

"Oh, I'm not in a rush. There's time. Thanks for checking, though."

"No problem. Whatever you prefer."

She seemed relaxed enough, in the rear-view mirror, while we waited at the traffic lights. Not on her phone, like most of my fares. Looking out of the window, a vaguely dreamy look on her face. A touch of nervousness in the way she was chewing her finger, maybe.

Perhaps she preferred to chat. I tried an anodyne question, to put her at her ease.

"Have you been to Caldecotte before?"

She sounded a little flustered by my mild query.

"Well, yes, once. He – we – I went for a lovely walk there last week. The weather wasn't great, but it was so pleasant. I think it's one of the most beautiful lakes in Milton Keynes, don't you?"

"Yes, it's got some nice circuits. Lots of wildlife. I park up there sometimes for my lunch break. Spending all day in the car makes me long for fresh air and exercise."

It was true. A favourite spot for me.

"I can imagine," she responded warmly.

"Where do you want me to drop you? In the pub car park?"

"Oh, I'm not sure. I think so. It was definitely a car park. I'll know when I see it."

She sounded pretty uncertain. Never mind, we would try the pub first.

But, as we drove slowly into the large car park towards the brick windmill tower, still impressive despite the loss of its sails, and past the deserted playground, she made a distressed sound.

"Oh no, this isn't it. It's not at all the same. Can we try somewhere else, please? I'm so sorry to be difficult. I didn't realise there was more than one car park."

There was quite unnecessary anxiety in her tone.

"Of course," I answered, calmly. It was by no means the first time someone had been unsure of their destination. Part of the job. I pulled into one of the many empty spaces to give us time to decide where to try next. I turned to look at her, smiling to ease her worry.

"What do you remember about the place? This is the biggest car park. The others are generally quite small."

She returned my smile gratefully.

"I'm so sorry I didn't get it right first time. It was definitely smaller. Near some trees. I – I think it was round, if that helps at all."

It did. I reassured her that I knew where the nearby circular car park was, and we zipped across the high speed dual carriageway and pulled in. There were only two other vehicles in what was often a busy set of bays. Not surprising. It was not a welcoming day for a walk. The angry wind was disturbing the surface of the lake and whipping the bare tree branches into a frenzy against a stormy and ominous grey sky.

"Oh, yes, this is it. Just as I remember it. Thank you so much. I'm really grateful."

"No problem at all. Part of the service."

"You've made me feel very safe. That's why I chose your company. Because you only use women drivers."

It was more than a gimmick. Some people did need that comfort, an extra sense of security. For all kinds of reasons, from religion to lack of social confidence or negative previous experiences. And it seemed to be working. My new venture was making a reasonable profit so far. We were never short of passengers, not all of whom were female.

"Thank you. I'm glad you chose us. Did you want to pay on the app?"

She shook her head determinedly.

"Oh no, he – I don't like to do that. It's not always secure, you know. I've been told that it's definitely safer for me to pay cash."

Most people did not seem to carry much cash these days and, to be honest, I preferred online payments. Much easier and no time-wasting tip calculation to be dealt with.

"I do have a card machine, if you would rather use that."

"No, thank you. Cash please."

She was quite firm about it. I agreed, hiding my reluctance, and told her the price. She rounded it up with a generous tip, avoiding the need for change. Refused a receipt.

"Have you arranged a return journey?"

"No, I – I hadn't thought about it. I suppose you will get booked up, though. It'll be about five o'clock, and that's a very busy time, isn't it? Can you book me in? I'd really like to go home with you personally, if that's possible."

She was sounding increasingly timid. Even needy. Quite surprisingly so. The shell of confidence she had tried to project was quite thin.

"Of course. Shall I pick you up here?"

"Yes, please."

"To return to the city centre? Sorry, I don't mean to pry. I need to ask, so that I can tell the office. They have to keep track of all the bookings."

"No, I'll be ready to go home then. To Giffard Park, please."

I smiled. While we did not do 'The Knowledge' like London taxi-drivers, we had all memorised the location of every grid square and major feature in Milton Keynes. Much better than blindly trusting a satnav.

"That's a nice easy journey. Straight up the V10. I'll see you here later, then. Have a good walk."

"Oh, yes, I'm sure – I hope I will."

The weather was already threatening to deteriorate.

"Do feel free to ring in if you want an earlier return. I'd hate you to get soaked."

She looked doubtfully at the glowering sky.

"Yes, I will. Thank you so much. You've been such a help."

She fumbled a little with the door, but managed to get herself out in the end. I saw her making her way rather slowly towards the lake path, as I reversed out and moved on to the next job.

I half-expected to receive a call asking me to go back earlier, because there was no doubt that the conditions worsened considerably during the afternoon. The wind had picked up, and heavy, drenching rain had set in. Not at all pleasant for walking, especially since Ms Smith only had a light coat and no hood.

I was kept quite busy, transporting people who had been caught out without coat or umbrella. Not easy driving conditions, either. Fountains of spray and rivers of standing water. School-run time was even more chaotic than usual, with harassed parents driving fast, and not always with due care and attention, in their haste to collect their precious children.

The torrential rain had eased off a little by five o'clock, when I returned to the little circle, next to a small grove of heavily buffeted trees. Unsurprisingly, the area was deserted by now; all the cars had left. I assumed my passenger was sheltering nearby.

I pressed the button to send the normal text message to inform her that I had arrived. There was no sign of her. I wondered if she had taken refuge under the concrete bridge and gave her a few minutes to make her way back. She had said 'around five o'clock', after all. But she did not appear. I rang Sally, in the office, to see if she had called to cancel.

"No, I'm sorry, Tessa, there was no cancellation. She used her phone to book, rather than the app, so I would have expected her to ring if she no longer needed you. I can call her back, if you like, just to check."

"Yes, please. I don't want to leave her out here if she's just mixed up the time."

Unfortunately, there was no answer at all from her phone. It went straight to voice mail. Perhaps she had run out of charge.

I did not know why, but I felt oddly anxious about her. She had been so insistent that she wanted me to take her home personally. I had taken the trouble to book it in specially with the office. I decided to go and have a quick look around, to see if I could spot her. It wasn't really a normal procedure, but we did feel a certain sense of responsibility towards our clients, some of whom were young, disabled, elderly, or otherwise vulnerable. I had, after all, brought her to this place.

I walked along the narrow gravelled path, which snaked its way towards the double road bridge under the H10. It was bordered on one side by overgrown bramble hedges, and a secret pool, stagnant between rotting fallen trees, and on the other by the bare spiky branches of harshly trimmed shrubs. I knew that she would not be visible from the car park, if she was waiting here. The weak illumination from the streetlights was flickering wildly, as the taller trees swayed before them.

I ventured under the dark bridge, roaring with racing traffic overhead, to the far side, but there was no one to be seen. Unsurprisingly, since the wind was strong enough to whip up white-topped waves on the inky surface of the lake, with cold spray striking viciously at my face. I turned back and went some way beyond the car park in the opposite direction, towards the inhabited areas, just to check, to be absolutely sure.

From the corner, under the lights, I could just about see across the curved bay in front of the tall townhouses of Monellan Crescent, as far as the bare, windswept willows on the other side. She was not there. No one was.

Oh well, there were plenty of inconsiderate clients who did not bother to cancel with us. She had probably made her way home hours ago.

Still, I felt a little uneasy as I made my way back to the car. Something did not feel right. I sent the 'trip cancelled' message and told Sally I was ready for my next fare, but it nagged away at the back of my mind. There was nothing I could reasonably do about it, however. Nothing to report, except an ordinary customer who had missed a booking.

I tried to explain to my sister, Naomi, why I was so concerned, later that evening. I was not on evening shift that day, and we were able to eat together, for once.

"I don't know why. I can't explain it clearly, but I just sensed that she was in some way vulnerable. That she might be doing something she was unsure about. Taking a risk. Oh, I know I'm being stupid. And there's absolutely nothing I can do about it, anyway."

She laughed, but gently.

"Well, no. I don't think the police would be very interested in a Miss or Mrs Smith from Giffard Park who didn't arrive to take a taxi home! You've seen too many crime dramas, Tess. It was probably the apocalyptic weather this afternoon – it's affected your mood. There's nothing to worry about. Sometimes nice people do just act in unpredictable and inconsiderate ways. I'm sure she's fine."

I accepted that she was right. Of course, she was right. It just did not feel right to me.

I did have one contact, in fact, who might be able to check things out for me. My ex-boyfriend, Rob, was a police officer, a detective sergeant. He would have access to the resources to follow this up. Check missing person reports. He would probably be delighted to hear from me, since he had never wanted us to part. That increased my reluctance to contact him, under the current circumstances – or any others.

I told myself sharply that I was worrying about nothing, and tried to banish her from my mind. With reasonable success. I had an early start on the following morning, followed by a frantically busy day, with a plethora of shorter journeys adding a sense of rush and urgency.

CHAPTER TWO

Missing

In spite of my enforced absorption with work, I was still occasionally niggled by concern about my missing passenger. I checked with Sally, and nothing more had been heard from her. She had tried to contact her once more, but her phone remained unresponsive. Somehow, each new fare I picked up caused me to compare them and their behaviour with her. By the end of the day, my head was throbbing, due to the unaccustomed tautness in my neck muscles.

My sister thought I was crazy to go on worrying.

"She's just a client. You didn't know her. It's not your responsibility. You're not her keeper."

I knew she was right. But the noise of heavy rain in the night poured reminders of that afternoon into my brain, and even the trees, waving wildly in the continuing stormy weather, seemed to be insisting to me that there was something badly wrong. And that I had to do something about it. If not me, then who?

I nerved myself to contact Rob. It risked opening up a can of worms, but was the easiest way for me to take some kind of action. Leaving it alone had become an intolerable option. I knew I could trust him, absolutely.

I still loved him, in fact. Breaking our relationship was the hardest thing I had ever done. He would happily have drifted on, changing nothing, keeping things light, remaining superficially contented.

I needed more. I wanted commitment, marriage, a family. He

was simply not bothered about any of that. His work was the central core of his life around which everything revolved. I was a pleasant distraction during off-duty time, that was all. I knew that I wanted and deserved better.

He had not understood. He had assumed I had found someone else. Betrayed him. He expressed anger rather than sadness. Why had I not told him I was going out with another man? I had made a fool of him. His furious reproaches stuck in my mind, poisoning my memories of our time together.

I could not make him see the truth, and after a while I gave up trying. Refused calls and stopped answering his messages, which had become increasingly plaintive, appealing for reconciliation. Muted notifications from him. It was easier not to see, not to look. To focus on my new minicab enterprise.

So making contact again was a wrench. And probably a mistake. Still, I could not let it rest. It had to be done. I had never been able to escape the persistent promptings of duty.

Deliberately not looking back at his previous, unanswered messages, I composed my own with care:

Hi, Rob. Hope you are well. I wondered if you had seen any missing person reports in the last day or so. I am a little worried about a passenger who missed her return journey on Tuesday. Just wanted to make sure she was OK. Tessa.

Polite, to the point, unemotional, and totally lacking in intimacy. No invitation there to start up a new social interaction, I hoped. Stick to business.

I felt much better when I had sent it. There was a faint grumble of anxiety, deep in my stomach, mainly about waiting to hear from Rob, wondering how he might respond, but I tried to ignore it. I had another busy work day. Plenty of fares. A number of repeat bookings, so we must be doing something right. We had a growing group of regulars, who used us for all their taxi trips. I was even thinking of taking on more new drivers.

Nothing from Rob yet. I kept checking my phone, whenever I stopped. I assumed that his silence must mean that my worry was a false alarm. He would surely have been in touch much more quickly, if my report had matched with a missing person.

Or did he still harbour resentments which kept him from replying? Definitely not. I knew him better than that. He was not that type of man. Not one to hold onto a grudge. I could relax.

Except that I could not. I had time off booked for the next day, and I decided that I would walk around Caldecotte Lake, by myself. Look for any signs of trouble, anything out of place. I was surprised at the relief I felt, once I had come to that decision. I did not inform Naomi. I knew she would tell me that I was overreacting again.

She was on night shift at the hospital that week, so I ate alone and sat watching television, finally feeling less tense. Made a shopping list, since it was my turn to restock the almost empty fridge. I even thought about arranging to meet a friend at the Caldecotte pub for lunch. To make the day a treat instead of a chore.

My phone buzzed. It was always on vibrate in the evening, so that my off-duty time would not be disturbed by trivial notifications or work emails. I took a look, just in case. Rob. My stomach lurched, but I ignored it and opened the message.

Can I ring, please, Tessa? It could be important. X

The kiss was probably automatic and certainly meant nothing. I had almost sent one to him, and it was so routine between friends that it had taken a conscious act of will to omit it. He seemed to be focused on business. I replied with a simple 'OK'.

He called immediately. I picked up.

"Hello."

My reserve was clear in the single word greeting.

"Tessa, it's lovely to hear your voice. I've missed you so much." Such warmth and pleasure in his tone.

I merely grunted. This was not supposed to be a social call. He got the message.

"Sorry, I know, you're concerned about your fare. Do you have any details about her? There is one report I'm following up on, although it's very early days at the moment. I'm keen to see if she could be your missing traveller."

"Thanks for calling me back, then. The name she gave us was Smith. She booked by phone and paid cash, so unfortunately I can't confirm that by matching it to a credit or debit card or a receipt."

That was something which had worried me. Had it been deliberate? Was she hiding her identity for some reason?

"Mm, our missing person has a very different name. Is there anything you can tell me about her? A description, perhaps?"

"Well, I think she lives in Giffard Park. She booked a return journey there, and called it home. I picked her up that lunchtime from the city centre."

"That sounds more promising. What did she look like?"

"In her mid-forties, I would say. She had a nice smile, pleasant face, but nothing very distinctive. Brown hair, cut short, in a straight bob. Dark eyes. No glasses or visible jewellery. I would certainly recognise her again, but I can't think of a more specific description for her. She was casually dressed and wearing flat, sensible shoes. She said she was going for a walk. I dropped her at Caldecotte Lake, and she mentioned that she had been there once before."

His voice had sharpened.

"It could be her. I can send you a photo which you might be able to identify, but I would really like you to come to the station and make a detailed statement. If this is the same woman, you may well be the last person to have seen her, before she disappeared."

Nerves and anxiety tightened my throat abruptly. The police station. A statement. It sounded frighteningly official, all of a sudden.

"I suppose I can do that. When do you want me to come in?"

"I'm sorry to ask, Tess, but I'd really like to see you now, immediately. This could be urgent. If she really is missing, we can't waste any time. I'm a bit worried that you dropped her at the lake. Too much scope for accidents – or other things."

Suicide. That was what he meant. Or a simple fall into the cold water. That could be deadly at this time of year. I would have to go. Duty called.

"OK. I'll come now."

"Thanks, Tessa. I'll meet you by the front desk."

Unfortunately, it meant I had to go back out. Into the lashing rain. Onto dark roads, with glaring headlights stabbing my tired eyes, idiot drivers provoking me into impotent rage. I took a deep breath, swallowed down the flood of useless self-pity, and picked up my keys again.

Feeling rather shaky, and definitely apprehensive, I hurried out into the wet, dreary night and set off in the car. Not a long journey, thank goodness.

I knew exactly where the police station was: in the centre, behind the magistrate's court. I had met Rob nearby, quite frequently, to go out for a meal or a drink, after he finished work. I had never been inside, though, and was slightly anxious at the thought of seeing him again, after all this time, in his own natural habitat.

No parking fees to worry about at this time of night, and there were plenty of spaces available. I hurried to the door, glad of my warm and waterproof coat. It was another deeply unpleasant evening, gusty winds hurling heavy handfuls of rain spitefully into my eyes.

As I entered, rather tentatively, I caught sight of him immediately. My insides turned to water. I had forgotten how good-looking he was, and what an impact his forceful presence had on me. The attractive way his dark hair flopped onto his forehead. His large, deep-set brown eyes, with the unfairly long lashes. The sensitive but sensual mouth above a determined chin. Memories of intimacy flooded through me and washed away my pretence of indifference.

He came forward, smiling, and I could not prevent my mouth from returning it. I thought for a moment he was going to kiss my cheek, but he glanced at the desk officer, thought better of it, and took my hand instead.

"Tessa! Thank you so much for coming out, especially on such a horrible night. I really appreciate it."

"No problem. I – I want to help, if I can."

"Come through. I've got some photos for you to look at and then, if it is the same person you drove, we'll take an official statement."

My breath was shortened with sudden tension. It simply sounded scary. Intimidating. He must have seen it in my face, because he hastened to reassure me.

"Nothing to worry about. Just tell me exactly what you did, saw, and heard. Then you can be on your way. We'll have someone type it up, and you can check and sign it tomorrow."

I nodded, still uneasy. He led my down an impersonal corridor lined with identical doors.

"We'll use an official interview room, because it's all set up to record your evidence. We don't want to miss anything. Even small details can be crucial. The first few hours and days are so important in a missing person case."

He was not reducing my anxiety. I hoped that I could be a good witness, but was far from confident in my ability to help.

The room was brightly lit, bare, and unwelcoming. Not an ounce of softness. An alien environment. Recognising the discomfort in my face, Rob offered me a hot drink. I hesitated, but then accepted, hoping it might ease my tension. He smiled sympathetically and hurried off to fetch it. I was left alone in that cold, pale place, huddled in my coat for comfort, counting the seconds, my mind flitting nervously, not settling anywhere.

He brought digestive biscuits as well as tea and suggested I sweetened my drink.

"I know you don't, normally, but it'll make you feel better. You look as if your blood sugar is low."

He had always been able to read my face, tell how I was feeling. I wanted to prove my independence, but I had to trust him on this. I was indeed still shaky, and calories would help.

Uncurling my hands from my pockets and wrapping them tightly around the plain, solid mug, I allowed the warmth to seep into me. It was a comfort. I sipped the milky liquid with pleasure, despite its over-sweet, bland taste.

"Better now?"

I nodded, trying to smile. His voice became brisker, more official.

"Right, I have several photos here of the person we believe might possibly be your fare. She was reported missing by a work colleague, yesterday, when she didn't turn up for her shift, and they were unable to contact her by phone. It was totally abnormal behaviour for her, so we took the details and made the report, even though it was too early to consider her to be missing, in the normal way, as an adult with no obvious vulnerability."

He slid some photographs, printed on normal thin office paper, across the worn, shiny surface towards me. They were clearly successive work profile pictures, rather than family photos. I picked them up and examined them carefully, half hoping that it might be someone else. But she was unmistakable.

"It's her. I'm absolutely sure of it."

He sat back, a mixture of satisfaction and concern on his face.

"That helps. OK, Tessa, I'm going to interview you, now, and we're going to take a recording of your evidence. They'll type up your statement from that, and you can come in tomorrow and sign it."

He turned on the machine and recorded a preamble, giving my full name, the date and time, and his own details. I felt slightly queasy. It was real. She was missing. My evidence was important.

"Please tell me, in your own words, what happened."

I took a moment to clear my head. Seeing her picture like that, knowing that I had been all too right, and she had actually disappeared, had shaken me.

"I picked her up at twelve-thirty on Tuesday lunchtime, from outside Marks and Spencer, in the city centre. She had booked with our firm by phone, under the name of Smith. A first booking with us. She wanted to go to Caldecotte Lake. She was a little hesitant, coming over to the cab, and it was busy, so I called out her surname."

I went through everything that happened, what we had spoken about. I tried, as Rob prompted me, to use her exact words when I could. I became aware, as I went through it, that she had twice said 'he' before continuing in the first person. I felt it could be significant. Was someone else involved?

"She definitely asked me to book her in for five o'clock, from the same place, to take her home to Giffard Park. I'm afraid I didn't ask for the actual address at that point. She said – she said I made her feel safe, and she wanted me to take her home."

"Interesting."

Rob asked me about my impressions of her, especially about her mental state.

"It's hard to say. She was quite dreamy, sitting in the back, but also nervous, I think. Possibly even excited. She was upset about not finding the right car park immediately, and very glad when we discovered it, at the second attempt. I – I don't like to presume, especially on a very brief acquaintanceship, but she didn't seem very confident in herself. Rather shy and anxious for such a mature person."

"I know you're perceptive, a good judge of character, Tessa. That's very helpful."

A few more questions, and then it was over, and he turned off the machine.

"All done. It wasn't so bad, was it?"

I shook my head. It was good to have got it all off my chest. Passed it on to where it might do some good.

"What is her name, if it isn't Smith?"

I was not sure that he would answer, but I had to ask. I had an intangible connection to her.

"Harriet Beckinsale. She works part-time in Central MK, at the library. A very conscientious and reliable worker, apparently, but quite withdrawn, especially since her divorce. An introvert, I suppose. Beckinsale was her maiden name. She went back to using it as soon as she separated from her husband, apparently. The split really knocked her confidence, according to her line manager. She was rather prone to anxiety, and stress, and they were a little concerned about her. Hence the unusually swift call to us."

"Oh dear, I do hope she's OK. She seemed such a nice person. But a bit vulnerable."

"I probably shouldn't be telling you all this, Tessa, and I will have to ask you to keep it confidential. It's just that you've been so helpful, reporting her movements like this, that I feel I owe it to you to pass on a few details. And I know I can trust you."

That gave me a warm feeling. Something still remained true between us.

"Have you been to her home yet?"

He nodded.

"That's where we went first, once we had the report from the library. We had her phone number from the library, but could not get through. It wasn't traceable, either. Switched off or damaged."

That was interesting. Worrying.

"We made a welfare visit, in the first instance, in case she'd collapsed or was unconscious. We found a neighbour with a key, fortunately, so we didn't have to break down the door. But there was no sign of her, no indication that she had been there overnight, and she clearly had not packed anything for a trip. Everything was in place, tidy, but lived in. The bathroom and bedroom were completely normal. All the essentials still there. She had a laptop and we're looking on there to see if there are any clues to where she might have gone. It was a bit of a mystery."

"But now – "

"Yes, now, thanks to you, we know she went to Caldecotte Lake, for some reason. Without a bag. Clearly not prepared for a night away. And that she may still be there. It completely changes the situation. Makes it far more urgent that we find her, find out what's happened. We'll start searching the area tomorrow morning, as soon as it's light. Beginning with where you dropped her. That's why I wanted to speak to you tonight."

It was concerning. And the lake was a large area to search. There was the river on the far side, as well. Fast-flowing, after the deluge of rain we had been collectively doused with.

"We'll make a public appeal for witnesses tomorrow. A lot of people walk and cycle there, and she may have been seen. That will help us to focus our search."

"I don't suppose I'm allowed to help look for her, am I?"

He smiled.

"Not really. It's best left to the experts. We need to keep any evidence as uncontaminated as possible. But I can tell you care about her. You have a big heart, always did. I'll keep you in touch with our progress."

I chose to ignore the more personal comments.

"Thank you."

He led me back to the front entrance. Turned to me, an unexpected catch in his smooth voice.

"Would you – would you be willing to meet me for a coffee tomorrow? I can let you know how things are going. And afterwards I can bring you in to sign your statement."

His suggestion was unusually tentative, from such a decisive person.

I hesitated. It was not ideal. Not what I had intended. It opened the way to a fresh start to a relationship I had put behind me, with a great deal of difficulty and heartache. I needed, however, for my own peace of mind, to know what was happening. Finding Harriet came first. That was more important than my trivial personal feelings of discomfort.

"OK. It's my day off."

We agreed to meet at the coffee shop in Waterstones, in Midsummer Place. It was generally less overcrowded and more tranquil than most of the cafés in the centre. At two in the afternoon. Our goodbyes were awkward. In the past, we would have hugged, maybe kissed. That would not be appropriate now. I gave him a vague, uncomfortable sort of wave as I left the station, and ventured out into the howling night.

CHAPTER THREE

Rendezvous

Next morning, I tried to sleep in, but as soon as I surfaced, my mind began circling intensely, far too active even to allow me to doze quietly. I got up, trying to avoid disturbing Naomi. She needed her rest. Long nursing shifts really took it out of her. We both worked pretty unsocial hours and had learnt, over the past few months together, to be mutually considerate. Sharing the house worked well for both of us, after her messy and painful divorce.

While I ate my toast, I checked the local news online, to see if there was any news yet about my fare. Harriet Beckinsale. It was interesting that she had such a distinctive name. It suited her. An ordinary person, in appearance, but not a Smith. She had reacted slightly oddly when I checked it with her on pick-up. Perhaps a delay in recognising that she was the person I was calling? A possibility I had only recognised in hindsight, looking back at all our interactions, in forensic detail.

There was nothing to see online. No appeal for witnesses yet, but it was early. I decided to watch the local television news. Not something I normally did in the morning.

There it was. Rob, on the television, looking tired but startlingly photogenic, making a familiarly formulaic statement. Showing a photograph of Harriet. A better one than I had seen at the station, presumably from a return visit to her house. Appealing for witnesses for that Tuesday afternoon. Anyone in the vicinity of the lake, or in the Caldecotte or Walton Park areas, who might have seen her, or noticed anything unusual. Anyone who might have seen her since or have other information. A number to call.

I hoped very much that she had been seen. There had been several incidents recently, which had made the national news, where people had disappeared by rivers or lakes and not been found for some time. Caldecotte Lake was extensive. They really needed to be able to narrow the search area. And there was so little daylight at this time of year.

I resisted the temptation to walk down and see for myself. It was not very far from our small house in Walnut Tree. Not a sensible idea, though. I would only be in the way. I busied myself with some essential cleaning and washing, to occupy the time until I was to meet Rob. I would do the food shopping afterwards.

I was glad that Naomi was still in bed, and I did not have to tell her where I was going. I knew that she would not approve. After her own difficult relationship break-up, she saw sinister motives everywhere, and she profoundly mistrusted the majority of men, and Rob, in particular, at this point. She argued that he had let me down, behaved and reacted unreasonably, and she had strongly encouraged me to make a clean break. Only the impetus from her persuasive pressure had enabled me to go through with it.

I could not help feeling a tingle of anticipation as I got ready. My life had been full to the brim with work, plenty of purposeful activity decorating our new house, and occasional meetings with friends, but absolutely no romance or dating. I never really met men any longer. My job was in a feminine world, and most of our clients were female, too. I must try to improve my work-life balance. I had left Rob because I wanted to settle down, with a family. I needed to find a way to make that happen.

I took more care than usual over my appearance, that day. I wanted to show him that I was managing fine without him.

That I was stronger than he thought. Independent. At least, that was what I told myself. I was certainly not trying to look my best to please him. Absolutely not.

I was fortunate enough to find one of the cheap rate parking spaces near the imposing, domed Cornerstone church and put plenty of time on the app. I could not be sure how long this meeting would take, as we would also need to attend the police station.

Incurably punctual, I was outside the shop more than ten minutes early. It was chilly in the draughts which whistled through the high open space of Midsummer Place. Rather than simply pacing up and down aimlessly, I checked on my phone for any updates about the case. I found that it was now in a position of prominence on the local BBC news, and there were pictures of police officers searching the ground near the car park where I had dropped Harriet, alongside the photograph of her. It made me shiver a little. I had set all this in motion. It was a responsibility.

A quick tap on my shoulder made me jump. Rob was there. Smiling at me, mainly with his eyes, which crinkled up attractively at the corners. He gave my shoulders a squeeze. I tried to look disapproving, but failed miserably. I had an urge to hug him, which I resisted firmly.

He insisted on paying for my coffee and buying us some chocolate cookies to share. We found a quiet table in the corner and sat down opposite each other. Did not speak for a while, as I fixed my eyes on the plate, slightly uncomfortable with the uncertain situation. Confused by the intersection between our past relationship and current meetings. Wondering what to say. When I raised my eyes again, I realised that he had been staring at me.

"What is it?"

"Nothing. Just – just looking at you. It's been so long."

His voice was deeper than usual. Lack of sleep, I supposed.

"Only six months. Not so very long. I haven't changed."

He lowered his eyes.

"No. Still the same Tessa. I – I've just missed you. I can't hide that. I wish – well, that we could at least be friends. Can't we manage that?"

I was surprised. I had not thought he wanted friendship. He had never offered it before. Just a continued relationship. Or conflict and separation.

"I – I don't know. Maybe. Now that we've had a break from each other. It might be possible."

His eyes flew up to mine, hope and pleasure plain to see.

"I would love that. Please, do think about it. I honestly have missed your friendship, your company."

I nodded. A little overwhelmed. Not sure what I thought. Could I cope with seeing him again? Were my feelings under tight enough control? I was uncertain. He still had the power to move me, that was clear. Waves of unexpected emotions, flooding me with warmth. My hands were shaking a little, so I hid them under the table and shut down that line of thought. Back to the matter of concern.

"So, how are things going? Any sign of Harriet? Has anyone come forward?"

"No reported sightings, yet, but it's early days, of course. I only made the appeal this morning. We've been back to her house, looking into her personal life, to see if there are any indications of her wanting to leave suddenly, or being in mental distress. Nothing, so far. Her laptop is security protected, so investigating its contents is taking longer than we would like. We need to check her social media, as that's often where we can find crucial clues to mindset in this sort of case. She didn't have a public profile, though, and a search for her name only brings up her employment at the library."

"That's a shame. It would really help to know more about her background, I imagine. Does she have a family?"

"We're trying to contact relatives, but it seems that she wasn't close to any of them. The people we've spoken to, so far, can't contribute much, even immediate family. It seems that they strongly and vocally disapproved of her husband, and, in return, he did his best to detach her from them. Even after the divorce, she had not chosen to reach out to family. Her parents haven't seen her for over five years. Cards on special occasions, but not even regular phone or email contact."

"She sounds like a lonely person. Solitary. Isolated."

He nodded agreement.

"You're right. That's the impression we're getting. I spoke to her work colleagues and they all said she was a bit of a dreamer. Very hard-working and conscientious. As you might expect for someone who works in a library, she's a real bookworm, like you. They said she had a preference for escapist fantasy, romance, even fairytales. She was someone who still believed deeply in love at first sight, happily ever after, that kind of thing. In spite of her own relationship problems."

"That's interesting. There was a kind of dreamy, nervous excitement in her, that day. As I've looked back, that's my strongest impression of her emotional state."

Rob took out a notebook.

"That could be helpful, Tessa. You didn't get the feeling that she was in despair, suicidal, at all, then? I know I asked before, but it's important."

I shook my head, decisively.

"No. Not at all. She was vulnerable, but in a different way. Hopeful. As if she was taking a chance, and that wasn't usual for her. I can't explain my feeling entirely, but she was looking forward to something, I think. I don't know what. Do you think she might have been meeting someone? She did say 'he' a couple of times."

"It seems like a strange place to have a date or a rendezvous, doesn't it? Especially on a miserable day like that. We're not ruling it out, but when we looked at your transcript, both the inspector and I thought the pronoun probably referred to her ex-husband, who seems to have been quite a controlling person."

That could be true. Particularly when talking about using the app to pay. The kind of thing an overbearing partner might conceivably disapprove of. And the type of rule and conditioning it might be difficult to shake off.

"Please, keep thinking back over your encounter, Tessa. Other little things may strike you and, in a situation like this, could be vital."

"OK. I can't get it out of my mind, anyway. I probably won't be able to, not until you find her. Safe and well, I hope, but it's looking less and less likely now, isn't it?"

He nodded, seriously.

"I'm afraid so. I think she would probably have turned up somewhere by now, even if only in hospital, if she were still alive. But we can keep hoping. Stranger things have happened. It could all be some kind of misunderstanding, and she may be perfectly fine."

I held on to that. It was important to me.

"I have something to ask you, Tessa. Officially. The inspector thinks we should do a reconstruction of what happened on Tuesday. As soon as possible. To jog people's memories, bring witnesses forward. She would like to run it tomorrow, with everything as close to your recollections as we can manage. We really need your participation."

I was shocked. I had not anticipated such a request, although I had seen similar things on the television. A very public re-run of what happened. I knew that it would be a very strange and possibly disturbing experience, but I had to agree. There was no choice. It was a matter of public duty. And I owed it to Harriet.

"OK. I'm working tomorrow, but I'll book out the time. The same timings and everything? So you need me to start just before twelve-thirty. Do you want me to reenact the attempted pick up at five o'clock, too?"

"Yes, please, although it'll probably be less helpful, at least in terms of witnesses. We already know you didn't see anyone! But it'll help us to visualise exactly what you did. As far as arrangements go, we'll find someone who looks like her, at least roughly, in terms of height, build and hair, but we need your guidance on what she was wearing. Colours and things. That's very important. It's the kind of thing people notice first."

He had his notebook ready. I thought back carefully.

"She had on a light coat, loose fitting and shortish, with no hood. I worried about that when it got so wet in the afternoon. Pale blue colour. Darker blue jeans, but not tight. Not jeggings, I mean. Flat black shoes, not trainers or walking shoes. Laced up. She didn't have a handbag with her. Her phone must have been in her pocket. That's where her purse was, too. She took it out to pay cash. It was black, made of leather, I think. She had quite a bit of cash on her, as I remember."

Rob grinned at me appreciatively.

"You've got such a good memory! I couldn't wish for a better witness."

I smiled ruefully.

"I find it hard to forget things, even when I want to."

There was a short silence. I was remembering past rows, which I would love to obliterate from my retentive memory, things I had tried in vain to explain, unpleasant accusations he had thrown at me in anger. Painful moments I did not want to relive. Looking up, I could see that he realised what was running through my mind.

His hand reached out for mine and gripped it briefly.

"Let's both make an effort to put things behind us. Make a new start. I – I accused you of some horrible things. I know, now, that they weren't true. Knew it then, I suppose. It was much easier to invent reasons to be angry with you than to accept my own failings or question my behaviour. I'm genuinely sorry. I – I know I've lost you, that our relationship is gone. But I would love to have you back in my life, as a friend."

I could not resist his emotional appeal. I, too, had missed him. His absence had left an empty hole, a vacuum I had been unable to fill. And I felt much happier with the idea of seeing him again, now that he had recognised that he was wrong and apologised so generously. A nasty scar might have the chance to heal.

"I'll try, Rob. I accept your apology, gladly. And I will try to forget the bad moments. I would like us to be friends. And I want to help, in any way I can, with this case. I feel responsible for her. I know I'm not, but I can't help it."

"I can understand that. It's an emotional connection and doesn't have to be logical. Don't worry, you've already been tremendously helpful. We wouldn't be anywhere near having an area to search if you hadn't contacted me. We couldn't even be sure that she was genuinely missing. Thanks to you, we have a chance of finding her, perhaps even alive."

His phone rang. He picked it up without hesitation and his voice reverted to its curt professional tone.

"Go ahead. Where was it? What state is it in? Do what you can. Are we sure it's hers? OK."

Intriguing.

"Right, Tessa, we need to go and get your statement signed, and I must get back to the station, and then join the search at the lake, I think. That was one of my colleagues at Caldecotte. They've just found what they think may be her phone."

He was in full police officer mode now, speaking crisply and with authority.

"Where did they find it?" I asked.

"Between the path and the water, under the bridge into the Walton Park section. It's pretty smashed up, and there's water damage, too, so I don't know how useful it will be. The case has her initials on it, so we can be fairly sure it belongs to her. We'll be able to match it to the number her employer passed on, anyway. Can you let us have the number she used to book the cab? Just in case it was different."

"I think so, as long as it's OK with GDPR. I'll check with Sally."

I was, however, deeply puzzled by the apparent site of the find.

"But – I walked past there. Looking out for anything which might possibly be a clue to where she was. I'm sure I would have seen it. I couldn't have missed it."

"Mm, that's strange. It was very dark, though, from what you described. Could it have been in the water when you went past and been thrown up by the waves? I don't know. We'll check tomorrow, when you do the reenactment. I can show you exactly where it was found."

I was sceptical about the wave theory. A phone is quite a heavy object. Yes, it had been windy, and the water had been forced up into waves, like the sea, but not under the bridge. And there was no tide. It seemed very odd to me. Unlikely.

Rob was in a hurry to get moving, however, so we walked briskly down to the police station. I could tell that his mind was entirely on the case, so I did not trouble him with small talk. In the station, I read the statement through carefully before signing it, but could not see any issues or inaccuracies. We agreed to meet there at around eleven-thirty on the following day, to finalise arrangements for the re-run of my movements.

"If you can put on the same clothes that you wore on Tuesday, that would be ideal. We want it to be as similar as possible, to try to bring forward other witnesses, even if it's just people who saw her at the shopping centre. I'll be publicising it on local media this evening, so there may be quite a few people watching, but just do exactly what you did last time. Don't let them put you off or distract you. There will be a television crew filming as well. Thanks so much for agreeing, Tessa. I really appreciate it."

He hurried me out of the building, eager to get back to work. Entirely focused. Pushing aside all peripheral considerations.

I hoped he would find time for rest. I remembered him missing out on that during previous difficult cases. Lack of sleep made for poor decisions, and possibly missing or misinterpreting important clues. He needed to take care of himself, but the pressure to find Harriet quickly would be enormous.

CHAPTER FOUR

Revisiting

In the morning, I managed to complete some taxi trips, before making my way to the police station. It was better to be working than fretting about what was to come. Nerves were rumbling in my stomach. I knew how important this could be and was concerned that I might do something wrong, make a stupid error. I had not slept much the previous night and was aware that I looked somewhat the worse for wear. I could only hope that my face would not be clearly visible from outside the cab.

After checking in with Rob at the police station, and being given basic instructions, I met the inspector, for the first time. She was a brisk, no-nonsense type, focused on the task in hand, rather than pleasantries, or putting me at ease. I knew from her first words that her expectations of me were not high.

"Please make every effort to do exactly what you did before, Miss Fordham. As precisely as possible, even down to the conversation within the vehicle, since that will help to ensure that you are following the same track in your actions, too. The police officer representing Ms Beckinsale will record what you say, as well as responding to it, but you can ignore that. Please tell her what she needs to do at each point. In as much detail as you can manage."

I nodded comprehension. I would do my best.

"It's unfortunate that you don't have CCTV in your cab," she continued. "That would have been extremely useful in the current situation."

I felt the need to apologise.

"I would like to have it, for the safety of my drivers, but we can't afford it just yet. We're a new company."

But the inspector had already turned away. Uninterested in my excuses. Rob made a wry grimace at me, and indicated silently that I should get moving. I walked back to my car, shivering slightly with apprehension.

He had been right. I did feel rather like a goldfish in a bowl. There were distinct groups and larger crowds of spectators standing around at the pick-up point, watching and commenting on everything I did, with evident curiosity. And a team with television cameras. It was rather intimidating.

The police had cleared plenty of space for me to pick up the imitation Harriet, so it was much less busy than usual, and I felt exposed. Normally the area outside the food store was a confusion of harassed hooting drivers, queues of impatient cars, and a few long-suffering taxis, picking up the tired and heavily loaded shoppers. Today, it reminded me of how quiet the area had been during Covid lockdowns.

It suddenly struck me as odd that she should have chosen this place to arrange to meet me. It was invariably frenetic and stressful, and she did not appear to have been shopping. Why had she not asked to be picked up by the library, just across the road? It would have been extremely familiar to her from work, and would certainly have made my task much easier. I made a mental note to mention it to Rob. With the altered name and the cash payment, it looked as if she had been aiming to remain anonymous, unnoticed, for some unknown reason.

I drew up where I had found her before, sent the confirmation text, lowered the window and called: "Taxi for Smith!"

The fake Harriet approached the car with less hesitation than the woman she was representing, and confirmed her name briefly. She climbed in quickly and we repeated the same conversation as before about where to go and which route to take. She had obviously read my statement, and attempted to respond with Harriet's words.

The tension in my shoulders began to ease, as I settled into my normal driving routine. My hybrid was so easy and intuitive to drive. It meant I could pay full attention to the traffic around and the unpredictable dangers it often posed.

The trip to the pub car park took approximately the same length of time as previously. Here, again, there were a few onlookers, staring intently at us, as we pulled into a space and discussed where to try next. Then it was off to the circular car park on the other side of the dual carriageway, diving across the hurtling traffic into the quiet side road. The area was completely devoid of vehicles, this time, but there were police officers standing watching, as well as a few members of the public, and the ubiquitous camera team.

I was able to use the identical space, and we discussed payment and the return trip as before. She exited the vehicle and walked towards the lakeside path. From behind, she resembled Harriet closely and her clothes were extremely similar. The coat was almost exactly the same colour. Her bearing was more confident, however, and she walked with a briskness my passenger had completely lacked.

I had not seen which direction she took at the end of the spur, and was annoyed with myself for not waiting an extra thirty seconds. It would have made the task of tracing her movements much simpler.

I was about to reverse and leave, when Rob opened the passenger door and got into the car beside me.

"Well done!" he said. "That went very smoothly. Exemplary timing. The inspector was pleased. And she isn't easy to satisfy."

I grinned.

"I rather gathered that. Do you want me to look at where the phone was found now, or at five when I come back?"

"We'd better do it later. We don't want to disrupt the reconstruction. And it was dark then, so it'll be more realistic. We've put a replica down in order to be able to judge if you would have noticed it, as you said. We're assuming she went that way, and sending our actor in that direction first, although we will try the southerly route too, afterwards."

I remembered to tell him what had occurred to me about the strangeness of the choice of pick-up location. He looked thoughtful.

"You're right. There seems to be a deliberate attempt here to obscure her identity. It doesn't fit with anything we have so far discovered about her life, unless it's to do with her ex-husband. Had he been stalking her? Made her afraid of being followed? We'll look into that. Especially as she did mention 'he' when talking about paying by cash."

"Mm. I still have the feeling she might have been meeting someone, a man. Perhaps a person who gave her instructions about keeping her identity secret."

I was a little frustrated that he did not seem to take this possibility seriously.

"You may be right, it's possible," he conceded. "And she might well want to keep that kind of rendezvous secret from her ex. But the inspector doesn't think it likely. Taking a taxi to meet a man friend by a lake on a winter's afternoon just doesn't seem very probable, in the kind of weather we had on Tuesday."

"Yes, but taking a cab to the lake, in order to spend several hours walking around it in the rain, also doesn't ring true. She didn't look like an outdoors type and certainly wasn't dressed for the conditions."

He put his head to one side, thinking.

"I see what you're saying. I'll put it to the inspector. If we can get onto Harriet's social media, we'll know more about her her intentions and habits. But the phone is really badly damaged, unfortunately, and her laptop doesn't seem to have much content on it. She didn't even have most social media apps installed. It's frustrating, almost as if she didn't want us to find her."

It was a conundrum. What had she been doing? Why was she going there? And, above all, what had happened to her?

Rob got out to talk to his officers, just as it began to rain, again. I was so fed up with the miserably wet month we were having. The river was already swollen and beginning to lip over its banks, trying to join forces with the massive deep puddles, which made the term 'dry land' laughable. And the heavy cloud filtered out so much light that it was profoundly depressing. I longed for some glimmers of bright winter sunshine.

I had agreed with Sally that I would go home between the two enactment sessions, and I was very glad to get back into the warm and have a cup of tea. Naomi was up and eager to know how it had all gone. I had confessed my meeting with Rob to her, including our decision to try to build a new friendship, the previous evening, before she went on duty.

As I expected, she had disapproved, but not seriously. She laughed at me.

"I knew you'd forgive him much too easily, Tess. You've always been too soft with him, too much of a doormat. Oh well, I tried to save you from yourself! You'll only have yourself to blame, if you end up right back where you started. He's always had the upper hand with you."

I protested that it was quite different, and we were only going to be friends, nothing romantic at all. Not a close or dependent relationship. She was having none of it.

"I'll believe it when I see it. You still go weak at the knees when you see him, don't you? You always did. There's definitely more than mere friendship between you, not to mention all the history you have together. You can't just pretend that it never happened. I just can't see you keeping it light. But it's your funeral."

I knew that she was right and flushed guiltily. I had felt the pull of attraction as soon as I saw him again. It was not going to be easy to keep him at arm's length. Unless he was genuinely only seeking friendship.

Naomi was keen to hear about how the reconstruction had gone. Now that it was clear I had done the right thing in contacting the police, she was fully absorbed in the case, although I kept my word to Rob, and did not share the private information he had passed on. She was a keen reader of detective fiction and excited to feel close to being part of a case herself.

"So, Tessa – accident, suicide, or foul play? What's your guess?"

"Oh, Naomi, I'm still hoping she'll turn up somewhere, safe and well. I can't get excited about the thought that she might be dead. Although I do recognise that she almost certainly is. It's a such a negative thought."

"Did she seem depressed?"

"Everyone keeps asking me that. No, not at all. Hopeful, if anything. I don't see her as a suicide, that's for sure. And all the paths are pretty safe, so accident seems unlikely."

Her eyes were alight with vicarious enjoyment.

"It would be so much fun to be involved in a real murder case, though, wouldn't it? Things like that never seem to happen round here."

I couldn't dampen her enthusiasm. She went on speculating until I had to leave for Caldecotte. I was glad to climb back into the car and leave her to it. I could still visualise Harriet's pleasant face very clearly. I wanted her to be alive.

It was dark, and drizzling heavily again, when I reached the car park. The cameras had gone, with plenty of footage to use on the news. No passers-by, now, just a few police officers milling around attempting to look purposeful, but no longer conducting the fingertip search, since the visibility was so poor. Waiting for my appearance. I realised that the car park was cordoned off, other than for their vehicles and mine, like a crime scene. They couldn't risk any evidence being lost or contaminated. Some poor constable would have to stand guard all night, presumably.

I parked as I had before, paused for the time I would have spent ringing the office, and then stepped out of the car, rather reluctantly. It suddenly felt ghoulish to go and pretend to look for her again, when I knew that she was missing or dead. I was surprised when Rob appeared out of the gloom, at my elbow. I thought he would have had more important things to do, and said so.

"No, actually your evidence is the best information we have so far. We need to get everything we possibly can from you. Can you walk exactly as you did then?"

I nodded and made my way, rather hesitantly, down the right-hand turn, over the wooden bridge, slightly slippery now in the misty drizzle. I hurried past the secret pool, with its deep shadows and mysterious shapes, and around the corner to the shelter of the double road crossing. Its gloomy grey concrete, scrubby vegetation, and damply dripping dreariness were the antithesis of welcoming. I had walked right through to the other side, I remembered.

As I passed under the second road, hearing the frequent thumping thuds as traffic passed over the expansion joints, I immediately spotted the phone they had placed there, on the concrete mesh between the path and the dark, turbulent water. I would not have missed it. It gleamed in the dim light. It had not been there that Tuesday afternoon, I was sure of it.

I told Rob, as we walked up to where I turned around.

"I'm sure I would have seen it that day, too. I was worried about her, looking around for anything which might show me where she was or had been. I wouldn't have missed it. It simply wasn't there."

He grunted, doubt evident in the sound.

"Honestly, Rob. Don't you believe me?"

It hurt, and that was reflected in my feebly pleading tone. His good opinion was so unexpectedly important. He turned towards me.

"Of course, I believe you, Tessa. It's not that. It's just that you were expecting to see something, this time. You can't be sure that, in your anxiety, you wouldn't have missed the phone on Tuesday. I accept what you say, and will put it to the inspector, but I have a feeling that she'll assume it was there all the time. I'm sorry."

I hung my head in embarrassment. It was probably just me being stupid, then. I hurried back the way we had come and showed him how far I had gone in the other direction. You could again see right over to the other side of the bay, in spite of the oppressive darkness, and the drizzle creating blurry haloes around the streetlamps.

The westerly wind was strengthening over the broad open expanse of the south lake, blowing in heavier bursts of rain, and I began to shiver. He sensed it and urged me back to the car.

"Time for you to go and warm up, Tess. Thank you so much for what you've done today. It's invaluable. Apparently we've already had a few calls from the public, and there'll be more after it's on television, I hope."

"Would you – would you be willing to let me know how it's going? Tomorrow or at the weekend?"

I was surprised at the meekness and hesitation in my voice. I really was not at all assertive with him. My sister was right about that.

"Of course. I'll message and we'll meet somewhere for a coffee again. I won't have much time off over the next few days, but I'll manage to fit you in, don't you worry. You deserve to know what's happening, after all you've done for us."

"Thank you, Rob. I – I hope you find her soon."

"Me, too," he agreed. I could see the tired lines of tension around his mouth and left quickly, so that he would be able to get away, too.

CHAPTER FIVE

Fifteen minutes of fame

I watched the segment about the case on the local news that evening. Rob speaking over the footage, patiently explaining what was going on. Plenty of film of my cab. More than I had expected. Our logo was nice and clear. I had not realised that I would be recognisable inside the vehicle, but I was quite wrong about that. It was very clearly me, tired eyes, frown, blemishes and all.

I was, therefore, not totally surprised when I began to receive messages from friends and even mere acquaintances, saying they had seen me on television. Asking what was going on. Wanting to know details of my involvement. Understandable curiosity, but it felt prurient and invasive to me. I tried not to be rude, but responded in the briefest of terms, if at all.

Sally rang and said that we had received a large number of new bookings, so the publicity was not all bad. Unfortunately, quite a number had asked for me specifically, and I realised that all my fares were likely to want to discuss the case in exhaustive detail. Everyone would have their own theory about what had happened.

She also warned me that there had been phone calls from reporters, wanting me to make a comment or be interviewed. Fortunately, she had not given any of them my private number, although they already had my name, probably from the company website. I was already in the public eye, without seeking it. The last thing I wanted was to be hounded by the press.

I thought about it for a while, and then typed up a comment, which Sally could give to any news outlets which chased her.

As a new minicab company, with a particular focus on women's comfort and safety, we would like to express our concern about the disappearance of Harriet Beckinsale, and hope that she will be found, safe and well, very soon. We have done all we can to support the police inquiry, from reporting the possibility of her being missing to the police, to participating in the reconstruction of her movements on Tuesday. Our thoughts are with her, and her friends and relatives. We will not be making any further comment on the matter.

I hoped that might be sufficient. I sent it off and tried to relax, without a great deal of success. In my dreams that night, I was tossed about by powerful waves of black water, sucking me down into the unknown and perilous depths.

By the next morning, the police investigation had clearly moved on. There was television footage of specialist divers arriving with their equipment, ready to begin their search as soon as it was light enough. The focus appeared to be the area around the road bridge. It suggested that they were fairly sure she had gone into the water, and was therefore dead.

It did not seem like the right move to me. I was an instinctive problem-solver and tended to try to analyse things logically. The choice of that place for a search seemed perverse. The path was not close to the lake at that point, and there was surely no chance of accident. A slip or fall would not have caused her to enter the water there. Even if she was avoiding a dog or a cyclist, there was plenty of space to move away without risk.

And it would not be a suitable place for a suicide attempt, I would have thought, since the water shelved relatively gently up to the edge. There were accessible spots with much deeper water, like the storm drain, or the weir, which would surely be more practical.

It suddenly occurred to me that she might have jumped off the road bridge, where the redway crossed the lake. There was a metal fence, but it could easily be climbed. In fact, I had seen teenagers jumping from there in the summer, at great risk to life and limb. I shook my head to rid myself of the thought. She had not been suicidal. I was positive about that. And surely she would have been seen. It was a busy road.

I tried to shake off my sense of discomfort, as I geared myself up for a busy day of work. I prepared, in my head, a casual, non-controversial response to the curiosity I was bound to face. Normally, I enjoyed chatting to my customers, putting them at their ease. Today, I would have welcomed stony silence.

The first few jobs were for regulars. They all seemed to have watched the television footage, and asked numerous questions, but were relatively easy to satisfy. Mostly, they were interested in how I felt about it all, and my personal impressions of the mystery passenger. They seemed to revel in the reflected glory of travelling in the same cab, with the same driver, as a missing person.

I tried to tell them how ordinary she had seemed, at the outset. But, if that were true, why had I been so concerned about the no-show in the afternoon? There must have been something about her which subconsciously told me that she was vulnerable and needed more care.

My fourth journey was different. A pick-up at the station, and the trip booked was to Caldecotte Lake. It had been arranged by phone, apparently in order to ensure that I was the driver. Sally told me it was a man called Soapstone. Strange name. We did not have many male passengers, apart from a few regular school journeys and a couple of very elderly men. I told myself that it was ridiculous to feel anxious.

The drop-off zone in front of the station was a churning swirl of chaos, as usual. Cabs, private cars, confused rail passengers, unwieldy luggage, idiots wandering in front of vehicles with faces glued to their phones. Fortunately, my fare was quick-witted and spotted my number plate, waved, and moved to a suitable place for me to stop. He even jumped in quickly, briefcase in hand so that he could slide easily into his seat.

My instinctive gratitude was short-lived, however. He asked to be 'shown the sights' before going to Caldecotte Lake, the type of vague request which is never appealing to someone who drives for a living.

"Can you be more specific?" I asked sharply. "What do you want to see? The city centre, the concrete cows, the Cock and Bull in Stony Stratford, remnants of ancient forest at Linford Wood, the Peace Pagoda, Bletchley Park?"

"Mm, I didn't realise there was so much to see in Milton Keynes. I've never been to the place before. I always thought it was just a concrete jungle with a surfeit of roundabouts and full of tents for homeless people."

As a long-term resident of the city, proud of its many amenities, I was rather offended. A less concrete city would be hard to find. And his upper-class accent was an irritatingly superior drawl.

"We actually have twenty-two million trees and thousands of acres of parkland," I responded, repressively. "And the Winter Night Shelter and the council have done wonders for street homelessness. Even the shopping centre is a listed building."

"Really? I suppose that's quite something for a modern place like this. Well, I don't know, can you just drive me around a bit so that I get a sense of the place? Please."

The politeness was clearly an afterthought, but however annoying, the customer is always right. And he was paying.

"Of course."

I took him to the centre and showed him the impressive, cathedral-like Cornerstone church and the end of the famous shopping centre, then went north, past Linford Wood, left towards the A5, up to historic Stony Stratford, back through the old workers' towns of Wolverton and New Bradwell, past Great Linford and down the V10 alongside scenic Willen Lake. Up to Campbell Park and down the V8, then left and into Simpson, where I stopped at the car park by Caldecotte Lake, popular with dog walkers, but totally empty on that wet and dreary day.

"This is Caldecotte Lake. Part of it, anyway. Just through those trees at the back of the car park."

I turned to look at the man, who had been quiet during our trip, responding only with rather unenthusiastic murmurs, when I pointed out some of the landmarks. His scowl seemed to be habitual, judging from the deep frown lines on his forehead.

"It doesn't resemble the footage I saw on television."

"Ah, you wanted the south lake, did you? You should have said."

I knew that I was being a bit naughty, deliberately misunderstanding him.

He stared at me hard for a moment and then laughed. It completely changed his appearance. He was quite nice looking, when there was a smile in his eyes.

"Didn't do my research, did I?" he said. "Silly me. I guess I deserved that."

I turned back, ready to make amends and set off towards the right end of the lake, but he stopped me.

"Don't go yet. Please. I would like to talk to you, and it seems quiet here. It's as good a place as any."

I fixed him with a stare and raised my eyebrows. He grinned sheepishly.

"You know why, don't you? There's no point in trying to deny it. And yes, as you guessed, I'm a reporter. Newspaperman. I want to do a piece on the missing woman, and you're the best person to talk to about her."

Now it was my turn to frown.

"I'm not doing any interviews or press. I don't want any publicity. I've seen what you reporters can do to people, how you distort what they say."

He smiled, assuming a candid air of confession.

"Our unfortunate reputation goes before us, as you say. I won't deny that press intrusion makes some people's lives a misery, because it's obviously true. I can't expect you to believe that I'm not like that. I would say that, wouldn't I?"

I nodded. At least he was not trying to pull the wool over my eyes.

He loosened his tie a little. He was very smartly dressed for a visit to a lake. I looked down at his highly polished city shoes and smiled internally. They wouldn't last long. He tried a different angle.

"It would be good for your business if you had a little more prominence in the media, wouldn't it? I'm not offering you money, but it would be free publicity for the firm."

I sniffed disparagingly. "We're doing fine as it is, thank you very much. I would not want to make money out of someone else's misfortune."

He regrouped for another attack.

"Look, I can make it a background piece, if you like. I don't even have to mention you by name. If I write something good, it might help to jog someone's memory, help the police to find her, or at least where her body is."

I did not want to hear those words.

"I'm still hoping she's alive. I know – it's unlikely. But it is possible."

"Well, then. Help me to write something which will make a difference. She's not the kind of beautiful young victim the tabloids will love to have on their front pages. It's not going to be easy to keep her in the news. This could be important. I'll even let you see it before we publish. I can't say fairer than that."

I paused to think. He was persuasive, there was no doubt about that. His voice had lost its sneering, contemptuous edge and was more natural, if still very clearly articulated. But I was still unsure.

"I don't know. I'm extremely reluctant to talk to you. Can't you get what you need from the police?"

He sighed.

"Oh, yes, the usual jargon and a series of useless facts. Nothing to make people really care about her, or want to find her. You met her. You know what she was like. You can make her human for me. Normally, I'd turn to her family or close friends, but they don't seem to be around."

That was true. As efficient as they were, and as urgently as they were working, Rob and the others did not have a personal connection to Harriet. I did. There was a definite bond. Perhaps I could make others see her as I had. As someone worth finding. I would have to keep quiet about the additional information I had received from Rob, but I could do that quite easily. This reporter would not expect me to know those details.

"Very well. As long as I am able to approve or reject what you write. What's your name? Which paper to you work for?"

His eye brightened.

"The name's John Soapstone. Call me John. What would you like me to call you, Miss Fordham?"

"Tessa."

He told me he worked for one of the broadsheets with a reasonably decent reputation, which was somewhat reassuring.

"Would you come and sit in the back here with me, Tessa? It'll be very uncomfortable for you having to twist round all the time."

I hesitated. It broke my rule, changed my role, modified my sense of being in control of the situation. I was deeply unsure about it.

He smiled. An understanding and attractive smile. It made a small dent in my defences.

"I know it feels wrong to you, but it really will be easier. I promise I won't bite."

Just then, I had a call from the office. Sally, wondering why this job was taking so long. Checking up on me, making sure I was safe. As per procedure.

"I'm fine, Sal. In the Simpson car park by Caldecotte lake. My current passenger wanted a guided tour and is now asking for more time, and he's paying, so I guess it's acceptable. I'll let you know as soon as I've dropped him off."

She agreed, but I could hear concern and reservations in her voice, despite the distortion on the line. I knew she would call back in half an hour, to make certain.

"Sensible. Telling her where you are. Just in case," he approved.

"There's a tracker in the cab, anyway, but I want to be sure that she knows what I'm doing."

"I do have my press ID here. Take a look." He seemed to understand, now, that security was an issue for me.

"OK. You are who you say you are. I'll come back for a few minutes. I need to return to work soon, though."

"It won't take long," he assured me, soothingly.

I took a good look at him, once I was in the rear seat. Quite tall, so that his short dark hair was almost grazing the roof of the car. Very neat and well-groomed appearance, rather like a lawyer. Not what I expected in a reporter. Intense, thick dark eyebrows, almost meeting above his nose, which gave his face a scowling look even in repose. Quite tanned. Obviously no stranger to winter sun. Very white teeth, like a television personality.

I realised that he was examining me, too, and flushed a little.

"What do you want to know?" I asked, rather brusquely.

"Hey, relax, Tessa. I'm not going to give you the third degree. I understand that you genuinely don't want your face plastered all over the papers. Although a very attractive woman like you could have made quite a bit of money out of a tabloid exclusive, you know."

I glared at him sternly. He raised his hand apologetically.

"Sorry, that's inappropriate. Forget it. Force of habit. Flattery is usually welcome. Anyway, it means that I'm very aware you are only willing to allow me to interview you for other reasons, not for personal publicity."

I nodded, still embarrassed by his unwanted personal comments.

"For Harriet. Because I'm worried about what might have happened to her."

"OK, then. You tell me, in your own words, what happened, and why you cared enough to report that she had failed to turn up for the return journey. Before her disappearance was public knowledge."

That was the crucial question. Why had I been so disturbed? So very worried about her that I could not let it go. Even days later.

I told him the facts, quite simply. What she had said. What we had agreed.

"I can't explain why I was so concerned about her. As you can imagine, we get plenty of no-shows. They're an occupational hazard. But she had seemed so very keen for me to take her home. As if we had bonded, somehow. She said I made her feel safe. Does that mean that she didn't usually feel safe? I don't know. I felt I had to get out and look for her, and when I couldn't find her, I knew, somehow, that it was all wrong. I tried to forget it for a day or so, but, in the end, I had to reach out to the police, for my own peace of mind."

"How was her mood? Do you think she could have been depressed, desperate, in mental or emotional distress? Is that why you were so concerned?"

I shook my head vigorously.

"I think the police have that impression, and I can understand why, under the circumstances. It's an obvious conclusion to draw. I did sense that she was vulnerable. Perhaps fragile in some way. But she wasn't feeling low, I'm sure of that. She was – dreamy, excited, a bit nervous. Looking forward to something, but not quite sure how it would turn out. A little wary. As if she was taking a risk and hoping it would work out."

"Interesting."

"I – I think, personally, that she was meeting someone, a man. The police don't agree, and I know it's just speculation. Perhaps it is unlikely, especially in that awful weather. I suppose – well, actually, I'm convinced that she's come to harm. Clearly the police are assuming that, too, if they're using divers to search for her. For me, though, there's something more. I believe that someone else is involved in what happened to her. That she's been taken or hurt."

"Can I put that in my article?"

I hesitated.

"Not under my name. Could you perhaps put it as a question? You know, *'Was someone else involved in this puzzling disappearance, or was it a mere accident?'* You know the type of thing."

He threw back his head and laughed.

"You really do have a good idea of how we work! How we manage to avoid getting into trouble, sometimes. I'll find a way to put it in. I think it could be important. It would help if people were searching their memories for her plus another, rather than just for a lone woman."

"Yes, you're right. I'm a bit frustrated that the police don't believe me, or don't think it's worth pursuing."

"I can understand why you feel like that. But they do have a lot of experience of this kind of thing. Most of the recent cases of this type have been accident or suicide."

"I suppose so," I agreed, grudgingly. "Although there was that nasty case here in Milton Keynes a couple of years ago. But I guess that kind of thing is rare."

It did not alter my perceptions, though. And my reactions were first hand, not based on the reports of others, or on previous events. Surely, that must count for something.

"OK, I think that's it for now, Tessa. I would like to thank you for your cooperation."

That sounded like a well-used formula. But he continued, more naturally.

"It's been really helpful. Can I please take your mobile number, in case I have any follow-up questions when I'm writing, and an email address to send the article to? I'll be staying in Milton Keynes tonight and should have it ready to go by late evening."

I was reluctant to pass on my personal contact details, although he assured me that he would keep them confidential. I wanted to trust him, but was not completely at ease. Part of me felt incredibly guilty about having spoken to him at all, especially without checking with Rob in advance, and I was also anxious about what he might write. Afraid that I had done wrong by Harriet, perhaps not portrayed her in the best light.

"Do you still want me to take you to the other part of the lake?"

"Yes, please. I need to see the scene for myself, get a sense of the atmosphere, maybe speak to the police there."

I explained that the car park was cordoned off, but I could drop him in the pub car park and he could walk back over the road bridge.

"Would you be able to pick me up again in about ninety minutes? From where you drop me off. I'll need a taxi to my hotel."

I nodded. Not totally happy about it. Why did it have to be me? I hoped he would turn up on time. It would be some indication of his trustworthiness.

Although it was not far away on foot, I had to make a considerable detour around the peanut roundabout under the A5 to approach the pub. He did not manifest any impatience, however. Expressed his thanks quite nicely when we arrived.

I made sure he paid before he left the vehicle. Just in case he was another no-show later on. He used the card machine and wanted a receipt, in order to claim it on expenses. It was quite a large bill, but he seemed happy with it. He must have been confident that the paper would reimburse him.

I gave him directions to the redway route across the lake and watched him begin to walk down the hill, smiling at how he tried to keep his fancy footwear dry, avoiding the numerous puddles and scattered piles of greenish goose droppings. Not well-prepared for the conditions here. But not such an unpleasant person, after all.

He did not look very happy, when I arrived to pick him up again. He was standing, ready and waiting, battered by the westerly wind and driving rain. His smart leather briefcase was very damp and his soaked city raincoat had no hood, so his hair was wet and thoroughly tousled. I grinned as he picked his way over to me.

"Stop laughing, Tessa!" he growled. "I know, I wasn't dressed for the occasion, was I? I needed full waterproofs and wellies."

I could not suppress a brief snigger.

"You do look a bit of a mess! I hope you're not completely drenched."

"Don't worry, I won't damage your cab! I'm not that wet. I stood in shelter when I could. But it's a foul day, and coming back across that bridge, I was really caught by the hurricane blasts you seem to suffer in Milton Keynes. I'm afraid these shoes are totally ruined, too."

I smiled. As I had expected.

"Did you manage to talk to the police?"

He paused, as if considering whether I was a trustworthy person to open up to.

"Yes, I talked briefly to a constable, and then the detective sergeant in charge came over. He wasn't exactly forthcoming, or welcoming, but he did seem to think that an article in the national press might help to unlock more potential witnesses, so he wasn't too off-putting. He told me a bit about Harriet. Where she worked, that sort of thing. Useful background."

My conscience was immediately eased. If Rob had spoken to John, I need not feel guilty that I had, too. And I had not betrayed any of his professional confidences.

I delivered him to the Holiday Inn in the centre, where he had booked a room. He looked very relieved at the sight of the reception area, promising warmth, light, and the metropolitan comforts to which he was accustomed.

"Goodbye, Tessa. Thank you for all your help. I appreciate it. You should hear from me, later, with the article. You'll have to look at it straight away, I'm afraid. I need to get it into print as soon as possible."

"Send me a text when you've forwarded it to me. I'll check it immediately and get back to you."

"Agreed. Can I have another receipt?"

"Of course."

We exchanged smiles as he left the vehicle. He had changed my view of newspaper reporters a little. At least he had a sense of humour and could laugh at himself. But I could not be sure that he was as honest as he seemed, not until I saw what he had written.

Naomi was already at work when I arrived home, so I was spared another inquisition. I made myself a quick omelette and settled down to relax in front of the television, with my laptop beside me, ready to look at John's article as soon as it dropped.

The local news had more coverage of Harriet's disappearance. Pictures of the poor divers, all working near the bridge area, in the most appalling weather conditions. Information about her phone having been found. A picture of it and encouragement to get in touch if it had been seen anywhere near the lake. Another clip of the reenactment and a good clear photo of Harriet herself. Very recognisable. A number to contact about any sightings or information. Rob stating that this was still a missing person inquiry, but that they were now deeply concerned for Harriet's safety. As was I.

My phone buzzed, and I assumed it was John. In fact, it was Rob, arranging to meet for coffee on the following day. Suggesting lunchtime, at Waterstones again. I agreed, a little surprised that he had not thought of The Caldecotte, or even the pub in Simpson. Perhaps he did not want his colleagues to see him meeting me. That would make sense. I had no right to the privileged information he was passing on.

Almost immediately afterwards, John contacted me, and the article arrived. It was better than I had expected. There was no explicit indication that he had spoken to me, nothing personal that I would have wanted to conceal. The direct quotes he used were only from the police. Combining their information with mine, he had written a nice portrait of Harriet, stressing how uncharacteristic her disappearance was, and he had included musings on whether foul play might have been involved. And finished with an exhortation from the police to pass on any information, however trivial, as soon as possible.

He rang.

"Have you read it? What do you think?"

"It's fine. Nothing for me to take offence at. A good article about Harriet. Thanks for keeping me out of it."

He laughed.

"Normally people are eager to have their name and photo included! But I kept to our agreement. It'll be in the paper tomorrow. The editor is happy, so it's a definite 'yes', as long as you approve."

"I'm glad. I hope it leads to more clues to what happened. I do want to find her, to know the truth."

"Mm. May I keep your details and stay in touch? You really changed my mind about Milton Keynes, and I would like to write an article about it one day soon. It's not what people think, even on such a thoroughly wet and miserable day."

"OK. You're right, it's a great place to live. I don't mind helping with that."

"Brilliant. You'll be hearing from me. Bye, Tessa."

I heaved a sigh of relief when he rang off. I was not cut out for this. It made me too anxious. I liked to remain in the background. Even at school, I had helped behind the scenes in productions, refusing the chance to appear on stage. I was pleased with the article, however, and genuinely hoped it might help the police investigation.

CHAPTER SIX

Surprising Clues

I was wearied by more curious and excessively garrulous passengers on Saturday morning, so I was glad to finish early, and have the prospect of an afternoon off, after my lunch with Rob. I was far less nervous about this meeting. We had decided to embark on a new type of friendship, so I felt less vulnerable, personally, and I was eager to hear how the case was progressing.

He looked shattered. His hair was an unkempt mess and there were distinct bags under his eyes, which were rather bloodshot. I insisted on buying him a sandwich to go with his coffee and cookie, and he ate it swiftly, obviously famished. I let him assuage his hunger, before beginning our conversation.

"Try to look after yourself, Rob. You're not going to make good decisions if you're this tired and hungry."

He looked up at me, grinning sheepishly.

"You know what I'm like, don't you? You're right. I need to get a better balance. We don't know how long this phase of the investigation is going to take."

Oh dear, that did not sound as if much progress had been made.

"Aren't you getting anywhere yet?"

He shook his head in frustration.

"Not really. The divers have found absolutely no sign of her near the bridge. Not the slightest indication of disturbance to the bottom of the lake. Obviously, conditions are far from ideal, and visibility underwater is very limited, but there's nothing to show that she was ever there. They have scanning equipment, and that hasn't turned anything up either. And then, the whole area is huge, and we can't rule out the river, or even the Ouzel Valley Park, as it connects to the lake at Simpson."

"I was hoping that there would be a few sightings to narrow your field."

"Nothing like that, at least not yet. A few people thought they saw her where you picked her up, in the city, but they had nothing useful to add. One thought she looked nervous and another said excited. She came from the direction of the library rather than the shops, but that doesn't really help, since we know she worked there."

He sighed.

"No one seems to have seen her down at Caldecotte. It wasn't exactly an inviting day, as you know. Very few people were out, and those who were, mainly dogwalkers, were aiming to get finished quickly, and escape the weather as soon as possible. Still, there was a good national newspaper article about her this morning and that may jog someone's memory. Not everyone looks at local news."

I flushed slightly, but he did not seem to notice.

"What we do have, now, is a purse which may possibly have belonged to her. Black leather, as you described. No cards or ID, only cash, and quite a bit of it. Not something you'd drop and forget about. It was handed in this morning. Some guys from the Red Bull campus, on their regular walk round the lake, found it yesterday lunchtime, and brought it to us today, having seen the coverage on television."

"That sounds more hopeful."

He grunted.

"It's not very useful, actually. They found it on the far side of the south lake, a long way from where her phone was, just lying by the path. I'll have to reprimand my constables. They were supposed to sweep the whole lake path on the first day of our search, and they obviously completely missed it."

"Mm. Like me and the phone." There was scepticism in my tone, but he was too tired to hear it.

"We need to try to confirm it was hers. It's very soggy and not a good surface for fingerprints. We managed to get prints for comparison from her house, but they're no help with this particular object. Would you mind looking at it when we finish here? It's not especially distinctive, but you did notice it when she paid, didn't you?"

"Yes. I think I might recognise it. I'll take a look, anyway."

"Even without any definite confirmation, we're moving our search over to that area of the lake. We have to try somewhere new. But the water's deeper there, and it's not going to be easy. It's close to the river, too, and I really don't want to have to start diving that, not if I can help it."

"I see what you mean. It's not at all straightforward, searching this kind of landscape. I can understand why they've had trouble in the past with this sort of disappearance."

He pushed the unusually lank lock of hair off his forehead and rested his chin on his hand. His eyes closed for a long moment. There was almost none of the normal fizz of energy exuding from him. He seemed to be close to exhaustion.

"I'm worried about you, Rob. Try to pace yourself. As you say, this could go on for days."

He groaned.

"Weeks. It's happened before with this kind of case. And then you'll get people trying to investigate for themselves, amateur sleuths, vloggers, that kind of thing. As it is, we can't close off the whole lake, and there are walkers, cyclists, runners, dogs, not to mention the wildlife … We tried using dogs to track her at the start, but it was hopeless. It's not exactly a pristine scene, especially after all the rain we've had. We just don't have the manpower to cover even half of it, either."

"Have you managed to find out any more about her? Or her ex-husband?"

"I've spoken again to one of her neighbours, the one who had the key. Harriet seems to have trusted her. Mostly, it was the typical 'she kept herself to herself' kind of feedback. It is clear, however, that she was planning to have a burglar alarm fitted, and that she was anxious about people hanging around the area, on the nearby redway. She wanted one of those security lights, too – the ones that come on when there's any movement. It all suggests that she didn't feel entirely secure at home."

I nodded.

"That's why she was so appreciative of being with me, then. She said I made her feel safe. It worried me that she didn't generally feel like that."

"Yep, there's something there, all right. But whether it has anything to do with her disappearance, we just don't know."

"And the ex-husband?"

He sat up a bit straighter and his voice took on a firmer tone.

"The inspector and I interviewed him together. Not a nice man, I would say. Quite a bit older than Harriet. I found him arrogant and rude, and the inspector did not take to him at all. Told me afterwards she pegged him as a chauvinist. He was very voluble about the divorce. All her fault, of course, as far as he was concerned. He was simply taking care of her, protecting her, sometimes from herself. She was too trusting, too naïve, and prone to wasting time and energy on useless lame ducks. He hated her family, called them spongers. Was actually proud of having detached her from them completely." There was a touch of sarcasm in his voice.

I shivered. It sounded like controlling behaviour. And Rob clearly did not like him.

"In the end, it seems, she rebelled against his domineering attitude, and left him, quite abruptly. Even went to a shelter for protection to start with. Completely unnecessary, according to him. He insisted he had never hurt her, not even when she was being childish and stupid. Some work colleague had encouraged her to leave. He was angry about that. Interfering cow, he called her. He fought hard to hold on to Harriet. Eventually, the divorce came through, and their house had to be sold. He was furious about it."

"I can imagine."

"She found a small place in Giffard Park to live in, apparently because there are good bus links to the city, and tried to keep the address from him. He settled in Woburn Sands. But, when we pushed him on it, he admitted to following her bus home from the centre and finding out where she lived. Keeping track of her activities. Even watching her in the shops, checking whether she was meeting anyone. He said it was for her own protection. He was worried about predatory men."

He laughed, shortly.

"That sounds like stalking!" I exclaimed.

He nodded.

"I agree. Suspicious and unpleasant. No wonder she felt unsafe. That kind of behaviour would be very frightening. If harm has come to her, he will definitely be a suspect. But it doesn't seem to tie in with what happened on Tuesday. Other than explaining why you felt she might be vulnerable. And possibly why she might keep her identity and her plans private."

He was right. It did explain some of her nervousness and the lack of self-confidence I had sensed in her. She had been through a lot. No one would come out of that unscathed. I could see that in my sister.

"Hopefully, you'll get some more sightings soon. Or she might even turn up. I'm still hoping, but it's becoming increasingly unlikely, isn't it? With all the publicity, she must know people are looking for her, if she's alive, and well."

He grunted assent.

"I'm afraid you need to face facts, Tessa. At this point, she's almost certainly dead. But we do need to find her body. And work out whether it is accident or suicide."

"Or murder."

He shook his head rather dismissively.

"I think that's unlikely. I know you feel sure that she was meeting someone, and it's possible that you are right. Not the former husband, though. I think we can be pretty sure of that."

I nodded. That would not fit at all. Rob continued.

"But even so, it's not likely that the person she was meeting would have tried to hurt her. That kind of thing is pretty rare, you know. It's possible that they had a sudden row, she became upset, ran off, and threw herself in the lake. The man would probably keep quiet about what happened, out of embarrassment or guilt feelings. That might explain the phone and purse being found so far apart. Perhaps they argued by the bridge and she went into the lake on the other side."

That was a possible explanation which had not occurred to me. It did seem to fit the facts, although I still felt, in my bones, that it was unlikely.

"That's what the inspector is inclined to think," said Rob. "But we're pulling out all the stops to find her, don't worry."

I nodded. I could see that from his evident exhaustion.

"Will you come now and check the purse for us? Forensics have had a quick look but it's at the station now, so that you can identify it, if possible."

"I'll do my best. I can't promise, though."

We walked down together, close but not touching. Silent, but engaged in shared thoughts. Both reflecting on the frustrating puzzle this case had become.

Another mercilessly bright room. The purse was in an evidence bag. Rob nodded to me.

"It's fine to take it out. We've checked it for prints. I'll take a DNA sample from you, for exclusion purposes, if you think it is hers, and get the lab to give it a more thorough going over."

Hesitantly, I pulled it out of the bag. It was still rather sodden. I closed my eyes for a moment, thinking back to the instant when she had taken money out of her purse to pay me. Bringing back the mental picture. It had a silver coloured clasp, rather old-fashioned, and quite distinctive. Zip section for coins, closed. Wallet slot for notes. They weren't folded, there was room for them to lie flat.

I looked at the purse they had found. It was identical. A similar wad of notes. Everything the same as the one that I had caught a glimpse of. A slight wave of nausea rose in my stomach. I knew it was not a good sign that this had been found. She would not have left it behind willingly. Unfortunately, I was now certain it belonged to her.

I looked up at Rob, surprised to feel tears in my eyes. I was not generally prone to them.

"I'm sure this is hers. The clasp, shape, the notes. All the same. You don't see many of this design nowadays. I – I suppose this means she's almost certainly dead."

My voice wobbled as I said the word.

Rob took the purse and returned it to the bag, before clasping my cold hand in his.

"I'm afraid so, Tessa. You knew it was likely. I'm so sorry."

I lowered my eyes, thinking of her. Sad for her. A stranger, but someone I might have liked. A booklover, like me.

"Thank you so much for your help, anyway, Tess. I'll send this off for DNA testing, although I have my doubts that they'll find anything, except perhaps her own under the clasp. We have that from her toothbrush and hairbrush."

The details were somehow revolting. She had lost all her privacy, all dignity in death, and yet she had seemed like a very private, self-contained person. Like me in that way, I supposed. The uncovered similarities were uncomfortable.

"We'll just quickly take your DNA and then you can go. You look as if you're ready for a rest." There was compassion in Rob's weary voice.

I looked up. He was also in need of a break, but I didn't suppose he would take one. I nodded acceptance and did the mouth swab DNA sample meekly, in silence.

"One more thing, Tessa. You mentioned that there were two cars in the car park when you dropped Harriet off. I don't suppose you noticed anything particular about them, did you? Even make and colour might help. They may be totally unrelated, but no one has come forward yet, saying that they were parked in the vicinity."

It had not occurred to me to wonder about them.

"I guess you're right. One of them may belong to the person who met her, and if not, they might possibly have seen her. At least they were definitely in the area. It's worth a try."

I closed my eyes and breathed deeply, trying to recover my memory snapshot of the car park when I arrived to drop Harriet off.

"One was a newish SUV, dark red, a Honda, I think, and 70 reg, but I don't know the rest of the plate."

"Wow – you really do have a good visual memory. And the

other?"

"That was older and more distinctive. Dark blue. Rather dirty and with a sticker about dogs on the back. That's what made me notice it. I think it was a Saab. Not sure of the number but it included a V and an E, I think."

I opened my eyes.

"Not much help, I'm afraid. If only I'd properly looked at the number plates. I'm so frustrated with myself. I missed seeing which way she went after I dropped her off, and now I can't even remember the cars properly."

"Hey, Tessa, most people wouldn't have any idea what cars they were. Possibly a colour, if we were very lucky. I suppose it's because cars are part of your job. You've been a big help. We can try to find out if any vehicles like that are linked to local addresses. It's a start."

I nodded, rather glumly. He was just being nice. I knew I should have done better.

"Would you like me to run you back up to the shopping centre?"

The kindness nearly blew my composure. I smiled weakly, nodded, and managed to express brief thanks.

It was strange, sitting in a car with him again. For some reason, it felt as if we were sitting much closer together, in that enclosed space, and I was much more aware of his strong physical presence. His intense personality filled the vehicle. I could smell his distinctive shower gel. I had always liked it. Being so near him was a little overwhelming, but quite comforting, too.

As he pulled up, his hand left the gear stick and clasped mine.

"Don't let it upset you too much, Tessa. We haven't found her yet. She could be alive. And you honestly have done everything you can to help. Try and forget it."

I nodded jerkily. I knew, however, that it would be impossible. The hope of finding her alive had made it all tolerable. Now, almost certain that she was dead, I was deeply upset, far more than I had expected. I had invested part of myself in the search for her, in attempting to rescue her. As if it were someone close we were looking for. Or me? Did I identify with her in some way? Possibly.

He released my hand, and we exchanged farewells. I could see sympathy in his eyes and knew that he understood how I was feeling. He had much more experience than I did of proximity to sudden death. And how it affected those involved.

"I'll call you in a day or so, to let you know how things are going."

I was grateful for that. I had to know what had happened.

CHAPTER SEVEN

Searching

Naomi could see, at once, that I was upset, and insisted on talking through the detail of what had happened. She prompted me with questions until it had all dripped or flooded out.

"Get it off your chest, Tessa. You'll feel better. And you know I'm interested. I promise I won't gossip about it. You can trust me to keep whatever you tell me confidential."

So I let it all go, all the worry and the puzzling details. When it was finished, I sat there motionless, like a lumpy sack of vegetables, with no energy or life left in me.

"For what it's worth, Tessa, I think you may be right about her meeting someone. But the police have far more experience than we do. Rob's right. Leave it to them. They'll do their best to find her. I'm afraid she's not likely to be still alive, though."

I nodded numbly. I knew. When it finally came, it would be bad news.

"Right, now we're going to try to forget all about it, at least for a while," said Naomi briskly.

She had time off that weekend and decided to arrange for us to go to the cinema and out for a meal that evening.

"You need a proper distraction. It'll do us both good. Bright lights and good food, after all the gloom."

I agreed, rather listlessly. Hoping that she was right.

The film did not do much for me. It was a romcom and amusing enough, in a light way, but it failed to hold my attention, which kept drifting away to Harriet, lying dead, in metres of cold, dark water. I had to force myself to focus on the story, for Naomi's sake. She was trying to help me.

We ate in the Xscape centre, at Namji. We both loved Indian food but rarely went out for it, so it was a real treat. The colourful décor immediately lifted my mood. We talked about summer holiday possibilities, and how to improve the miserably plain, wildlife desert of a garden we had inherited with our house. What kind of bird feeder to buy. Nice things, looking forward, to better times. I relaxed properly and felt the warmth of spice and conversation creep into me. Fell asleep, that evening, thinking of summer.

Sunday was a brighter day. It was wonderful to glimpse the sun after so much dull monochrome. I was determined to make the most of it and get some fresh air and exercise. I would go for a long walk. Spending so much time sitting in a cab, I valued any chance to stretch my limbs, get the blood pumping, and breathe deeply in unprocessed air.

The best place for that in the vicinity was Caldecotte Lake. I swallowed hard, and decided that I would walk all the way round it. It would be good for me, mentally and physically. And, somehow, I felt that I owed it to Harriet. Naomi was still in bed, so she was not there to dissuade me. It felt right to me. I was not rubbernecking, or ghoulishly curious, just paying my respects to her, as best I could.

And, secretly, hoping to find some clue to her whereabouts. It was possible, after all. Such a large area could not have been meticulously searched. Rob had mentioned a lack of manpower. I might spot something others had missed. I felt a desperate need to contribute somehow to the investigation, to make a difference to the search for my passenger. My missing person. It might seem egocentric or arrogant, but I sensed that I was intangibly linked to her, and that I still had a part to play, however small.

I dressed up warmly and put on my comfortable old walking boots, a lasting legacy of lockdown. Took the redway alongside the Heron schools and on towards the lake. Turned left at the bottom, past the pond area, thickly edged with feather-headed reeds in their beige winter colours, and then onto the winding path which led between the trees to the south section of the park.

Despite the bare branches, brownish water, and squidge of damp leaf mould on the paths, it was rejuvenating to be in such a wild environment, even so close to a main road. The traffic was thundering past up above, but I was in a different world, echoing with joyfully piercing birdsong. The robins and wrens seemed to be revelling in the blue sky, too. It lifted the soul. That part of the route was deserted, and sheltered from the keen wind. The solitude and sunshine exactly suited my reflective mood.

When I came to the road bridge, from the other side, my heart lurched suddenly. I could not help wondering if Harriet had actually died here, where her broken phone was found. There was nothing new to see, other than a haphazard pile of debris and rotting weed from the lake floor, stacked untidily by the side of the path. The smell of stagnant water and fermentation it released was unpleasant. I marched on quickly, eager to be back in the sun, away from this clinging shadow world.

As I rounded the corner to the wooden bridge, I could see that the circular car park was still cordoned off and full to bursting with police vehicles and equipment. It must have remained their base. I hurried past, my gaze averted, along to the corner where I had checked for her presence that afternoon.

The wind was strong on this exposed point. Seagulls floated jerkily on it, their plaintive calls transporting me to the seaside in winter. The cormorants were hanging their wings out to dry in their crowded colony, on the tall denuded branches of the wood at the end of the promontory. Their collective guano had painted two of the trees a ghostly white, glowing in the pale sunshine. Some flew past, like fast black winged arrows, heading for the open water to fish. A greylag goose honked mournfully, while the mallards' mocking laughter jeered at its sorrow.

As I allowed my eyes to drift over the open expanse of water, drinking in the rare sunlight, I could not avoid seeing, in the distance, incongruous police activity on the far side of the lake. Divers in the water, a boat, a van or two, police officers standing around. I wondered if Rob was with them. I turned away. The spell was broken.

The act of walking itself was, however, soothing my sadness, allowing my mind to meander more peacefully, instead of constantly circling the same painful images. I allowed my thoughts to float freely, drifting on the wind, basking in the unaccustomed glow of sun and exercise.

I pushed on past the sailing club, urged to pick up the pace by the rhythmic metallic jangling from the masts of the stored boats. I was largely ignoring the increasing number of walkers I encountered. Some of them smiled at me, as I would expect in this area, but others were far too engaged in their own loud and often tasteless conversations. The snatches I heard were not pleasant and I tried to shut them out. Malicious slurs, excited enjoyment of tragedy, unpleasant sneers.

"I bet she killed herself. Waste of time for the police to use their resources to find one stupid suicidal woman."

"Do you think she was murdered? Oooh, that would be so exciting. I'd love that. I do hope they find the corpse soon."

"I don't know why everyone's worrying about this. She's probably gone off with some new boyfriend and just not bothered to let anyone know."

Fortunately, the glare of the low sun hid their faces, turning them into vague dark silhouettes. I did not want to see the sneering mouths, avid eyes, and contemptuous expressions I could hear in their voices.

I knew that I was frowning, upset by the facile judgements and hasty conclusions. I consciously smoothed my forehead and tried to regain my former peace, looking out for the bobbing brown rabbits I had often spotted between the end of the lake and the railway line. None were to be seen. Too many people and dogs. Far more than usual. Like the crowds which had flocked to the area in Covid times.

As I passed the turn-off towards Fenny Stratford, weaving my way between groups and couples oblivious to my presence, and trying to avoid the self-absorbed speeding bikes, I saw uniformed police constables on both sides of the path, speaking to all the walkers and cyclists. I slowed obediently.

"Excuse me, madam, did you happen to be walking here last Tuesday? Or the previous week? We're looking for anyone who may have seen this woman, perhaps with a companion."

He thrust a copy of Harriet's photo under my nose.

I shook my head.

"No, sorry."

He had obviously not recognised me, and I was not going to try to explain how I was related to the case. It would be more trouble than it was worth. Better to let him get on with questioning others. I continued along the narrowing path, which had an awkward camber sloping towards the lake, making it more difficult to keep a steady pace. I kept my eyes on the route I was following, deliberately looking away from the police activity I was trying to pass. Today, it was not my business.

"Tessa! What on earth are you doing here?"

It was Rob's voice. He appeared beside me and gripped my arm, turning me towards him.

"I just had to come. Walk round for myself. For Harriet."

The anger faded out of his face.

"I should have known you wouldn't just be trying to nose out what we were doing. Sorry. I overreacted. There have been so many tragedy tourists, insisting on voicing their repellent opinions and theories, not to mention the press, bloggers, curious locals, and goodness knows who else. It's not a pleasant side of human nature."

I nodded.

"I can imagine. I heard some of what they were saying as I walked round. I tried to block it out, but without much success."

"Come over here, out of the way. I was going to ring this evening, anyway, to update you."

We moved to the far side of the police van, closer to the lake, out of view, and sheltered from the icily penetrating westerly.

"Any progress at all?" I asked.

"Not a lot, I'm afraid. One probable sighting, but not from last Tuesday. From the previous week. In this area, where the path is quite narrow."

"Was she alone?"

"That's where it gets a little more interesting. People often have to walk in single file here, to allow others past, and, apparently, there was a man in front of her and also one close behind. She might have been alone, or with one or other of them. Or even both! Unfortunately, the witness can't give us any description of them at all, not even general height or build. She remembered Harriet only because of her beaming smile. She looked so radiantly happy, on what was a fairly gloomy, dull day."

"Mm, that is interesting. What a shame we can't tell if she had a companion! Or what he was like if there was one."

"I know. That's police work for you. Still, it's one small step forward, in that this sighting confirms what Harriet told you, and explains why she might have wanted to return, given her evident enjoyment of the walk. But it's no real help in finding her."

It was disappointing. I took it, however, as further validation of my theory that she had been meeting someone. Rob gestured towards the lake and its unusual surface decoration of small boats and divers' heads.

"We're focusing our search over here now, since the purse was found in this area and she was seen here, even if not on the same day. It's taking a very long time, however, because visibility underwater is extremely poor, after all the rain we've had, and the lake is very full."

"Do you now think she was on her way to see someone?"

He grinned ruefully.

"Yes, we think you're probably right about that. Sorry we didn't take you more seriously, at first. But whether she did meet and walk with a man, missed him and walked alone, or didn't walk at all – whatever actually happened, all our ideas on that are pure speculation, I'm afraid. We are asking people if they might have seen a couple, though. Not just a lone woman."

That was progress, at least.

"What about the cars? Any luck there?"

"We have managed to trace the Honda driver, in fact. He hadn't seen any of the publicity or requests for witnesses. But he hadn't noticed anything, either. Not exactly an observant bloke, unfortunately."

He sighed.

"He did return to his car, about twenty minutes after you dropped her off, though, from the road bridge side. Since he says he didn't encounter her, or anyone else, we're tending to think she went in the opposite direction, now. Despite the phone. I suppose someone might have picked the phone up further along and then discarded it under the bridge, once they realised it was broken."

That seemed to me to be a convoluted and unlikely explanation for its presence.

"I'm sure it wasn't there on Tuesday, anyway. Perhaps you're right. Someone found it and then got rid of it a few days later when we started searching for Harriet."

Rob looked sceptical, but I was sure of my memory on this. It had been left or placed there later.

"Any luck with DNA on the purse?"

He smiled faintly.

"Again, one tiny step forward but no real leads. We put a rush on it, as you'll imagine. Her DNA was found inside the purse and on some of the money. And yours, of course. But there was an unknown trace under the clasp as well. Not on our databases, unfortunately, so it doesn't take us anywhere. But if we were to find the man who seems to have been involved, we'd be able to check him against it. So it could prove useful in the end."

Some clear confirmation that I had been correct in identifying it as belonging to Harriet, at least. That was a relief. Rob pushed his hair back off his forehead and sighed.

"You were lucky to find me here, actually. I'm spending most of my time following up leads elsewhere and on the phone. I'm off back to the station now. Do you want a lift?"

I shook my head, determined to complete my circuit.

"No, I've still got quite a long way to go. I think it'll be quieter on the north lake. I'll be able to think better. Remember her in my own way. Good luck with your leads. I really hope you find her soon. I have to know what happened to her."

"I can understand that. I'll keep in touch. Bye, Tessa, love."

"Bye, Rob."

I moved off. My brain felt a little foggy, but I had been startled by him calling me 'love'. That was the way he used to say goodbye. It shook me. I persuaded myself, however, that it was like a kiss on a message, and meant nothing. We were, after all, only friends now.

I was right about the north lake. Once I was past the busy pub, the swarms of passers-by swiftly thinned out, and I was able to recapture my reflective mood. Only a few brightly clad runners to avoid.

There were plenty of wild fowl and songbirds to spot on the lake and in the bushes, whose bright red and yellow branches brought welcome colour, even in the depths of winter. I relished the twists and turns of the path which lent this route a pleasantly rural atmosphere. Each corner exposed a new vista and a different angle on the cleverly landscaped parkland.

The weir was roaring, as I passed it, torrents of brown water pouring through, down to the already flooded river. It often burst its banks here, out onto the flood plain next to Simpson village. I was stunned by the power of its flow, its ability to evade all human efforts to control it.

A moment of enchantment, as I spotted a mature heron, standing in the edge of the muddy floodwater, its pterodactyl-like head cocked and neck stretched as it looked for prey. I stood and watched it for several minutes, fascinated by its incredible stillness. When I first lived in the area, they were a rare sight, and they had never lost their magic for me. I'd even seen little egrets, their pure white cousins, by the river, on several occasions. They always seemed to me like harbingers of good fortune, bringing delicate delight on soaring wings.

Transported by the peace of this part of my walk, I prayed silently that Harriet would be found soon. As well as the man she had been meeting. He had to be held responsible for all this uncertainty, worry, and distress. He should, at the very least, have responded to the calls for information to tell what he knew.

Of course, he might have chosen not to do so, because he was guilty of some crime, and had hurt her in some way. Even killed her. Rob did not seem to think it was likely, but to me it appeared to be a disturbing possibility.

CHAPTER EIGHT

More Questions

The local news that evening again majored on the search for Harriet. The purse was displayed, and I was surprised to hear the junior officer, who seemed to be running the update that night, state that it had been identified by 'her taxi-driver, Tessa Fordham', and confirmed by DNA traces. Not what I wanted or expected. I had not given permission for them to publicise my name in that way. I must speak to Rob about it.

Back at work that Monday, I found the constant questioning even more tiresome. There were also a good many more male passengers, a number of whom had, according to Sally, asked for me specifically.

"I think we'd better stop accepting that kind of request, Sally. It's not how we normally work. Tell them that they are booking a cab, not a particular driver. I don't particularly want to be driving sensation-seekers or amateur sleuths, let alone reporters."

"That makes a lot of sense, Tessa. I've been a bit worried that I might be putting you at risk, accepting those particular bookings. There are all kinds of weirdos out there, and I don't want you to be stuck in your taxi with one."

I shuddered at the thought. Unlike traditional black cabs, our cars had no protective screens for the drivers. Time to do something about it.

"We've been doing well for the last month or so. I think we need to look into installing CCTV in all our cabs. We're all women, and it would give us some extra protection. Up until now, most of our fares have been people who feel vulnerable themselves, and mainly female, but the clientele seems to be changing. I don't want any of us victimised or, God forbid, anything awful to happen. Harriet's disappearance has brought home to me how precarious everyday life can be. And it might make some of our passengers feel safer, too. Can you research the costs for me, when you have time?"

Sally's voice was full of relief.

"I'm so glad you said that, Tess. I've been starting to get really concerned, not just about you, but the others too. At least when people book through the app there's some information about them on the system. But we're getting a lot of phone bookings at the moment and that's much less secure for us."

"Yes, you're right. They can give a false name, like Harriet did, and pay by cash, and then we're none the wiser. They become untraceable. Find out how easy it will be to set up and we'll get a system installed, as soon as possible. And I think you can stop special requests for individual drivers from now on, unless it's one of our regulars."

"Agreed. I feel much happier about that. Thanks, Tessa. I'm afraid you've got two more special trips this afternoon, but that'll be the end of it."

I would be very relieved when they were done. I definitely felt more exposed, when I knew a male passenger had requested me personally. All the publicity around my role in the case had made me a target.

I avoided social media personally, but Naomi had spoken of nasty comments, and even threats she had seen online, and Sally had been forced to remove the ability to comment on the company's Facebook posts. I had chosen not to look, but apparently quite a few trolls had been emboldened to comment on my personal appearance and make disgusting propositions. I had been lucky with John, my friendly reporter. He could have been someone much more threatening.

The first of my afternoon requested trips was another reporter, from a local radio station. He was quite pleasant about it, and I did not feel unsafe, but I refused to allow him to record an interview, and answered his questions with brief, unemotional statements, similar to my prepared written comment. He was disappointed. I could hear that in his voice.

"I'd just like to give a personal angle to this story, Miss Fordham," he said, pleadingly. "We know almost nothing about this Harriet Beckinsale. It would be so much more compelling if we had an exclusive interview with you, about her, and about how you feel, personally, about the whole thing. Give it a bit of human interest."

"I understand what you are saying, but I'm afraid the answer is still 'no'. I don't want that kind of cheap publicity. The focus needs to be on finding her, not on me. I'm only involved incidentally. Why don't you get an interview with one of the detectives? They'd have more to tell you, I should think."

I laughed inside at the thought of the short shrift he would receive from the inspector.

"I have tried. They were rather insulting. About me and my programme. Said it would be a waste of their time, for such a small audience."

"Oh dear, that doesn't sound very polite." I was unable to keep the amusement out of my voice.

He alighted at the city centre, obviously disgruntled. Probably going to try for a *vox pop* or two among the shoppers. Any personal reaction would be better than none.

The final one was different. A middle-aged man, with very dull black hair, which I suspected was not his natural colour, given his light brown brows and eyelashes, and rather pale grey eyes.

Trying to disguise grey hairs, no doubt. He was very polite and respectful, and I began to relax my guard a little. He asked to be taken to Caldecotte Lake.

"I'm afraid I can't take you to the car park where I dropped Harriet Beckinsale, you know. It's still cordoned off by the police."

"Thank you. That will not be a problem. You may drop me nearby, on Monellan Crescent."

This one had obviously done his research. Looked at the map. Or knew the area well. He had not, so far, asked any prying questions or demanded an interview. I was curious about why he would have requested me as a driver.

"Do you mind me asking why you wanted me to drive you today? Why you asked for me specifically?"

There was a lengthy pause. I felt myself flush slightly. It was not my place to ask. He was the paying customer.

"Not at all, Miss Fordham." He evidently knew my name from all the reports. "I was interested to see the woman who was so central to the police investigation, that's all. Mere personal curiosity, I suppose you would say. You haven't chosen to be interviewed on television and seem to be an instinctively private individual, so taking your cab was the only way for me to satisfy my interest in you."

"Oh," was all I could think of to say. I was distinctly uncomfortable with this line of conversation.

"It seems that, without your remarkable intervention, the police would have had no idea where to look for the missing woman. They haven't exactly done well in their current attempts to discover her."

There was a slight sneer in his voice at that point. A touch of contempt.

"But it would have been a much greater challenge if they had been searching across the whole city. In fact, they could not have been certain that she had not left Milton Keynes altogether. Or that she was actually missing."

"I suppose that's true. But anyone else would have done the same and reported it, I'm sure."

"I don't think so. You seem to have contacted them proactively, well before there was any publicity about her being missing. Not many people would have made the effort to do that."

I shook my head a little. It sounded like a compliment, but was delivered in a cold, almost critical tone.

"I was concerned about her. I'm sure other drivers would have felt the same. We have a kind of duty of care towards vulnerable passengers."

He laughed. A slightly mocking tone.

"You have a very idealistic view of your job! Most cabbies are only focused on earning as much as possible, in my experience. They might have been annoyed at the lost fare, but that's all. You responded very differently. And now, having seen and spoken to you, I understand why."

I mumbled something non-committal. I did not want to hear his opinion of me. Probably as a meddling busybody. Or something worse.

We turned into Caldecotte, and I drove slowly around the curve of Monellan Crescent.

"Anywhere here is fine, thank you, Miss Fordham."

I pulled up.

"I would like to pay cash, please."

Oh dear, not another one.

"If you prefer."

He gave a good tip, rounding the fare up to fit the note he proffered. No receipt required.

"Thank you, Mr Brown."

That was the name he had given when booking. Another very plain one.

He smiled suddenly, what looked like genuine amusement lightening his impassive face.

"You're very welcome."

He stood still, waiting, on the pavement until I was completely out of sight. I saw that in my mirror. So I had no idea where he was going. Did he live in the area or was he visiting the lake to see for himself where the drama had happened? He had spoken of interest and curiosity, yet there had been none in his tone of voice. He was a strange one, that was for sure.

For no particular reason I could fathom, I chose to use the circuit offered by the road pattern to double back on myself, driving past the spot where I had left him. He was gone. There was no sign of him at all. A mystery wrapped in an enigma.

My last fare that day was one of our nicest regulars, an elderly lady, who had given up her car the previous year, and used us several times a week. We gave her a special rate. It was a real pleasure to see her benevolent face again.

"How are you, Tessa, dear? I saw you on the television. It must be difficult being involved in such a prominent case. I've been praying for you, and the missing woman."

"That's so kind of you, Mrs Brettham. It has been quite stressful and, as you say, the publicity is difficult for me. I've never enjoyed the limelight. And I – I've been very worried about Harriet Beckinsale. I hoped, for a long time, that she would turn up, alive and well. But I don't think that's likely any more. It's so sad. She seemed like a very nice person."

"It sounds as if you did everything you could to help. I'm sure the police are doing their best. I know Caldecotte fairly well. Used to enjoy walking there with my husband. It's such a large and difficult area to search."

"Mm. And I can't forget it, or put it behind me until she's found, and we know what has happened to her."

"I'll pray for that, too, dear. Try not to worry too much. If she's already dead, nothing more can hurt her, after all. It's just a body now, not the real person."

What a strange way of looking at it! But comforting, in a way. Harriet would not be aware of being in the water, of decomposing, or being swept along by dark tides. She was safe, in a sense, her spirit gone from her body.

I was grateful to Mrs Brettham. It was a very different perspective, which helped me to deal with the uncertainty better. I still wanted her found and her story told, but it was less urgent. The situation could not become any worse for Harriet personally, whether that took days, weeks, or even months. She was beyond pain and distress.

CHAPTER NINE

Shocking Discovery

Several days passed without any encouraging developments. Rob informed me, apologetically, that the search was to be scaled back.

"It's just such a vast area, and we can't possibly know where she entered the water. Or even if she actually did. She could have walked anywhere, or been transported to the other end of the city by the friend she met. We have a couple more days with the specialist teams and then we'll have to cut it down. We'll keep it an open investigation, but with no body, no sightings, and no more leads, we have to move on to other cases, with more chance of resolution."

I was deeply disappointed. He could see it on my face. Tried to rally my spirits.

"We still may find traces in the next few days. Or something may come to light, as the water levels drop. We're due for a few days of drier weather, it seems."

"It just feels so wrong to give up on her like that. If – if it was Naomi, or a friend of mine, I'd be devastated if we never found them."

His eyes were full of sympathy.

"I know. I – I've sometimes caught myself thinking, 'what if it were Tessa?' It's a horrible idea. I know my colleagues feel the same. We've all got families and can imagine how we'd feel. But our resources aren't infinite, you know that."

"I suppose so." My voice was very subdued.

"Will you still meet me for coffee, sometimes, Tessa? I've loved having you back in my life. Someone I can talk to, even about cases, and know for sure that you'll keep it confidential. You have no idea what a precious thing that is."

There was longing in his tone, and a naked vulnerability in his face that I had not perceived before. I was surprised that he felt so strongly, but had to admit that my own pleasure in his company was very real.

"I – I suppose so. I've found it good to talk to you, too. My job makes it difficult to meet up with others at normal times and Naomi's shifts are even worse. It's been nice to have you as a friend."

He reached over the table and clasped my hand. I was shocked to feel his fingers trembling a little, and his skin was clammy and cold.

"Are you OK, Rob? You feel as if you might have caught a chill. It's not surprising, having to be outside all that time, in such dreadful weather. Please look after yourself. You could make yourself really ill."

He smiled, a little tightly.

"You care so much, don't you, Tessa? About everyone. Even people you barely know. It must be exhausting."

I did not understand what he meant. Of course, I cared, and especially about him. We had known each other for years and had recently been very close. My puzzlement must have shown on my face, because he spoke again.

"Don't worry, love. Nothing for you to be concerned about. I'll be fine. I'll give you a last update before we close down the search, and then we can arrange a purely social meeting."

I nodded, still uncertain, and confused by his odd reactions. I wanted to hug him as we parted, to make him feel better. His expression was so sad and lost. I compromised by touching him gently on the shoulder.

"See you soon, Rob. Try to take it easy when you can."

His mouth tightened, as if he were in distress or pain and wanted to conceal it.

"Bye, Tessa, love."

He turned away, abruptly, and marched off determinedly. Did not look back. I had a lump in my throat. Concern for him, of course. Nothing more.

The local obsession with Harriet's disappearance was finally beginning to abate. Work returned to normal, more or less, although the upturn in business persisted. I was frustrated that we had no answers, but there was nothing at all I could do about it. Only hope that, one day, the truth would come out. My mind no longer circled the case constantly. Just at night, when I closed my eyes for sleep.

Then, as the search was about to be called off, I received an unexpected phone call from Rob. His voice was intense and very serious.

"Tessa. Good, I've reached you. Please can you cancel any jobs for the next few hours and come to the Open University. I need you."

My instinct was to obey without question, but I felt the need to ask. I was not his subordinate, after all. I must learn to be more assertive.

"Why? What's happened?"

A slight pause.

"I'll tell you when you get here. Come along from the new roundabout near Simpson and pull into the first car park on your left. You'll see us."

Without more ado, he rang off. Curt to the point of rudeness. I knew it must be genuinely urgent. Sally agreed to find alternatives for all my rides, and I made my way south through Milton Keynes, past the busy bustling Willen Lake area and on down Brickhill Street. I tried to keep my mind on the driving and ignore the bursting bubbles of trepidation in my stomach.

It was late afternoon and already the darkness was closing in. I detested the gloom of winter, and this year, we had missed out on sparkling, cold, bright days. Stormy, wet and drab, instead. We were all yearning desperately for the first signs of spring.

It was the first time I had turned right at the new roundabout with its odd slope, and I had only rarely been into the Open University grounds, most recently for a Covid jab. I spotted the car park he had mentioned without difficulty, and could, indeed, hardly ignore the police presence at the far end of it, with vans, equipment, and blazing white floodlights. I drew up some way away, and nerved myself to leave the cosy cocoon of my cab.

I was glad that I had taken the time to put on my coat. It was cold, and sharp gusts of wind pushed against me as I walked over, rather hesitantly, unsure of what I might find and who to report to. The lights were quite blinding against the glowering sky. It felt as if I was walking into the darkness and peril of an interrogation room. I could not even make out the ground in front of my feet. I raised my hand to provide some protection from the glare.

From just behind and to the left of me, I heard Rob's comfortingly familiar voice. Something to hold onto in the waves of apprehension which flooded through me.

"Tessa. You made it. Come with me."

I turned obediently towards him.

"What's this all about, Rob?"

He did not answer, but took my arm and hurried me over to a dark blue marked van, inviting me to sit in the front seat, but turned towards the open door. I was increasingly puzzled. He stood facing me, his expression extremely grave, examining me carefully, for some reason. I could not help feeling even more nervous.

"I'm sorry to bring you in like this, Tess. I don't feel that I have an alternative, and the inspector was quite insistent. She – she said you were a tough cookie, underneath, and would cope."

Cope with what? That sounded even more intimidating. I began to shiver, more from anxious tension than chill. His voice became lower, almost a growl. The words shot out, rapidly.

"I – I'm afraid we've found a body. Well, it wasn't us, actually. A dog. It dragged the corpse half out of the river, near the bridge here, before its owner could call it off and pull it away. He contacted us straight away, thank goodness. We've brought it out onto the bank, for now, but obviously we need to take it in for further examination."

I was dazed by the fast stream of words, not taking in anything other than the word body. And it. Not her.

"Is it Harriet?"

The words burst from me unbidden.

He paused.

"That's why we've called on you. We believe that it is her. I'm sorry."

It hit me quite hard. A shock of stunning coldness, like being doused in icy water.

"What do you need from me?"

He spoke a little more gently.

"We need a decent identification. Some certainty. We'll call on a family member, later, and use DNA for confirmation, but you're the only one who saw her recently. I know we could ask a work colleague, but choosing, contacting, and getting hold of someone, right now, would not be easy. The inspector thinks you'll be the best person. You've been very helpful so far."

"Are you sure? Can't you just identify her from the photograph?"

He shook his head.

"We need to be positive. And you can identify her clothing, as well."

"OK. I suppose that's true. I'll do it."

I could not prevent a shake in my voice. He reached out a hand and took hold of mine, wrapping it in his warm grasp.

"I knew we could rely on you. I'm afraid it's not going to be very pleasant, however. It never is, seeing a dead body, but it's much harder if you know the person. And – well, as you know, she's been missing for quite a while, and probably dead for all or most of that time. And immersed for a lengthy period in water."

The reality could not possibly be worse than the grotesque image which swelled in my mind. I swallowed down the nausea which rose inside me.

"Can we please get it over with?"

I was pleased that I sounded relatively firm. More confident than I felt.

He nodded, compassion in his dark eyes, which were glittering brightly in the reflection of the powerful light. He helped me out of the van and took me to the end of the car park, lighting my way with a torch. We walked down a pathway almost overshadowed by high hedges, past a small churchyard, ominous with shadowy gravestones in the darkening twilight. On down to the riverbank, where a small white tent stood out against the gloom, familiar enough from news footage and detective programmes.

I realised that I was holding my breath. Stopped for a moment, outside the tent, trying to gain control of the currents of unruly emotions surging through me. Rob turned to me, eyebrows raised.

"Ready?"

I nodded.

"Can you put these covers on your shoes? We don't want to add any more trace evidence to the mess we already have."

He supported me as I put them on, then followed my example. He lifted the tent door aside and urged me through it.

Inside, intensely bright lights banished the shadows, dazzling me for a moment. I blinked twice.

"Is this her? We need to do this quickly, sergeant. Once out of the water, immersed bodies decompose much more quickly, and I need to begin the autopsy as soon as possible."

The brisk voice, emanating from a man almost totally enveloped in white protective gear, steadied me. I had a job to do. An important if unenviable task.

"Come forward, Miss Fordham."

"Tessa, please."

Why did I say that? What did it matter what he called me? We were never going to be friends.

I advanced hesitantly. Part of me afraid even to look. But needing to see, to find out the truth.

Still lying on the wet, grassy bank, head askew, mouth gaping open, filled and smeared with viscous brown sludge, her eyes mercifully closed and concealed, was Harriet. Despite the state of her body, battered, filthy, liberally strewn with entangling strips of weed, she was unmistakable. I had seen her face so often in my mind's eye since her disappearance.

My eyes were glued to her face, exposed to the pitiless, revealing light. A strange sort of horror gripped me. There was a rushing in my ears and a sudden heave in my stomach.

"Quick, sergeant, she's either going to faint or vomit."

Rob's reassuring arm came round me, bringing me out of the

trance. I was not sick, but did retch unpleasantly, before apologising.

"Don't apologise. I – I felt it myself, and I'm used to this kind of distressing sight. I have to ask, Tessa, is it her?" he said, compassion and gentleness in his tone.

As if it came from a long way away, I heard my voice speaking clearly and with deliberation.

"That is the woman I drove to Caldecotte Lake, who called herself Smith, but whom I now know to be Harriet Beckinsale."

"Exemplary."

The gowned man seemed to be impressed by my clarity.

Emboldened, I dared to look more closely, to examine the rest of her body.

"She – she's not wearing the same clothes. Completely different. She was in jeans and a coat, not a dress."

Despite being sodden and stained, it was evident that the material was patterned, floral. Not the style of thing she had chosen on that Tuesday. It was rucked up, exposing the top of her poor thin white legs. My eyes slid swiftly away to her feet, which were naked under their patina of foul sticky mud. She had not been dressed for winter.

"Interesting," said the white-clad figure, almost camouflaged against the bright tent.

Rob nodded thoughtfully.

"Indicative. A strong confirmation."

I ignored their cryptic words.

"How did she die? Do you know yet? Was it here that she went into the water?"

Important questions, but it was not my place to ask them, not really. I expected to be shut down or given some brief, non-committal, professional answer.

"I don't have a definitive cause of death yet. That will have to wait for the post-mortem. But she did not drown, of that I am quite certain. She has not been in the water for more than two or three days, although she has been dead for much longer than that. Since soon after she went missing, I would estimate. Then kept, or rather stored, somewhere cool. But not frozen, I think. That's pretty clear from the condition of the skin and the body."

There was a strong sense of relief alongside the instinctive disgust at the details. If she had been alive all that time, it would have been terrible to think that we had not found and rescued her. And to imagine what she might have been suffering. Why would anyone hold onto her dead body for so long, though? That was definitely odd. The calm, analytical voice continued.

"She is likely to have gone into the river recently, some way upstream from here, and been carried along by the strong current, since it is in flood. As you will gather, I do not consider this to have been a death from natural causes or a suicide, especially given the date when she was first declared missing. It is, therefore, essential that I am able to carry out the post-mortem without delay, so I am most grateful to you for agreeing to identify the body for us. It means that we can proceed immediately and begin a thorough search of the area, here and upstream, for any indications as to how she came to be in the river."

I blinked again. I was amazed to receive such a detailed answer, which seemed to be directed at Rob as much as me.

"Thank you, doctor. That's very clear. I'll send the team down to move the body and we'll begin searches, as soon as you've cleared the way."

His arm still around my waist, Rob led me out of that terrible bleached-white place. I stumbled as we entered the enveloping darkness and would have fallen without his support. The cold air seemed to hit my stomach, and I retched again, turning away to vomit, as far from his shoes as possible.

A constable appeared and took his place, standing next to me, while Rob hurried off to pass on the vital messages to his colleagues. Embarrassed, I gradually managed to calm my spasms and straighten up, slowly.

"Feeling a bit better, now, Miss? Come with me, then. Do you need to hold my arm?" The voice was sympathetic, not disdainful.

I shook my head, wiping my mouth with a scrunched up tissue from my pocket. I would have liked the support, but felt the need to demonstrate some semblance of dignity and self-control. He seemed to sense that I was feeling ashamed of myself.

"Don't worry, Miss. We've all been there. It's a natural physical reaction. Come along. I've got a torch."

Staggering occasionally, I managed to follow him back up the dark path. At this point, the presence of the church and graveyard was comforting, rather than threatening. It provided a strange kind of appropriate dignity for Harriet in death. Something denied her by the killer.

The inspector was addressing her troops when we got back to the car park, distributing jobs with practised efficiency. She nodded an acknowledgement to me, as I stumbled past. Rob appeared beside me, to relieve the constable. He put his arm around my shoulders. An intimate gesture which I found immensely comforting.

"I'm so sorry I let myself and you down, there, Rob. I just couldn't help it. It suddenly hit me so hard, and I couldn't keep it down."

He squeezed me tighter.

"You did nothing of the kind. I'm really proud of you. The inspector is pleased, too. She – we both understand it was a big ask. She's told me to drive you home and make sure you get a hot cup of tea and something to eat before I come back to help."

"You don't need to do that. I can manage. I'm fine, now."

Even to me, it sounded like a token protest. I was feeling far too shaky to drive myself safely. Although it felt like midnight to me, in reality it was early evening, and the roads would be full of tired workers eager to reach home. Rob ignored my words.

"We can send a car to bring you back to collect your cab, tomorrow."

"It's no problem. One of the girls will bring me. Thank you, Rob. I have to admit that I'm feeling pretty off balance."

"It's entirely understandable, Tessa. I'm sorry to have had to ask you to do it."

"I'm glad I was able to do one last thing for Harriet."

It was true. There was a lasting stain of guilt on my conscience, although I knew that it was unmerited. It was not my fault. I just wished I had not been the one to leave her there, to meet someone who seemed to have been a brutal murderer.

Seeing again, in the over-sharp focus of my memory, her poor battered face, her swollen body, dumped like that on the riverbank, like a pile of rubbish dragged from the flood, I was suddenly overwhelmed with sadness, and tears came in a torrent. Huge sobs, quite uncontrollable. We had arrived at Rob's car, but before we got in, he put his arms around me and held me tight, his mouth pressed against my hair, soothing me with meaningless inanities, until the shakes and desperate crying eased.

Eventually, some semblance of calm returned, and he helped me gently into the vehicle. Took off the muddy shoe covers. Insisted on attaching the seatbelt for me.

He had to ask for my address. He had never seen the Walnut Tree house. It had been part of my supposed new start. Like me, he knew his way around the city, and had satnav for the minor roads, so I did not need to direct him. I entrusted myself to him and closed my eyes, letting go completely. He turned the heating up and the warmth gradually relaxed my tensed muscles.

"Can I pull onto the drive?" he asked, quietly, as we arrived.

I stirred myself to look up, seeing our new home through his eyes. Small, or rather compact, as the estate agent had put it, but attractive, the red brick warm in the glow of the street light outside. Semi-detached, with a garage and, importantly, plenty of space on the drive for two cars. The kind of place Rob and I might have chosen together, if we had progressed to marriage and a family. Very unlike the rather poky, dingy rented flat I had lived in, alone, when we were still together. Sharing with Naomi had meant we could afford a little more space and privacy.

The windows were darkened, only the porch light was on. She must be at work already. I was glad of that. I did not feel able to tell her, yet, what had happened.

He switched the engine off. Turned to look at me, frowning slightly.

"Will your husband or boyfriend mind me coming in?"

My mouth fell open. Had we really not talked about this? I shook my head slowly, in puzzled disbelief.

"I – I share this house with Naomi. My sister. You must remember her. She's split up from her husband. I thought you knew. I was sure I'd told you, talked about it."

He reddened.

"I don't think so. I would definitely have remembered. I – I just assumed that you would have settled with someone else, by now. I thought you must be living with him, as you had moved."

I gaped at him.

"It's only been a few months. That would have been quick work."

His face turned a darker red.

"I'm so sorry. I wasn't trying to judge or insult you. I know I was wrong when I accused you of seeing someone when we split up. You would never do that. But I thought you wanted to settle down, have a family. I assumed – I hoped you would have found someone nice by now."

It was my turn to blush.

"This isn't the right time or place to talk about it, but – I haven't even dated anyone yet. I've been focusing on work and sorting the house out with Naomi."

An embarrassing admission. No one had even asked me out. I hurried on.

"So, no, you won't disturb anyone. She's at work at this hour. Anyway, are you coming in?"

He nodded. His face was still flushed.

"I've had my instructions. Thank you for not being angry with me. I'm sorry I got it all wrong again."

I struggled out of the car, a little faint and dizzy. It was too much emotional turmoil, all at once.

He hurried round to offer me his arm.

"You're still feeling shaky. It's only to be expected."

I fumbled with the keys but managed, eventually, to open the door, and put on plenty of lights, to make it feel more welcoming. We had kept some fairy lights in the living room after Christmas, unwilling to give up their comforting twinkle in the depressing long nights of January.

"This is really nice, Tessa. I like it. It's very you. Where's the kitchen?"

I took him through. Fortunately, Naomi was a tidy person, and she had cleared her things away, before going to work. It was a small kitchen-diner, with a simple wooden table and chairs at one end.

"You sit down. Just tell me where things are. Tea or coffee?"

"Coffee, please. I think I need a caffeine boost."

I pointed him in the right direction and watched as he made us both a drink and found some nice chocolate biscuits, leftover

Christmas presents. He brought it all to the table and sat down with me.

"I've put sugar in, Tess. I know you don't often take it, but you really need to, today. And so do I. It's been quite an afternoon for both of us."

"Can you tell me about it? I think it might help me to rinse some of the worst images out of my head."

He looked searchingly at me, then seemed to make up his mind that I was right.

Eyes focused on his coffee, he began.

"Well, as you know, we were about to give up on the intense search. There was no more money to keep it going, and we really had very little hope of finding her in such a large expanse of water. We hoped – this doesn't sound nice, but it's true, I'm afraid – that when her body had decomposed enough it would float to the surface and be discovered by a rower or dog-walker."

I shivered. He smiled at me, sympathetically.

"I know. It's a revolting thought. But it was all we could hold onto, at that point. The inspector was irritated about it, but we had no clear indication that Harriet's death was anything other than accident or suicide, so it was simply not worth the quantity of resources we were putting into it. She might even have been alive somewhere, oblivious to what was going on here. It's happened before. We were getting some very negative media comments and questions, too."

I sighed. Why were people so uncaring? Perhaps it would have been different if she had been part of a loving family, keeping her name and personality in the news. But maybe not even then. Complaining was a national pastime. Compassion went by the wayside.

"We weren't happy about it," Rob continued. "And there was a distinctly sombre atmosphere down at the lake. I'd gone over for one last look. Nothing. No sign at all. I could sense the bitter frustration in all the searchers. No one was talking. Then we got the call. I told you how she was found, if you remember."

"I didn't take it in, I'm afraid. I heard the word 'body' and that seemed to shut out everything else for a while."

He touched my hand gently.

"I'm sorry. I should have given you more time to grasp what was happening."

I shook my head.

"No – it had to be quick, to be of any use. The pathologist said so."

"You're right. We were in a hurry. But I could still have given you a moment. Anyway, what happened was that a young man was on that path by the church. It's a nice area to walk in, when the sun's up. Feels rural but also ancient, somehow. His dog, quite a big one, was off the lead, running ahead. He realised that it had gone into the edge of the water and called it back. It wouldn't come, so he hurried to get it. The river's very fast-flowing at the moment, after all the rain. He was worried the dog might be swept away."

I nodded. I had noticed how strong the rush of the brown water in the river was, when I had walked around the lake.

"The dog had grabbed something large and was pulling it out of the water. It had been wedged against a tree trunk, apparently, on the bend. He thought it was a bundle of clothes and tried to pull the dog away, then saw a face. Apparently, he fell backwards with the shock and – well, let's just say that your small pool of vomit will not be the only one."

I tried to laugh with him, but it was not funny. I felt sorry for the man. What a foul thing to see, so unexpectedly! At least I had been given some idea of what was coming. Rob sobered up quickly.

"Anyway, he managed to get the dog off and put it on the lead. He didn't touch the body himself, but it was firmly stuck anyway, half out of the water. After a short while, he pulled himself together enough to call 999. They realised it could be Harriet and contacted our team. We were able to get there very quickly."

He looked down.

"Even for us, it was a pretty ghastly sight. We had her photograph so clearly in our minds. Felt we knew her, I suppose. We were pretty sure it was Harriet. It felt like – like a failure. We'd spent so much time searching, but in the wrong place. We should have found her much sooner."

His voice had dropped an octave. It was obviously a bad moment.

"We did the normal routine things, called the pathologist in as soon as possible. But we all felt very low. Depressed. Until he said he thought she hadn't been in the water long. It wasn't our fault, after all. She hadn't been there to find. It made us feel better, somehow, but also even more determined to find out what had happened to her."

We never really thought about the impact of all this on the officers involved. They were human beings too, not machines. As prone to stress and depression as the rest of us. Affected by the dreadful stories they became part of. The remnants of those moments of deep misery were still evident on his face.

"Then, we needed a quick ID so that we could proceed on a firm footing, and the inspector suggested you. I was reluctant to put you through something as upsetting as that, but she insisted. Said you were well up to it and I shouldn't underestimate you."

That validation gave me a warm feeling. I had only met her briefly, yet she respected me.

"I don't know if she's right. I did overreact, I suppose. But I'm glad I could help in some way, do something to aid the investigation."

"You didn't overreact. It was a normal bodily response. I've had it happen to me, before now. Especially in hot weather, when there's a hideous smell as well. And you've honestly been a tremendous help, all along."

I smiled weakly.

"I still feel guilty that I was the one who dropped her off there. I know it isn't really my fault, but I can't help it."

He put an arm round my shoulders.

"You shouldn't let that feeling get on top of you, Tessa. You did your job, that's all. And went well beyond the call of duty in reporting her missing and then giving us so much useful evidence. I'm going to have to get back to the search now, I'm afraid. We'll have to comb both banks going upriver, and it'll be all hands on deck. It's a murder inquiry, we know that. Will you be OK? I can try to fetch someone to be with you, or call the hospital and get Naomi back, if you like."

"I'll be fine. Thanks for staying as long as you have. I feel much better now. Good hunting. I hope you find something which leads to finding the killer."

He gave me a brief hug, an unexpected peck on the cheek, and left, his face back in official mode, and mind on the job in front of him. That was why he had kissed me. He was on auto-pilot and had reverted to former habits. It meant nothing. Nothing at all.

CHAPTER TEN

Investigations

Although I was mentally and physically exhausted, I knew that it was far too early to try to sleep. I turned on the television, switched to the news channel. Breaking news. It was all about Harriet. What they were now calling the *'tragic find of a woman's body in Milton Keynes'.* There was not much footage yet, but plenty of unfounded speculation about what might have happened. Most still imagining the death to have been caused by an accident or suicide. Some suggesting negligence or incompetence in the failure of the police to find her sooner. The idea of murder had not surfaced yet.

After a while, I switched it off. It was strange, being in possession of more knowledge than the media about what had happened. It made me realise how much of what you see is guesswork, misinformation, and rumour. Speculation to fill the void in the rolling news output.

I attempted to distract myself with a book. Not a murder mystery, that would be too close to the mark. A fantasy adventure set on another planet. It did not work. My brain would not allow itself to be deceived. In the end, I took a warm shower, had a hot drink, and climbed into my comfortable bed.

Sleep would not come. The over-bright, stark images of Harriet's body returned, every time I closed my eyes. I put on soothing music. It made no difference. I yielded to the force of what was occupying my mind, and allowed myself to go over what had happened, one frame at a time. I had to process it, somehow. In the end, I drifted into an uneasy, disturbed sleep for a few hours.

My alarm brought me back up to the surface with a painful jerk. I suddenly remembered that I had an early shift today. I was glad to have clear tasks to undertake, but recalled that my car was still at the Open University. I would either have to cancel my first job and walk there, or get one of my drivers to take me. It was still very early, so I decided to dress first and then make my decision.

As soon as she could hear me moving around, Naomi called up. She must have recently returned home from her shift and wanted to talk to me before going to bed.

"I'll get a drink for you. Tea or coffee?"

"Coffee please. Nice and strong."

I dressed hurriedly, grabbed my phone, and tumbled down the stairs, still not in total control of my limbs. Or my brain.

"I thought you were out, when I didn't see the car. Is everything OK?" Naomi asked.

I stopped dead. Of course, she did not know. For a moment, I could not think where to begin. Shook my head in helpless distress.

"Have you heard, then? It was on the radio when I drove home. They've found your Harriet's body at last." Naomi sounded pleased.

I could not prevent the tears from coming into my eyes.

"Sit down, Tess. What's wrong? You wanted them to find her, didn't you? I know you said so."

I sipped some coffee. Then explained to her what had happened. How I had been involved. Her eyes opened wide. She thrust her toast at me and turned to make some more.

"Poor Tessa! What a horrible thing to have to do. No wonder you're upset. Are you really up to work today?"

I nodded, numbly.

"It would be worse, just sitting around. Nothing to distract me. I can't get her poor face out of my head. I need to work. Would you mind taking me to pick up the cab this morning?"

"Of course I'll take you. That's no problem. Whenever you're ready. I just don't want you to overdo it. I can tell you had a difficult night."

I tried to laugh.

"Do I look that bad?"

She shook her head at me. I knew that was not what she had meant.

"Yes, you're right, I haven't slept much. Very bad dreams, too. But I'll be OK. I'll finish early if I need to. But I want to do the first pick-ups. It's not fair to drag someone else out of bed for that, not when it was my turn."

Naomi agreed, somewhat doubtfully, made sure I forced down some more breakfast, and drove me to the nearby Open University. The car park had been fully taken over by police vehicles, officers, dog teams, and mysterious bulky equipment shrouded in tarpaulins. My cab had been engulfed by the creeping spread of it all, but I remembered where I had left it and made my way over, picking my way between the obstacles. I had refused to let my sister come in with me.

A junior police officer approached me pre-emptively, as I walked over.

"Sorry, Miss, you can't come in here today. Police incident."

I explained who I was and why I was there.

"Oh, I understand," she responded, more warmly. "We might need to get them to move a couple of vans, so that you can get out."

She accompanied me to the cab and arranged for a few vehicles to be shifted, so that I could leave. Before I set off, I saw the inspector in my mirror, marching over purposefully. I lowered the window.

"Miss Fordham!" she said. "I'm glad I caught you. I just wanted to thank you for your assistance with the identification last night. It was a great help. I'm sorry that it was such an unpleasant task."

"It certainly was, but a necessary one, from what I heard."

"Indeed. It's enabled us to move faster and make better progress, both with the search and the autopsy. So, thank you. I would like to interview you again, tomorrow ideally, just to see if we can glean any further useful information, now that we know for certain it is a murder inquiry."

An unpleasant prospect, going through it all again. Another small task I could perform for Harriet, though. I had to consent.

"OK. Your sergeant has my phone number. Feel free to text or message with a time that suits you. I'll make sure to be there."

She nodded in acknowledgement and charged off again. A busy person. Not given to pleasantries or small talk, so I appreciated the fact that she had made the effort to thank me. Even if it was simply a preamble to asking for another interview.

All my passengers, that day, had heard about the body being found. I did not speak about the identification, but expressed my sadness at her death. It was the best I could do, while keeping my emotions under control. It was certainly not my place to explain that she had been murdered. I responded non-committally to any such speculation. Most of them assumed it had been suicide, however. I found it more difficult not to refute that.

As promised, I finished early and went home, drained, and ready for a quiet evening alone. I knew Naomi was on duty again, and I would have the place to myself. I was settling down with a hot drink when my phone rang. I assumed it was Rob or the inspector, but it was John, my tame reporter.

"Hello, Tessa. I hope you don't mind me contacting you. I gather that the missing person case has moved on suddenly. The body's been found and a little birdie told me that you identified it – I have my sources down at the station. And that it's now a live inquiry."

"Mm." Ironic that a dead body would spark a live inquiry.

"I would really like to interview you properly. Get a handle on the case. You know you can trust me to write it up without sensationalism. I think you could give me the insight I need to be able to compose something more effective. Would you be willing to do that?"

I took the time to think through his request, which was relatively tentative, as if he expected a refusal.

"I suppose I might be. For Harriet's sake."

His enthusiasm was evident.

"Brilliant. Thank you so much. I'd much rather speak face to face. Can I come up and meet you tomorrow? In the morning, if possible."

Tomorrow was shaping to become a rather intense day. Which was better than idleness, in my current state of mind. And both meetings could conceivably help to find the killer.

"OK. If you text me when you know which train you're on, I'll collect you from the station. Where do you want to go?"

I was not going to invite him to my home. Or even to give him my address. I needed to be more careful than that. I was learning to be wary.

"To the pub by the lake?" he suggested. "It looks quite big, so there must be some quiet spots. It's a bit awkward speaking in the car."

"OK, that sounds feasible."

"I'll look forward to it."

He actually sounded as if he meant it.

No sooner had he rung off, than I received a message from the inspector.

Is tomorrow afternoon a possibility? Preferably at your house, since the press is camped outside the station.

OK, I replied.

2.30?

I accepted. I wondered if she would be alone, or if Rob would come with her. I hoped he would be there. It would be less stressful to have a friend present.

I warned Sally that I would have to take the day off, apologising for the disruption.

"Don't worry, Tessa. I was amazed you worked today, at all, after what you've just been through. It was on the news that you were asked to identify the body. It must have been awful."

Her voice contained sympathy, and a hint of curiosity. Now I was glad that I was not going to work next day. I had not realised that my role had been made so public. It would have been purgatory, having to rehash it repeatedly. But Sally deserved an answer.

"It really was. You can imagine. A very difficult moment. Shocking and distressing. And I can't get some of the more horrible images out of my mind. I may have to take a couple of days off to get my head straight, but no more. Don't forget to take your time owed, as well, Sally. You seem to have been doing an awful lot of hours recently."

She laughed.

"You're right. Rachel is having dreadful morning sickness and has needed me to cover, but don't worry, I'm having the weekend off. The extra money does no harm in January, anyway."

I was so lucky in my staff, both in the office and the drivers. They were all extremely reliable and trustworthy. There was no one who needed micromanagement or any kind of close supervision.

Everyone was ready to help out and work as a team. My father had always told me that trust breeds trust, and he was right.

I was too exhausted, that night, to be anxious about my forthcoming interviews, but the shocking image of Harriet's face still intruded, every time my eyes closed, and I tried to relax. I tried my standard remedy of reading fiction again, an old favourite this time, and it helped a little. Took me into a happy space and a safer world. In the end, I fell asleep in the middle of a familiar page.

I heard Naomi return in the early morning and crept down to talk to her. I wanted to brief her on the inspector's visit.

"That's fine, Tessa. I'll be sleeping, I hope, but I'll keep out of the way in any case. She won't want anyone else listening."

She looked worn out. Shadowed eyes in a drawn, white face. Several tough shifts in a row. She would need her rest.

"Rob might be here, too. I don't know."

She smiled.

"Easier for you if he is, I guess. Don't worry. It'll be fine."

I did not tell her about John, the reporter. No need. Or was I secretly not confident that she would approve? I opened my mouth to begin, saw how shattered she looked, and left it. For now.

Wide awake, I did not try to go back to bed. Naomi had the en suite, so I was free to shower in the main bathroom and take my time over getting ready for a stressful day. Over breakfast, I looked at the news channel again, keeping the sound low so as not to disturb my sister's sleep.

Sally was right. I was clearly mentioned as having identified the body, and they had used my profile picture from the website alongside the information. Just the kind of invasive publicity I had been keen to avoid. Unfortunately the photo was in the public domain, so I could do nothing about it. At least it meant that I need not feel guilty about talking to John. Some kind police officer had obviously released information about me to the press, without my permission or knowledge.

There was still no indication from the police that they had begun a murder inquiry, but their renewed activity had provoked considerable speculation, based on the size of the investigation team and the number of senior detectives involved. It would not be long before everyone knew.

I experienced a slight sense of *déjà vu* when returning to the Caldecotte pub car park with John. At least there had been no prior sightseeing trip, this time, and the weather was far less hostile. He had dressed more casually, on this occasion, and would be a less conspicuous companion.

There was no sign of the sneering sarcasm of our first encounter. He was smiling from the start, and seemed genuinely pleased to see me. I was somewhat surprised to realise that I reciprocated.

We both decided to have a light brunch and sat in a quiet corner, with a stunning view over the beauty of the north lake. Today it was celestial blue, with sparkling diamond highlights where the breeze ruffled its calm reflection of the heavens. Swans, sailing serenely along, wings proudly furled, might almost have been added deliberately for scenic effect. John kept glancing out of the window, his eyes drawn by the image.

"What a beautiful setting! I would never have linked a view like this with Milton Keynes. And the contrast with the other week, in that miserable weather, is disconcerting. It's like a different place. I can see now why you say it's a great city to live in."

As a proud Milton Keynes inhabitant, this comment made me very happy. It was always hard to explain to outsiders how amazing the mix of convenient urban facilities and thriving parks, countryside and a natural environment was. How it benefitted the mental, as well as physical health. It had been a lifesaver for some during lockdown, quite literally.

Down to business. I had another appointment that afternoon.

"So, what did you want to ask me?"

He asked if he could record me on his phone, so that he could refer to it later. It would make our conversation less stilted if he was not trying to write notes. I agreed, a little hesitantly. I hated hearing my own recorded voice and could not imagine that it would anything but painful to listen back to.

"You will run the article past me before publishing, won't you?"

"Of course," he assured me. "You have no need to worry."

To my surprise, he went right back to the very beginning, from picking Harriet up in the city centre, all the way through to the distressing experience of identifying her body. I tried to keep a lid on my emotions, but at times my voice wobbled or deepened, as I relived difficult moments. At the end, I felt somehow lighter, as if it had actually been a cathartic experience to unload the full story.

"Thank you, Tessa. That was excellent."

"I'm just not clear what kind of article you're intending to write using it."

He looked a little shifty. My suspicions rose.

"Well, there are several ways I can approach it," he proffered. "Ideally, I would like to tell the story of your involvement in the case. You're a special person, Tessa. I'd like other people to hear your voice."

I glared at him. Just what I had been afraid of.

"Definitely not, John. I absolutely refuse. That's not what I want at all. You should know that by now."

He sighed.

"OK, OK. I suppose I expected that reaction, after what you said last time. The other way to do it, is to use your testimony, and other elements I've been able to collect, to paint a picture of

Harriet, talk sympathetically about her story, and explore what seems to have happened to her."

"Mm. That sounds much better. Can you wait a day or so?"

"Why?"

I paused. Could I really trust him?

"Look, I'm privy to certain information from the police which I haven't shared with you. And won't share with you. But the nature of the investigation is going to become clearer in the next day or so. It may change the tenor of your piece."

He looked searchingly at me.

"I think I understand you. You mean it's going to become a murder inquiry, don't you? I know you can't tell me, and you don't want me to jump the gun. But you're right, that would change the tone of what I write. More than just sympathy. Anger at what has been done to her. The need to find the killer, before they do it again."

I did not nod. That would be going too far. I did smile encouragingly, however, and he indicated his comprehension.

"Can you message me the minute it's revealed publicly, even to a few people? Then I can get my article in. I'll send it to you anyway, so that you've already approved it – hopefully. I wish you'd let me put you in, though. It would give it a sharper focus. Make it more interesting. Help it to stand out."

"No, it's impossible. I would hate that. I already detest having my photo and name on the television. A more personal account would be even worse."

He held up his hands.

"I get it. You're a private person. You just don't realise how rare you are. Everyone else seems to want their fifteen minutes of fame, or more if available. Your attitude is refreshing, in a way, even if it does frustrate me, professionally. Personally – well, I find it very attractive, appealing. It's so nice to talk to someone who will genuinely keep what you say confidential."

I could feel myself blushing.

"I'm sorry, Tessa. I've embarrassed you. May I stay in touch with you? I'd still like to do that article on the many and varied charms of Milton Keynes. In fact, I'm going to take a photo of this amazing lake view today. It would be a perfect teaser."

"Of course."

After a pause, he leaned forward a little.

"Do you mind me asking why you became a taxi-driver, Tessa? It's an unusual choice for a woman."

I looked down. Should I give him my stock answer about enjoying driving and wanting to be in control of my working hours? I sensed that he would see through that. He had been straight with me. I owed him something closer to the truth.

"It's complicated, John. And a long story. I won't tell you all of it now, if you don't mind."

"You don't have to tell me any of it, Tessa. It's none of my business."

I shook my head. Looked down at the table. It was not easy to know where to begin.

"No, I don't mind. I – I was very academic at school. An all-rounder. I wanted to be a doctor, so I knew that I needed top grades in everything. And was doing well, in fact. On track. Then things started to fall apart. I was badly bullied for being a swot (not that they called it that). Lost all my confidence. Got very low. Couldn't make it into school."

I paused, remembering the pain of that time, which had never entirely left me.

"My parents and Naomi were great. They saved me. And books, I suppose. Escaping into another world. I wouldn't have made it this far without them. But I didn't get much in the way of qualifications. Oh, I could have tried for university, taken an access course, I suppose, but I wasn't at all sure I'd cope, emotionally."

It had been a tough decision.

"So, after trying various things, working in a coffee shop, attempting an apprenticeship, retail work, I had a go at driving a cab. Liked it. Oh, not the weird hours and weirder passengers, but the autonomy. The independence. And now I've managed to start my own business, one I'm really proud of."

I finally raised my eyes, uncertain of his reaction. I could read sympathy in his face. I did not want his pity, so I gritted my teeth for an embarrassing response from him.

"Thank you for telling me that, Tessa. I appreciate your confidence. I'm glad you've found a career that works for you. And with your obvious intelligence, I'm confident that you'll make a great success of it."

Not what I expected. I was grateful for what he said. Somehow, he had known that feeling sorry for me was neither necessary nor wanted. I smiled at him, hesitantly. Surprised that I had told him about my past, even a short version. It was normally kept strictly private.

He insisted on paying for my meal.

"It's on expenses, like the taxi fares. And you've definitely earned it."

I did feel quite drained afterwards. I dropped him back at the station, and he waved cheerfully, as if he were a friend rather than a reporter, before he was swallowed up by the maelstrom of rail passengers hurrying to and fro.

CHAPTER ELEVEN

Deep Dive

I was beginning to feel nervous about talking to the inspector. She was a very different character, much less easy to please, and I was not sure that I would be able to answer her questions satisfactorily. In a way, rehearsing some of it with John might have helped, though. It had brought all the sights and sounds back into my mind very clearly, whereas I had deliberately tried to park them in my subconscious, over the last few days.

I kept an eye out for a car so that I could avoid a ring at the doorbell, since Naomi was still sleeping upstairs. I heaved a sigh of relief when I saw Rob arriving. I was glad he would also be present. Why did I feel like that? I was unsure, and was not ready to examine my reaction. The cold fact was that he made me feel a little more secure, and that was sufficient for now.

I opened the door before they could knock, and quietly invited them in. Offered refreshments, but the inspector refused. I was not entirely surprised. She did not come over as a relaxed person. Sharing food and drink would make this a more informal occasion. I led them into our living room and they took seats, facing me. Rob checked with me that I was happy for him to record me. The inspector spoke first.

"Thank you for agreeing to see us here, Miss Fordham. I did not want to expose you to the scrutiny of the media gathered outside the station. I know you tend to avoid personal publicity wherever possible."

"Thank you for that. I was somewhat surprised to see that someone had informed them that I identified the purse and even the body. Without my knowledge or permission."

She reddened slightly.

"I'm sorry about that. I do apologise. It was an error. A junior press officer passed on the information to his contacts and added it to a briefing, before I realised what he was doing. He's very apologetic, but unfortunately the damage can't be undone."

"OK. I'll accept that. As long as it wasn't deliberate. I really don't have any desire to be in the papers or on the news. Rather the reverse."

She nodded understandingly.

"I'll try to ensure that nothing like that happens again. Anyway, let's get on with our main business. I would really like you to go through every tiny aspect of your interaction with Harriet Beckinsale. I know it may feel that you've already told us everything, but, this time, I'm happy for you to go beyond facts. Your impressions could be very important."

I know my face expressed a touch of my inner incredulity. She justified her statement.

"You are perceptive. You realised that the phone had been planted later, not dropped, and were sceptical about the discovery of the purse, too, I believe. I wish we had paid more attention to your instincts at the time. I'm told you always believed that she was going to meet someone, a man. You seem to have been proved right, and it is most probable that the person with whom she had a rendezvous was, in fact, involved in her death in some way, either as the killer or as a provocation to her former husband."

I was embarrassed at her rather formal expression of praise, but it did encourage me to speak more freely, which might have been her motivation. I ran through it all again, slowly. Stopping to think about my subconscious thoughts and feelings, and put them into words where I could.

At the end, she expressed herself highly satisfied with what I had said.

"Now, this may seem like a strange question, Miss Fordham. Is it at all possible that your taxi was followed from the city centre on that Tuesday?"

It certainly was an unexpected query.

"Followed? Deliberately, you mean? Well, I wasn't looking out for anything like that. Milton Keynes is not exactly a hotbed of espionage! So it's possible. It could have happened in the city centre, I suppose. There was quite a bit of traffic going my way. It wouldn't have been obvious if anyone was following the cab."

I paused to think.

"I don't think I would have noticed a car behind me, when I was driving into the pub car park, either. Again, it was nowhere near empty, and there are frequently vehicles entering and leaving. I think I would have been aware of being followed close to the circular car park, though. It was very quiet, as I said. I suppose someone might have come after me over the dual carriageway but continued down into the estate, but I don't think so. I would have spotted them at that point."

"Mm. So, it is possible that someone might have been able to see that you were heading for the Caldecotte lake area, if they had driven behind you?"

I was bewildered by this line of questioning.

"I guess so. Why? I don't understand."

Rob shifted in his seat. He intervened for the first time.

"Look, Tessa, our top suspect, so far, is clearly her ex-husband. He's a nasty piece of work, a stalker, and obsessed with Harriet. Obviously, he can't have been the man she was meeting that day.

But he might have spotted her in the centre and followed you down to the lake. Seen her with another man. That's the kind of thing which would enrage a possessive bloke like him. He could have taken her, once she was alone again. Perhaps kept her at his house until he chose to dispose of her."

My mouth dropped open. It sounded over-complicated, too cleverly calculated. Like a detective story. But it might fit the facts we had.

Rob continued. "He lives in Woburn Sands, so he's probably familiar with this end of the city. It's the best explanation we have, currently. We need to get a search warrant, have a chance to check his house and car, but we don't have sufficient cause currently. We've invited him in for interview tomorrow. We didn't ask for an alibi when we spoke to him before. We weren't thinking murder, and it wasn't likely that Harriet was meeting him, so we didn't bother. Now we will."

I sat back. A new theory. I was glad that things were moving forward, even if I feared that this might be a red herring. Wouldn't the man who had met Harriet have come forward, under those circumstances, if he was not involved in her death? Perhaps not. The circumstances might make him very reluctant to raise his head above the parapet. Still, Rob was correct. It had to be worth checking.

"We'll ask for a DNA sample, too. Ostensibly to rule him out, but we can try to match it with the traces on the purse."

The inspector cleared her throat.

"Has anything else happened which you find odd, Miss Fordham? Since the disappearance, but before the body was discovered. I know you've been to the area a number of times. Anything at all could be of value."

"Well, I've faced a great many questions from my passengers about the case, including from a couple of reporters. You would expect that, I suppose. But I did have one rather unusual fare. He asked for me specifically on the phone. We've put a stop to that now. You're ordering a cab not a driver."

"Sensible," approved the inspector.

"This man was not a reporter. I took him to Caldecotte Lake from the city centre, as requested. When I told him the round car park was cordoned off, he said it was fine to drop him on Monellan Crescent. Before we were anywhere near. So either he knew the area well, or he had done his research. I can't exactly put my finger on it, but there was definitely something off about him."

"Can you be a bit more specific?"

"He said he was curious to meet the woman who had been, as he put it, 'so central to the police inquiry'. He said that, without my report, the police would have been looking all over Milton Keynes, and would have found it much more difficult even to be sure that she was still in the city. Or missing at all. Something like that."

"It's true, of course, but I agree that it's rather an odd thing to say, and a strange motive for wanting to ride with you."

"He said it was personal curiosity. Yet he didn't ask me a lot of questions or even sound that interested. He said that, having met me, he understood why I had acted as I did. I didn't ask him to elaborate. I guess I was afraid of what he might say. That it might be insulting. But it seemed odd."

The more I reflected on it, the stranger his attitude seemed to me.

"I dropped him by the pathway through to the lake, between the three-storey townhouses, and he stood and waited until I had left, before making a move in any of the four possible directions he could take from there. As if he didn't want me to see where he was going. I – I don't know why, but I circled round and came back the same way soon afterwards. He was gone. I have no idea where he went."

The inspector looked at Rob.

"There just might be something to this. She was right about other things. She has strong instincts."

He nodded.

"She's a good judge of people, I know that."

It was strange to hear them discussing me, as if I was not there.

"What was his name?" asked Rob.

"Brown, he said. But he paid in cash, like Harriet, so it could well be a pseudonym, I suppose. That was another thing which struck me. The similarity of their approach. Phone booking, cash payment, ordinary name. He laughed when I called him Mr Brown."

"That settles it. We'll look into this, Tessa. We could do some house to house in the Caldecotte area, see if we can track him down or find someone else who spotted him. We were thinking of going around to ask if anyone had noticed Harriet, anyway."

The inspector nodded.

"Can you give us a description to work from?"

I thought back carefully.

"The most obvious thing was his very black hair. I thought it must be dyed. A home dye. It was very matte, dull. I would put him around fifty, I think, although the hair might have been an attempt to hide his years, so he could be older. His eyebrows and lashes were a very pale brown and his eyes were a light colour, too. Grey, I think. It was a strange combination. He had rather full lips and a thin nose, I think. Very smooth, unwrinkled skin. A bland face, almost expressionless."

The inspector smiled.

"You're a good witness, Miss Fordham. Would you work with an artist to produce an impression, something we can give to our officers?"

"Of course. I'd like to help. And it would be interesting."

"I'll send someone round later today, if that's OK with you. While it's fresh in your mind. I want to make progress on this. We'll aim to start knocking on doors tomorrow. Alongside formally interviewing the ex-husband. Two possible leads. We hope one will take us in the right direction."

I was impressed with her proactive attitude. "Do you have any other suspects?"

Rob grunted.

"Other than the ex, not really. He's a vindictive person and could be violent, I think."

"Poor Harriet. No wonder she was trying to find someone better."

"That's an interesting comment, Miss Fordham. Do you mean that she might have been searching for romance? I think perhaps we need to look at dating websites. See if she was registered anywhere." The inspector sounded pleased to have another lead to pursue.

"Could she have met a man in the library? It might be worth talking to her colleagues again."

This suggestion was from Rob. A good one.

I had one more question. Something I had been putting off.

"Would you be able to tell me the results of the post-mortem? How she actually died? It's not morbid curiosity. I just feel I have to know what happened."

The inspector had already turned off the recording. She looked searchingly at me and nodded.

"I think, by now, I know that I can trust you to keep it confidential. Most of the results confirmed the doctor's initial impressions. She had been killed between eighteen and forty-eight hours after you dropped her off. After so much time, it wasn't possible to be more precise. She was not disposed of in the river, however, until much more recently. Probably about two days before the body was discovered. The indications are that she was kept somewhere cold before disposal, which had slowed decomposition."

The words were matter-of-fact, but the image they conjured up was unpleasant. She continued.

"We know that she must have been killed indoors. As you noted, her clothing was different, and she was not dressed for being outside."

An unwelcome image of the filthy dress where it had ridden up on her legs intruded. I gulped and tried to focus on her words, not the pictures they evoked.

"As for the cause of death, it was not drowning, as must now be obvious. She was suffocated. Probably smothered. One single fibre was found right inside her nasal cavity. Normally we would expect more traces, but immersion in the river had a powerful impact on trace evidence. There were characteristic petechiae in her eyes. But there were no other obvious injuries evident, apart from extensive post-mortem damage, although the pathologist did insist that there appeared to be some mild bruising on her lower arms and the upper parts of her legs."

She cleared her throat.

"It appears that she may have had sex some time before she was murdered. It's not clear whether this was consensual. The tox screen showed traces of a strong opiate, so she was probably heavily drugged before being killed."

That was a relief. She would not have suffered horribly. I hoped. A more peaceful death than what happened to her afterwards. Less distressing than it might have been.

"Thank you. That helps. I – I'm glad it wasn't a more violent ending."

My voice shook a little. Rob smiled reassuringly at me and thanked me again for my help. The inspector nodded.

"You've been a very valuable witness, Miss Fordham."

I felt extremely relieved when they left. It had gone more smoothly than I had feared, and my suggestions had not been ridiculed. I tried to picture Mr Brown clearly in my head, preparing for the artist's impression.

Naomi was up and about before the artist arrived. She was very excited about seeing the process, delighted that it was to take place in our home.

"I think artist's impressions work much better than those identikit things. Those never look like real people."

"Mm. As long as I can describe him sufficiently well."

"You're very observant, Tessa. Always have been. You notice things I haven't seen at all. And you have an almost photographic memory. There's a good chance you can get a likeness."

The artist was a somewhat unexpected character. I had expected an earnest young man, for some reason, yet she was a middle-aged woman, with a comfortable smile and reassuring manner. We sat together at the table, with Naomi hovering in the background, listening eagerly, while she made tea for us both.

The swiftness and sure line quality of her sketching were remarkable. Just watching the pencil move over the page was fascinating. We began with the overall shape of the head, length of hair, form of the brow and chin. She asked me detailed questions which prompted me to examine carefully my mental picture. Then we moved on to the position of eyes, nose, mouth, and then their structure. The first sketch was not quite right, but the second one really had a look of the man I had seen for only a few minutes, some days ago.

"That's amazing, Elizabeth. You're so talented. I actually think I might recognise him from that picture. Thank you so much."

She smiled contentedly.

"I've enjoyed it. To be honest, I don't often have a witness who has such a clear picture in their head. Often they've only glimpsed the offender, or not looked properly. You have a good eye, as well as an exceptional memory. Do you draw, yourself?"

I shook my head.

"I always enjoyed art in school but haven't touched a pencil or paintbrush since I was fourteen."

"You ought to give it a try. Eighty percent of good drawing is looking properly and you have that skill already."

I flushed, flattered by the praise. Perhaps I would get a sketchbook and give it a go. It would be a good hobby to take up. If another rather solitary one.

Naomi studied the picture.

"He certainly looks like a real person, but not anyone I've met, unfortunately. I was hoping I'd recognise him!"

"The chances are that someone will, though," I said. "It's got to be better than nothing. The police don't seem to have many other suspects at the moment."

Elizabeth thanked me and whizzed off to get the sketch scanned and distributed.

"I don't photograph them, because it's too easy to distort the perspective. A scan is more accurate."

I knew the mysterious Mr Brown might prove to be entirely harmless and totally unconnected with Harriet's death. It might all be a waste of time. It felt good, however, to be contributing to some kind of progress in the case.

CHAPTER TWELVE

Interlude with books

The artist's impression was prominently displayed on the television news on the following morning.

"The police would urgently like to speak to this man, possibly known as Mr Brown, in order to eliminate him from their inquiries. If you think you recognise him, please call us immediately."

It looked very convincing to me. The startling impact of the straight, jet black hair and pale brows was clear. I hoped it might jog someone's memory. And if the officers going door to door had it, there was a chance that they might find him, or someone who knew him. I was not sure that the name of Brown was genuine, however. It was too similar to Harriet's false name of Smith.

The report also clarified that the investigation was now a murder inquiry.

"Following the post-mortem, it has become clear that Harriet Beckinsale was murdered. We have a large team investigating her death, but we need help from the local community. We would like any members of the public, who may have been near the Ouzel river or the Valley Park, three or four days ago, to reflect on whether they saw anything suspicious. This could be a person acting strangely, some unusual debris on the bank or in the water, damage to the surrounding area's plant life. Even an unusually strong scent your dog picked up. Please check dash-cams for any footage in the Simpson area. We believe that her body was dumped in the river near the Simpson car park, probably under the cover of darkness."

The investigation seemed to be moving on fast. I began to have real hope that the killer might be found.

I sent a message to John, informing him that it had now been announced that she had been murdered. He rang me back.

"Thanks for letting me know, Tessa. Actually, I had a tip-off from a police contact that it would be public knowledge today, so the article is in this morning's edition, on the front page. Thanks for your help with it and for approving it so promptly last night. The editor is very pleased. We've got in ahead of the other papers and that's always good."

He had sent his draft over in the evening. I had no hesitation in accepting it. It painted a sympathetic picture of Harriet and what appeared to have happened to her, including the distressing discovery of her body. His source in the police station had obviously passed on some additional details, which made it even more gripping. It even mentioned the clothes she had been wearing, which I had thought would probably remain confidential.

"You're welcome, John. I just hope this and the artist's impression make a difference."

There was a pause.

"What artist's impression?"

"They have it on the news this morning. I had a rather odd passenger a few days ago, who might possibly know something. It came up at my second police interview, and I worked with the official artist yesterday afternoon to put together a picture. They're going house to house in Caldecotte and Walton Park from today with it and her photograph."

Another pause.

"I wish you had told me about it last night, Tessa."

He sounded very disappointed in me. Let down.

"I'm sorry. I didn't think. Obviously, I didn't mention it when we met, because it hadn't happened yet. Sorry. But you should be able to get a copy from the police."

I was surprised that my voice sounded so emotional.

"I will. I'm sorry, too. I didn't mean to sound censorious. You're under no obligation to me. I just would have liked to put it in, that's all. As it is, even our front page seems out of date already."

"I'm so sorry. I should have told you yesterday evening."

There was an embarrassing catch in my voice.

"Don't be. It's not a problem. Honestly. Can you tell me why this passenger seemed suspicious to you? I can write something up for tomorrow."

His voice sounded warmer. He seemed to have forgiven me. It was more of a relief than it should have been.

I went into detail about the strange disappearing Mr Brown. He, too, agreed that it could be a useful lead, and promised to write it up and send to me for checking that afternoon.

"You might need to check with the police, too. I don't know how much of this they want to make public. They – they have another possible suspect, as well. I don't think I should tell you about him, but they might be willing to, if they want to put some additional pressure on him."

"You're right. I'll speak to them. It would be good to get their perspective as well, anyway. Thanks, Tessa. You're a star."

I was glowing with an odd sense of pleasure at his approval. I valued his good opinion.

"You're welcome, John."

I looked forward to further interactions with him. He was much nicer than I had imagined a pressman could be. And not the contemptuous upper-class twit he had appeared to be when we first met. Perhaps even a future friend.

Rob rang at lunchtime to update me.

"The inspector is very pleased with the picture, Tessa. It looks like a real person. We've already had a couple of possible identifications from shopkeepers, which we are following up, and the officers have started going round the estate, beginning with the townhouses by the lake. Unfortunately, a lot of people are out at work during the day, so we're going to have to return to those places in the evening."

I felt encouraged, all the same. His appearance was so distinctive, so memorable, that someone must know him or have seen him.

Rob's idea of talking to people at the library had taken hold of my mind and I decided that I would see if I could interview anyone there. I knew the police would also follow it up, but felt that perhaps a friend of Harriet's might be more open with me than with someone official. Especially with any confidences they had shared.

I had not been into the central library since childhood and was flooded with nostalgia as I approached the impressive red brick building, with its tall architectural pillars. And the amazingly lifelike bronze of girls whispering to each other outside, which had fascinated me as a child. Inside, it was as cavernous as I remembered. Like a modern cathedral of books.

I recalled how gripped I had been by the enormous mural on the stairwell. It was an astonishingly convincing, yet somehow fanciful image of the early days of the new town, with young people at the heart of it. It was probably the first real artwork I had admired. Our family had never been gallery visitors. That painting had confirmed my sense that this was a truly optimistic place. The library and the city.

It had always felt like a privilege to go in and browse the books there. And the library had been the birthplace of my lifelong passion for reading. Being permitted to take out ten free books at a time had seemed like paradise. I was immensely grateful for the inspiration which had given me so much pleasure and escape over the years. Another link between my life and Harriet's.

I went to the desk and asked to speak to someone about her. The receptionist looked doubtful, but then recognised me from the television footage. There had to be some compensations to having your face plastered all over the media.

"Oh, you're the lady who reported dropping her at Caldecotte Lake, aren't you? You helped to keep her story in the papers, too. We were really grateful to you. I'm afraid people would just have forgotten about her, otherwise. I'll just ask my manager to come out and talk to you."

"Thank you so much," I said, relieved that it was easier than I had feared.

After some consideration, I was ushered into a back office to chat to the manager. I explained what I was doing there.

"I just want to help to find out what happened to Harriet. I know the police are doing their best, but it's important to me personally. I feel responsible, after leaving her at the lake. I want to do whatever I can to investigate."

The manager in no way resembled my mental image of a library official. No half-moon glasses, no hushed voice, no grey hair in a bun. A smart, modern woman with a great air of efficiency, combined with a caring manner.

"I would like to do all I can to assist you," she responded. "I'm happy to answer any questions which don't interfere with Harriet's personal confidentiality, and I'll invite her closest work friend, Imogen, to talk to you afterwards. Would that be useful?"

"That would be perfect. Thank you."

I asked Mrs Bromy about Harriet's personality and work. Whether she ever saw personal friends when on duty. Whether she herself had ever seen her chatting to one of the library's clients.

"She was one of my most reliable workers, I have to say. A model employee. Extremely punctual, conscientious, focused. Flexible, too. And she always rang in or sent a message as soon as possible, if she became ill. Without fail. Excellent attendance. That's why I was so worried, when she didn't turn up, and I received no phone call. And then there was no answer when I rang her. It went straight to voice mail. It just wasn't like her. She rarely took time off, anyway, and was always willing to take on an extra shift if needed."

"It's such a good thing you did report it. Without that, my information would have been useless. We wouldn't even have known her name."

The tension in her face eased somewhat.

"Thank you for saying that. I was very unsure. I didn't want to get anyone into trouble. But it was so out of character. That's why I felt I had to contact the police. I sensed that something bad had happened to her, although I could never have guessed that she would be murdered. I was thinking she might have collapsed at home, perhaps had a stroke. She lived on her own, so no one would be there to call for help."

I could understand why she had been concerned. The unauthorised absence must have stood out starkly against her good record.

Her smile was rather twisted.

"Unfortunately, neither of us managed to change her fate. In spite of everything, she died. Was killed."

I bowed my head.

"I know. That's why I'm so determined to bring her murderer to justice."

She took a deep breath, and then continued.

"You mentioned chatting, and that's something she rarely did in work, unless a vulnerable client needed support and encouragement. She liked to focus fully on her work. She did sometimes take part in story time for the children and was excellent at reading traditional fairytales and books for very young children. They responded so well to her. But not so much with the more modern children's books for the older ones, which can be a little gritty. They didn't suit her personality at all. You could see that she disapproved of some of the language, as well as the more realistic settings."

That echoed some of the feedback Rob had passed on to me, as well as my own fleeting impression of her. An idealistic person, with a strong fantasy life. And a belief that good would triumph over evil.

Imogen, Harriet's friend, gave a somewhat different perspective.

"I've known her for about ten years, now. We never met socially, but we always looked out for one another here, and enjoyed a quiet talk over lunch when we could. I suppose we were quite close, really. We shared a lot. Were able to be honest with each other."

That was a true friendship. And very rare.

"I definitely miss her," she said, sadly. "I keep looking round for her, to tell her about silly little things that have happened at home or in the library. And it hurts that she's not there any longer. There's an emptiness, a void. Work is less enjoyable. I – I hadn't realised that she had become so important to me."

That was the most emotional response to Harriet's death that I had yet heard. I warmed to Imogen. She sighed deeply, and then went on.

"I knew how desperately unhappy she was in her marriage. She was deeply reluctant to leave that horrible man, because she believed in 'till death us do part', but in the end she saw sense. He was very controlling, aggressively so. I could only see it ending in tragedy."

"He apparently insisted to the police that he never hurt her."

"Huh! That's definitely not true, from what she told me. He certainly damaged her psychologically, and I know that there were several occasions when he did hit her, even injured her. She kept it pretty quiet, and I know she didn't even want to mention it in court, but she did tell me. I saw the bruises, on her arms and once even her neck, although she tried to cover them up."

Anger coloured her voice.

"He was really sorry afterwards, or so he said. There was always some kind of reason or excuse. Sometimes he even persuaded her it was her own fault! That she had goaded him beyond bearing. She would always forgive him and let him off. But it was getting worse. He wouldn't let her do anything on her own and got angry if she was even five minutes late home on the bus. It was time to make the break. I could see it escalating to something really serious if she stayed."

It sounded depressingly familiar. The cycle of worsening violence behind so many killings.

"Were you the one who suggested she went to a shelter?"

"Yes, we found one locally together. It took a lot of persuasion. She kept changing her mind and giving him one more chance. Until it happened again. So, when she finally agreed, I drove her to the shelter, straight from work. Without any luggage or personal things. Just to be safe. I was afraid of how he might react if he knew she was leaving. It was lucky that there were no children to worry about."

"Yes, that would have really complicated matters. I'm sure you were right to push her to take action. You hear such awful stories."

"Mm. She'd always wanted kids, but he utterly refused. Didn't want to share her with anyone, not even their own children. It shows you what kind of guy he was, doesn't it?"

I nodded. It certainly did cast him in a very negative light.

"He never let her learn to drive, either. Told her she'd be a danger on the roads. All to make her more dependent on him, I think."

Hence the reliance on buses and taxis.

"How did she respond once she was properly free of him, in the end?"

Imogen sighed again.

"She struggled a lot with it. And with living alone. She felt guilty, to begin with, as if it was all her fault, as he insisted in court. It tormented her. Then she realised he was still trying to follow her. He'd found out where she lived and used to hang around nearby. She felt really intimidated by him. She got quite a lot of calls which hung up immediately, as well, and she was convinced they were from him. She started to feel genuinely vulnerable, but was worried that people would just think she was paranoid. I told her to go the police or get an injunction, but she wouldn't."

I could understand that. It would mean yet more trauma for her.

Imogen's gentle face was full of sadness.

"I encouraged her to try dating, go on the internet, but she was afraid to. Too many strange people online, she said. Too much of a risk. You could never be sure who they really were."

"I can see her point. It's worked out to be very dangerous for some."

"Yes, I know it's a bit of a minefield. But she wouldn't even try. I did notice that she seemed a bit happier in the last few weeks before she disappeared, though. She wouldn't tell me why, but there was a bloom on her face and a sparkle about her. As if she had an exciting secret and couldn't or wouldn't tell me about it."

"Did you ever see anyone talking to her at the library? A male borrower, maybe."

"Not really," she answered, with some hesitation. "I did half see her, once, around the corner, talking intensely to someone, a man, I think. She was looking up at him. I couldn't really see him, though. He was behind a stack of books. Now that I look back at it, either he or the conversation must have meant something to her. She looked full of – joy. Almost blissful. As if she'd been kissed by Prince Charming, as she always dreamed. She had a bit of a Cinderella obsession."

This could be important.

"Did you tell the police about this?"

"They didn't really ask, and I wasn't about to volunteer extra information. I didn't want them thinking she might have invited something bad to happen to her, as if it was her fault somehow. As if she'd taken a stupid risk. You know how they can be. There's a whole lot of victim blaming."

I could understand where she was coming from. She was trying to protect her friend's reputation.

"I don't suppose you saw what he looked like."

"Not really. He did have longish, very black hair, though. I saw him from behind later on. It looked dyed to me, to be honest. Not many people have hair like that naturally."

I nodded. My thoughts exactly. It sounded like Brown.

"Would we be able to try to spot him on CCTV? Or find a library card for him?"

She looked surprised.

"We might have been able to, but we don't keep our CCTV for more than thirty days, I'm afraid. Data protection and all that. So I don't know if we could connect him to a library card. Or even if we'd be allowed to. Anyway, I don't remember exactly when it was. About five or six weeks ago is the best I can do."

She must have seen the disappointment in my face.

"I'm sorry. At the time, I was just happy for her. Glad that she might have found someone she seemed to really like. She deserved a bit of happiness. And now, it's too late."

"Never mind. Thank you so much. You've been an enormous help. You've confirmed something for me. And that's important. I really want to help to find her killer."

She gulped and smiled.

"Me too. If I've been at all useful, I'm glad."

With thanks to all involved, I managed to extricate myself from the library. But decided that I would return and get a library card for myself, soon. I had forgotten how much I loved the place.

I rang Rob, straight away, and told him about the dark-haired man and the possible connection to Brown. And also the indications that Harriet's ex-husband had been violent towards her on more than one occasion, in addition to his controlling behaviour.

"Tessa, that's brilliant. Thank you so much. She never told us anything about that. It confirms that they have to be our top suspects, at the very least. We'll persevere with the house to house and see if we can catch up with Brown. And we'll see if we can ask for a warrant to get hold of all the Browns on the library system, especially any who live in the Caldecotte area. You never know, we might get lucky and find an address."

"If it's his real name," I responded doubtfully. "But I really hope you do. She sounds like such a nice innocent person. And had already suffered so much with that nasty ex-husband. How did you get on with interviewing him?"

"He doesn't have a strong alibi. Says he was shopping at the DIY store for part of the time and absolutely denies following her. We'll try to check their CCTV. But the inspector is still very unhappy about his story, and is pushing for a search warrant. He won't let us in without one and asked for a lawyer. So he's probably got something to hide. If we can get into his house, we'll soon find out if she was ever there. He refused to give a

DNA sample, which is even more suspicious."

"You really don't like him, do you? I have to admit, he sounds like a prime suspect for a violent crime. And usually the killer is someone close to the victim. He may have lost his temper, after seeing her with Brown. Taken it out on her. I would have expected a more physically violent response, though, rather than smothering."

"Maybe. It doesn't seem that she had been attacked or beaten, according to the pathologist. But he's definitely a possible killer."

"And if it was Brown, he must be the same kind of possessive predator, I suppose."

"Mm. So sad that she might have fallen for a bad guy all over again. Unfortunately, it's a pattern we see, all too often. But we'll get him, Tessa. Whichever one it is. Don't you worry about that. We won't give up on her."

"I know."

There was a slight tremble in my voice. It was emotional for me. Such a sad story. Such a lonely woman. Just seeking some small solace in a cold and uncaring world.

That evening, John rang about the article he had written. It was well put together, and he had checked with the police what he was allowed to put in.

"Is there anything else you can tell me, Tessa? I really do want to do my best for your Harriet. You've made her real to me. She matters. I would like to be part of catching her killer."

"I've been at the library this afternoon, talking to her manager and a close friend. Found out some more about her ex-husband, who sounds like a nasty kettle of fish, and violent, too. He's the other key suspect I mentioned to you. Could be our murderer. Shows all the signs of being potentially aggressive enough."

It was true. He matched the profile of many wife-killers. "But he would have needed to follow us from the centre. I don't know how likely that is, even for an obsessive stalker."

Yet he had discovered where she lived by following her bus home. It did match his modus operandi.

"The other thing I discovered was that she was spotted at the library, talking intensely with a man, some time before she disappeared. He was only seen from behind, but he had dyed black hair, like my Mr Brown. I don't think you can really use any of that in an article, but it does mean he's a much stronger suspect, now that we have a more definite probable contact between him and Harriet."

"You really do go above and beyond, don't you, Tessa? All that sounds very useful. I think I can include an oblique reference to your information. Mention a probable sighting of them together without being specific about where. Emphasise the need to find him and include the artist's impression again."

"I suppose that could work. I just don't want to get anyone into trouble for talking to me."

"I understand. Thank you so much for being open with me. We must meet for lunch sometime soon. I'm quite missing your beloved Milton Keynes. It's got under my skin."

I laughed.

"That's quite a turnaround from our first meeting."

"It certainly is. It's your influence, you see. I miss you, too."

I was flustered. That was unexpected. Personal. "I'm sure we'll meet again soon."

"You can count on it."

Was he trying to flirt with me? Or start some kind of relationship? I did not know, and was not sure how I felt about it. Or him. There was no doubt that it was pleasant to have a new friend, though. Was that how Harriet had felt about the elusive Mr Brown?

CHAPTER THIRTEEN

Reckonings

I had decided to work as normal on the following day. I felt recovered enough from the shock of the identification, and Sally had told me that we were unusually busy. The increase in regular business was proving more long term than I had expected. It was encouraging.

A number of older people, who were sometimes uncomfortable with the app, were ringing to book. Often saying that they had seen our company on the television and wanted to give us a try. And sometimes paying with cash, which was less advantageous, but we never wanted to exclude people, especially the elderly or disabled. Most of our vehicles would take a normal wheelchair, and we had one van which could be booked for more bulky mobility equipment.

I always tried to walk during my lunch break. Ideally in one of the parks, or along a wooded redway. Nature was so reviving. Sometimes, however, especially when the weather was inclement, I would park at one end of the shopping centre and go up one side and down the other. It was less relaxing, but at least it was movement and a change of position. Driving was not the healthiest of jobs, and I wanted to resist its impact on my body as far as possible.

That day, it was wet outside, and my previous trip had brought me to the city church end, so I took the decision to walk inside. The bright lights and buzz of excitement did counteract the external gloom, but weaving around self-absorbed shoppers and avoiding those who had stopped mid-walkway for a chat or to look at their phones was irritating. I tried to shut out the distractions and focus on the movement. Let my eyes relax and flit around, and switched off my brain.

Suddenly, near the John Lewis end, there was a loud exclamation and I felt hands on both my shoulders. Someone had stopped right in front of me and halted my forward movement. Annoyed, I stared at the man, with some hostility. He had no right to touch me.

"What do you think are you doing?" A peremptory question. Why would he think he had the right to touch me?

"You're Tessa Fordham, aren't you?" he asked, anger in his voice.

There was no real point in denying it. My name and face had been all over the media. I nodded and examined the man obstructing my way. He was quite tall, and somewhat flabby, despite exuding an impression of great physical strength and confidence. His eyes were slightly bloodshot and he looked rather dissipated, his florid face bearing the marks of repeated over-indulgence.

He actually grabbed me again and pulled me to the side, by a quiet shop doorway.

"How dare you touch me?" I was angry, too.

"I – I have to speak to you. It was necessary to get your attention. Make you stop and listen to me." The words were conciliatory, the impatient tone was not.

"Huh!" was my only response. I did not have to listen to him. I shook myself free of him and turned to leave.

"Please," came a slightly less arrogant request. "I'm sorry if I was too rough. I'm Ralph Jordan, Harriet Beckinsale's husband. I must talk to you."

"You mean ex-husband, don't you?"

His face was suffused with red rage for a moment, then he controlled it, with an obvious effort.

"I guess so. But I – I never stopped loving her, caring for her. She was always mine. And I'm sure she loved me too, underneath. Other people just got in the way, interfered. Tried to take her away from me."

"That's not what I've heard." I did not want to betray confidences or reveal sources of information. Not to this intimidating bully. But I was not going to acquiesce to his fantasies. "But it's irrelevant, now. Unfortunately, she's dead. And we need to catch her killer. It could be you, for all I know. Most victims are murdered by people close to them."

I did not know why I spoke to him like that. All my pent-up frustration was poured into anger at this man who had treated poor Harriet so badly.

He actually flinched, as if I had slapped him.

"I would never do that. Never hurt her. Not like that. I've been trying to protect her. Keep her safe from people who might exploit her, take advantage of her innocence."

He spoke as if he really believed what he was saying. Even though I knew he had been violent towards her. His voice hardened in accusation.

"It's you who took her to that lake, left her there. It's your fault she's dead."

Now it was my turn to be hurt. He was voicing what I had heard in my own head, so many times. But it was not true. I had to stand up for myself.

"She ordered a cab and I took her where she asked me to. That's my job. I even searched for her when she did not turn up for the return trip and then reported her missing. I'm not responsible for her murder. Her killer is."

I turned to leave him. My break was almost over and I had to return to the taxi. He touched my arm, as if to prevent me from moving, then removed it, as I fixed him with a hostile stare.

"I'll walk with you," he said.

"I can't stop you," was my response.

"Look, I'm sorry. I didn't mean to blame you. I know it's not really your fault."

The words were apologetic, but his tone was not. "But you could help me. The police think I – I followed you to the lake. You can tell them I didn't."

I shook my head.

"I can't tell them that, because I don't know if it's true. I didn't see you following me, but I don't know what car you drive and I wasn't on the lookout for stalkers."

He spoke through gritted teeth, with a sudden rage I found all the more intimidating because it was tightly controlled.

"Don't call me a stalker. I'm not a stalker. You don't know me."

I took a slightly shaky breath.

"No, I don't. But I've spoken to people who say you did stalk her, that you followed her around, even to her house. Watched her. Scared her. Now, just leave me alone. I have to get back to work."

"Talking to me is more important. I'm Harriet's husband. You'll stay with me until I say you can leave."

I stopped and gave him the full glare. Unfortunately, it was not very effective, since I had to look up at him.

"You're not her husband. And you have no right at all to control what I do. I know there's really tight security and plenty of CCTV in this centre. If you continue to harass me, I will scream and get help. You'll be arrested and you'll look even more like the guilty party in Harriet's murder."

For a moment, I thought I had gone too far, and he would strike me. His hand was raised, fist clenched. Then the truth of what I had said reached his brain, dissolving some of the fury into baffled frustration. He backed off a little. A very little.

"You're very confident in yourself, aren't you? That you're safe here? But I'll find you. I'll talk to you for as long as I want to, but somewhere else, where there's no security and no CCTV. You just wait. I'll be round a corner, where you don't expect me. And then we'll see how brave and confident you really are."

He hissed his last words viciously at me, turned on his heel, and marched off. Other people moved swiftly out of his way, leaving him a clear path through the crowd.

I stood there, trembling with anger, emotion, and, yes, fear. I had provoked a very dangerous man. That much was clear.

"Are you all right, dear? I thought that man was going to hit you for a moment. Come and sit down with me."

It was an older black lady, her friendly face showing genuine concern. She took my arm, led me to one of the metal seats and sat beside me, patting my hand until the shaking stopped.

"Thank you. You're very kind. Most people would have just walked past."

"Oh, no, I couldn't do that. I was afraid for you. He looked so angry, so violent."

She was right. He had looked frighteningly ready to use force. On me.

"I – I might have to report this to the police. Would you be willing to be a witness?"

I knew it was unlikely. I had heard from Rob that few members of the public were willing to act as witnesses these days, and she surely would want to avoid possible retribution from that highly aggressive man.

"Yes, I would, dear," she said, quietly, after a thoughtful pause. "I've never done anything like that before. But I think he needs to be stopped. And that murder case in the papers makes you realise what awful things can happen. I'll give you my name, address, and phone number, and if you contact the police, you can pass it on to them."

My heart melted with gratitude. What a lovely person! So courageous, too. Impulsively, I gripped her hand.

"Thank you so much. You've restored my faith in human nature."

She smiled and shook her head.

"I'm sure most people would do the same."

We exchanged contact details. She recognised my name.

"I knew you were familiar. I thought you looked like the taxi-driver from the television. Well, dear, I'm all the more ready to support you, if needed. Look after yourself, won't you? There's a murderer out there, he knows your name and face, and where you work, and he won't be at all happy with the help you've given the police."

I stared at her in surprise.

"Do you really think I could be in danger?"

She smiled, understandingly.

"I know, it sounds crazy, doesn't it? And I can't know for sure. But, yes, I think you could be in danger. Either from that nasty man who just threatened you or someone else. You've made the killer's life much more difficult. So please, do take care."

"You're so kind. Do you mind if I give you a hug?"

"Not at all, my dear. I thought you looked like a nice person from your photograph, and I was impressed that you cared enough to report that poor woman missing. Now I've met you, I can see that I was right. Let me know what happens, if you get the chance."

"Thank you so much, Sylvia. Your kindness has turned what

promised to be a horrible day into a much better one."

I gave her a quick hug and hurried back to where I had parked. I called Sally to explain why I was late.

"You need to report that, Tessa. He sounds dangerous. Do it now, and contact me for a fare when you've finished."

I knew she was right. His threats had been genuine enough, that was clear. I knew he had been violent towards Harriet. And possibly even killed her. I shivered. The phrase 'as if someone had walked over my grave' took on a new, more personal meaning.

I took a deep breath and called Rob. His voice was curt, as if he was in a hurry to get back to something important. A little impatient with me ringing him, disrupting his work.

"What is it, Tessa?"

"I'm sorry to disturb you, but I just had a nasty experience in the shopping centre. Harriet's ex-husband approached me, well, grabbed me, made me stop and speak to him."

"What? Are you serious?"

"I'm afraid so. That's what comes of having my name and picture on the television and in the papers."

I told him what had happened, how unexpected and upsetting the confrontation had been, and how scary his final threats had seemed.

"Are you OK, Tess? That must have been very frightening."

His voice was full of concern.

I told him about Sylvia helping me and being willing to be a witness for me.

"That's brilliant. So unusual, too. Sometimes people will help out at the time, but they normally melt away as soon as the police are mentioned."

"Can you do anything about it? Arrest him? Keep him away

from me, at least?"

"I think so. We can charge him with threatening behaviour, that's for sure. There's amazing CCTV coverage in there, as you told him. And with a witness, too, who's willing to come forward. It gives us a good reason to search his house and take DNA, as well. That could be crucial to our murder inquiry. Can you come down now and give an official statement? I'd like to get him into custody as soon as possible, before he causes any more harm."

I agreed. I had suddenly become painfully aware that my job made me quite vulnerable to someone like him, and I did not like the thought of him waiting for me around some unexpected corner. Perhaps following me obsessively, as he had Harriet. I had been granted an unpleasant window into her life. No wonder she had been keen to hide her identity. No wonder she had been happy to meet Mr Brown, if that was his name.

I drove down to the police station, and was able to find a convenient parking spot. Rob met me in reception, put a comforting arm around me, and took me to another bleakly bright interview room, where he plied me with welcome tea and biscuits, and took my statement. As I went through the detail of what had been said, his face darkened with anger.

"That bas – horrible man! How dare he threaten you like that? Don't worry, he'll get what's coming to him. Even touching you the way he did could constitute an assault."

"I don't know if he killed her, though, you know. Why would he draw attention to himself like that if he had? Why would he want to talk to me?"

Rob shook his head.

"Who knows what goes through the head of nutters like Ralph? He might even have persuaded himself that it was all your fault. Or simply been angry with you for helping our investigation. He goes straight to the top of the suspects list, for me, and I'm sure the inspector will agree. We'll arrest him for threatening behaviour and then really get to work on him. Find out what makes him tick. And test his DNA."

I nodded. I supposed he was right. He had more experience with this than I did. I shuddered.

"I'll be glad when you've got him," I said, slightly tremulously, to my shame. "Murderer or not, I can't help being a bit afraid of what he might do, if he got me on my own."

Rob's hand came out and held mine.

"We'll take him into custody as soon as possible. Give him a bit of a scare. See if we can set bail conditions which keep him far away from you. He's probably bluffing, anyway. But do take care."

"Sylvia said I could be in danger from whoever the murderer is. Do you think she's right?"

Rob lowered his eyes and flushed slightly, then met my gaze.

"I'm afraid she may be. It's not something we considered before, but you have – you have become one of the public faces of the investigation. It puts you in the line of fire. I'm sorry. But we'll arrest him in the next few hours, don't you worry. Then you'll be safe again."

I gulped.

"If he's really the killer."

I still had my doubts, even after meeting him. A nasty, vindictive, aggressive man. If he had seen Harriet with another man, he probably would have reacted violently. But would he have been following her that day? Would he have taken her and stored her body for all that time? It seemed a little far-fetched. Unless he was totally obsessed with her.

"I'm confident he is. Don't worry, Tess. But if you're feeling at all anxious, maybe you should go home this afternoon. Not go to work."

I shook my head firmly.

"No, I won't let him intimidate me. And I won't cower at home waiting for an attack that may never come. I'm done with running away from bullies. They're not going to ruin my life again. You just get him as soon as possible. I trust you. I know you'll do your best to keep me safe."

He took both my hands in his and looked right into my eyes.

"I promise I'll look after you, Tessa. Do everything I can to protect you. Always. He'll be off the streets very soon."

I gave him a slightly forced smile and prepared to leave. We hugged outside the station as we said goodbye, and he repeated his promise to take care of me. Back in the car, I sat for a while, still shaken by recent events.

I had talked bravely enough about not being intimidated, but the truth was that I did feel quite intense fear when I thought of meeting him alone somewhere. I was not physically powerful or trained in self-defence. I was a bit of a coward. That had been proved before. So, the only thing to do was put it right out of my mind. Pretend it had never happened.

It was a busy couple of hours and, after a while, I forgot to worry about each new passenger possibly being Harriet's former husband, Ralph. I was confident, in any case, that he would have been arrested by now. There was no more need to worry. Rob had my back.

In the late afternoon, I received a last-minute booking to pick up a new passenger called Johnson from the Simpson car park by Caldecotte lake. He had asked to be taken to the city centre, to the John Lewis end. An easy journey. It was to be my last of the day. I was glad to be on the home straight. It had been a tiring shift, with too many inconsiderate or speeding drivers making the work much more stressful. On top of the emotional strain of what had happened at lunchtime. My energy was drained. One more trip and then home.

It was very dark, already, when I pulled off the narrow road into the parking area and chose a space about half way down. There was a small silver van parked at the bottom end, ghostly in the dim light, but otherwise the place was deserted. Although there were streetlights on the road and the redway, the car park itself was in dappled shadow. I shivered a little. Harriet had been dumped in the river near here. The deepening darkness oozed ominously towards me.

I gave myself a good shake. One more job and then home. There was nothing abnormal to worry about here. Ralph, the ex-husband, would be in the police station by now.

There was, however, no initial indication of a passenger waiting for me. I sent the text message to say I had arrived. All of a sudden, I made out a pale arm, waving rather feebly above one of the larger bushes at the far end and immediately got out to see what was going on. Perhaps my prospective passenger had fallen. I did not want another drama to deal with, but I moved nearer.

"Could you please help me to carry my bag? I dropped it, and I hurt my shoulder, when I fell over."

It was a rather quavering voice, with a marked Scottish accent. Definitely not Ralph. It was safe.

"Of course. I'm coming. Don't try to lift it, I'll help."

I hurried over to the bottom end of the car park and round the corner. I could see a long fat green bag, lying unattended in the centre of the redway and stooped immediately to pick it up. I sensed someone standing right behind me and was about to look up and smile reassuringly, when I felt a tremendous blow on the back of my head and a tide of blackness surged up, unstoppably, to devour me whole.

CHAPTER FOURTEEN

Trapped

I regained some level of consciousness in complete darkness, compression, and semi-suffocation. I could not move my hands up to my face. My arms seemed to be pinned immovably to my sides. It was a nasty sensation and my nose immediately began to itch, simply because I was unable to scratch it. The frustration was ridiculously intense.

My knees were folded right up against my chest and held there tightly. I could not move them. My back hurt, and my muscles began to spasm due to the unnatural position. Breathing was a struggle and rather painful. I focused on trying to calm myself, fighting down the stifling panic, which surged through my body like a tidal wave. There was no room for fight or flight in this constricted space. The adrenaline had nowhere to go.

I gradually became aware of a truly revolting stench invading my nostrils, which induced me first to retch uncontrollably, and then be sick. There was no room for the sickness to escape to, my head seemed to be encased in something quite tight. I felt as if I was being slowly smothered and was terrified that I would choke on my own vomit.

I managed to calm my stomach and focused on the basic but essential activity of breathing in and out. Slowly and carefully. Through my nose. Mouth closed. The panic subsided a little, but I was completely disorientated and desperately frightened. The utter darkness was profoundly oppressive.

Slowly, I realised that I was being gently shaken, by a vibration under my body. Something around and beneath me was moving. Listening carefully, I could hear an engine noise. Suddenly there was a jolt, then another one immediately afterwards. A speed bump?

My brain was finally beginning to work rationally. I was in a vehicle, being driven somewhere. The bag on the path had been an ambush. I had been knocked out and captured. Abducted. Kidnapped. The dramatic language seemed ridiculous, but here was no other way to describe it.

Was it Ralph after all? Had he disguised his voice? My stupidity in allowing myself to be tricked disgusted me. He had said that he would be waiting around some corner. I had not even thought to be wary. Had walked right into his trap. And now I was at his mercy. If he had taken me like this, he must be the killer. I knew he would have had the strength to lift me.

I began to shake. Fear, rather than cold. Was I about to be tipped out into a river or lake, like poor Harriet? The images of the dark, turbulent water under the bridge, the brown flooding torrent over the weir, the huge lonely expanse of the south lake came unbidden into my mind. The thought of drowning, trapped in the blackness, all alone, was petrifying. I tried to struggle against what held me, but could not move appreciably. Tears threatened to suffocate me.

The tormenting period of despair seemed to last for hours. I tried to pray. *Out of the depths.* But the enveloping fear was too strong. In the end, my mind simply said: 'please', and repeated it, like a mantra.

I realised that the vehicle had stopped, and the engine tone changed its note, before it ended abruptly. I worked out that we must be inside somewhere. Then a much louder noise, as if a metal door was being opened. Whatever I was imprisoned in was soft and flexible. It was pulled and dragged in the direction of my head, then dropped down some distance. The pain as I landed brought a groan from me. I almost blacked out again. There was silence. I did not try to speak. I was frozen with terror.

The darkness became a little less complete. Vague greenish light pierced my black prison, through small gaps and thinner spots in my tight shroud. Suddenly, there was a dragging feeling. The tightness around my arms and knees released a little, as if some additional binding had been removed. Then a zip was pulled swiftly down my back and white light flooded in, dazzling me. Cold air reached my nostrils and I sucked it in, greedily.

A strong hand rolled me onto my back. I was helpless to resist it. My knees fell sideways, untethered, of their own accord, and I was conscious that I had absolutely no control over them. They began to tremble pathetically. My arms were free, but numb and useless. I was half-blinded by the harsh glare of a strip light above me.

"My poor dear! I thought you would be unconscious until I made you comfortable. I'm so sorry. That must have been a little unpleasant."

The words seemed nonsensical and I tried to shake my head to clear it. The pain in my skull surged and I nearly lost consciousness again. I kept as still as possible, very aware of the foul vomit all over my face, dripping back now into my hair. The smell of it was nauseating, but less repellent than the other odour, which had overcome me with its penetrating putrid power.

"Don't try to move. You're concussed. I'll fetch something to clean you up a bit."

Again what was said was surreal. It was not Ralph's voice. That much was clear. But there was no connection between the words and my reality. I tried to move, when I heard footsteps walking off, but the effort was too much for me. Very quickly, the feet returned and I felt a warm wet cloth on my face. I closed my eyes. It was pleasant. There was a floral soap smell from the flannel, driving out the other disgusting odours.

"I was going to carry you in the bag, but that won't do, now. If you lie very still, I'll use a fireman's lift to move you. Don't struggle or you may fall and worsen your head injury."

The voice was sweetly reasonable, and I instinctively obeyed. It was also familiar, and it gradually seeped into my confused and battered brain, that my strange kindly kidnapper was none other than Mr Brown. Or Mr Johnson. I had been right about him all along.

He was much more powerful than he had appeared. Being moved made me intensely dizzy and I had to close my eyes, but he heaved me over his shoulder with no apparent difficulty. My head knocked uselessly against the wall once or twice, but he did not seem to notice. I drifted into a dark faint as he began to move upstairs.

When I woke again, I was lying on a softer, more comfortable surface. A bed? A white ceiling above me. Warm lamplight. It did not hurt my eyes. Some relief.

But something was wrong. My arms were up above my head, tied to something. I could feel bonds on my wrists. And one ankle, too. I struggled and tried to move my aching head.

"Don't do that, my dear. You'll feel much better if you lie still. It will take a while for you to recover from your concussion. Don't worry, I'll look after you. Help you to get better quickly."

"Why am I here? What do you want from me?" I managed to whisper, with great difficulty.

"I don't think you're up to hearing the whole story right now, Tessa. Yes, I know your name. You've been a very troublesome girl, interfering with my plans, and I was really quite angry with you, for a while, but I've forgiven you now. We're going to get along very nicely together."

He was right about one thing. My brain felt like wet cotton wool and I could not gather my thoughts. Struggled to comprehend what he was saying.

"I've only tied you up temporarily, my dear. Just until I can explain the situation to you and show you your options. You're not capable of understanding, right now. I can see that in your poor vague eyes. I'd like to get you washed and showered, but that's not feasible either. So I'll just bathe your face, and fetch a nice cool drink for you, and then let you sleep."

Befuddled and frustrated, I turned my head towards the voice, ignoring the shooting pain and the flashes of light before my eyes. It was indeed Brown. He looked different, however. No black hair left. It was cut much shorter and bleached blond. Darkened eyebrows and eyelashes. No one would recognise him from the picture now.

That made me feel intensely sad, although I did not quite remember why. Tears blurred my vision. He leant over me and gently brushed the disgusting hair from my face, washing the area around my mouth, nose, and eyes with what appeared to be a blue fluffy flannel.

"There, you look much better now. You're really a very pretty girl underneath. I can see we're going to have a good time together."

He must have seen the instinctive recoil of fear in my eyes.

"Oh, don't worry, Tessa, my darling. I'm not going to hurt you or force you. I'm not a rapist. You'll soon see. Just relax. I'll be back in a minute with a nice drink. It'll take the nasty taste out of your mouth."

I simply could not think straight. Confused and uncertain, I gave a tiny nod. Drifted vaguely away on a wave of grey until he returned. He slid his arm under my shoulders and gently raised my head, so that I could drink. It was cold and refreshing as it slid down my throat, with a strongly bitter aftertaste.

"Yes," he said. "I've drugged it. Just to help you sleep and recover. The sooner you're better, the sooner we can talk things through.

And you'd like that, wouldn't you? You want to know what's going on."

"Yes," I muttered.

I was laid back on the pillow. Even its soft pressure hurt my head. He turned on some quiet, soothing, classical music. I heard him sit down, somewhere out of my sight. I could not fight it. I let go, and allowed the darkness to overcome me like a tide.

CHAPTER FIFTEEN

Explanations

Slowly, consciousness returned. My eyes felt gummed together, but I could not rub them. My hands were still tied and my arms felt heavy, numb, bloodless. With an effort, I managed to force my eyes half open. The ache in my head was crushing and there was a dry metallic taste in my mouth. I tried to swallow, but it was difficult.

As feeling began to return, I was humiliated to realise that I must have wet myself. Burning shame swept through me. It brought home to me the completely helpless and vulnerable position I had been placed in. Tears trickled down my cheeks and I could not suppress a sob.

The quiet music was still playing, but it had no calming impact. A sense of hysteria built in my chest and I could barely restrain it. I looked around wildly for some means of escape, ignoring the shooting pain in my head and neck. Saw solid white shutters on the window, closed to the outside world. Opened my mouth and tried to scream. Only a pathetic dribble of sound emerged.

Suddenly the door, beyond the foot of the bed, opened. He hurried in, carrying a glass of water.

I could barely hear my own cry, but I made an effort to continue, hoping desperately that, eventually, my throat would clear and I would be able to increase the volume. Someone would hear me.

"Tessa! You're awake. I'm so glad. Please don't try to scream. You'll only hurt yourself. I don't think anyone will notice, but I would have to gag you, just in case. See, I have a cloth to go in your mouth and strong duct tape here, all ready to use. You don't want that, now, do you? It would be quite unpleasant for you. Close your mouth, like a good girl."

The contrast between his gentle remonstrating tone and the violent threat of gagging me, silencing me, was confusing, frightening. I could not cope with being further imprisoned, with having even less control over my own body. I might not be able to breathe properly. My nose was quite blocked. I shut my mouth as instructed.

"That's better. I really didn't want to gag you. I want to look after you. I understand why you were crying out, however, my poor dear. You probably feel extremely disorientated. You're not sure where you are or what happened. Don't worry about it. You've had a very long deep sleep. You'll soon feel much better. Let me wipe your face for you."

As if I could stop him.

Nevertheless, I suffered his ministrations without struggling, although I hated the sensation of his warm breath on my face, invading my space.

He became aware of the wetness on the bed, on my clothes. I turned my face away, deserving the punishing stab of pain, feeling the heat of the deep flush, humiliated to my very core. I bit my lips together to hold in the sob.

"Oh, Tessa, don't be embarrassed. It's not really your fault. You couldn't help yourself. You were so sound asleep, like a baby. Never mind. There's a plastic sheet underneath you, so the mattress won't be wet. I'll change the bed for you while you're in the shower. You'll soon be nice and clean again."

There was kindness, gentle consideration in his voice. Patronising, as if I were a small child who had suffered an accidental urination. As vulnerable as I felt, it was comforting, and I could not restrain the gratitude.

"Thank you," I whispered.

"Now, Tessa, before I untie you, let's just set some ground rules, shall we? Look at me, please, dear."

Reluctantly, I turned my head to look at him. It set off fountains of sparks in my eyes, accompanied by shooting stars of pain.

"I'm much stronger than I look, Tessa. You know that, now. I follow a strict workout regime and have very powerful muscles. I can overpower you, especially in your current state, very easily. I can quickly throttle you into unconsciousness, if I need to. And I have a knife for insurance. See? Not large, but extremely sharp, and I know how and where to use it."

I stared in horror at the stark pointed metal blade, glimmering evilly in the lamplight.

"I don't want to threaten you, or to talk like this. I want us to be friends. I'm just making plain to you that you mustn't even think about trying to get away. Once we've had our little talk, I'm sure you won't even want to. But, just for now, I want to show you that you are entirely in my power, and you must, absolutely must obey me. In everything and immediately. Without hesitation."

I looked from the knife into his implacable steel grey eyes. There was no doubt or uncertainty in his voice. I had to respond.

"OK."

"Good. Now, I'm going to unbind you in a moment and take you to the shower room. The window is locked and so is the shutter. I'll give you a dressing gown and a towel, and you can clean yourself up, get rid of the foul smell of the vomit and the urine from where you have unfortunately soiled yourself."

Hearing the words brought back the intense shame and embarrassment. His voice was even, but there was an undertone of him subtly taunting me with my physical inadequacy, emphasising his absolute control over me. Only with his consent could I be clean and continent.

"When you're nice and fresh again, smelling a bit better, you'll be able to come back in here, and change into some lovely clothes I have for you. A fetching deep blue dress covered in beautiful white flowers. I'm sure it will fit perfectly. It's all planned and ready, everything bought in advance. All my preparations made for you, as my honoured guest. When you come back, I'll have changed the bed, and you'll be able to rest some more. We'll have a nice cup of tea and then talk things over."

I agreed meekly, my muddled mind beginning to reflect on what I could do in the bathroom. If it had a lock... His saccharine voice interrupted my thoughts.

"I can see that you're still not understanding your position, my sweet. There is a lock, for your privacy, so that you can feel comfortable and relaxed. But I can very easily open it from the outside. There's no bolt. I would be loath to disturb you during your ablutions, but I will if I have to. If I hear any excessive noise, I'll have to come in and gag you. Do you see, now?"

Tears came into my eyes. He had thought of everything. The powerlessness was almost physically painful.

"Don't cry, my dear. It's really not so bad. I won't hurt you unless you make me. I thought I would want to punish you, to see you suffer, for making my life so difficult, but I find that I have quite forgiven you. The head wound, the vomiting, you wetting the bed – these are quite sufficient, for now, to chastise you and correct your uncouth behaviour. You've made amends, even though it was involuntary. Paid your price. Taken your punishment. We can now be friends."

He actually patted my poor bruised head in a strangely avuncular way.

The thought of being a friend of this terrible man was revolting, but it would do me no good to say so. I vaguely remembered that it was a good thing to remain on the right side of your kidnapper. They would be much less likely to hurt you. Or kill you. I could not, yet, bring myself to talk to him, but I might have to overcome that reluctance.

It took some time for me to be capable of movement, even once he released me. The sharp tingle of returning blood in my arms was unpleasant. My head was still intensely painful and dizziness overwhelmed me the first time I tried to sit up. I was forced to accept his help and support to make it onto my feet and be able to move slowly and unsteadily out of the room.

To my relief, the small shower room was spotlessly clean and comfortably warm. There was shampoo, good quality shower gel, soap. A white toilet and sink. A modern, powerful shower. It was such a pleasure to be able to wash away the disgusting residue of vomit and remove the befouled clothing. There was even a toothbrush, still in its packet, and a new tube of toothpaste.

By the time I stepped out of the bathroom, I felt like a new person. I could even think a little more clearly. Washing my hair had been a painful business due to the wound on the back of my head, but it was so good to rinse away the smell and the stickiness. The deep headache was still there, but less debilitating than before. And clean teeth make such a difference to the morale.

The fluffy dressing gown felt soft and gentle against my rather bruised body. I had unstiffened somewhat under the reviving flow of warm water.

He was waiting for me.

"Good girl. You look much better. Leave the old, soiled clothes on the floor. I'll dispose of them for you. Come and get changed. I'll be just outside the door. I think I've remembered everything you'll need."

Immensely grateful that I did not have to change in front of him, I hurriedly began to put on the clothes he had laid out for me. My balance was still precarious, so I sat on the clean bed most of the time. There was underwear, more or less in my size. A rather pretty dress, very girlish, not my style at all. A woolly white cardigan. I caught sight of my reflection in the long mirror on the wall. I looked quite unlike myself. It was disorientating. Alienating. Especially with my head swimming whenever I moved it too quickly.

He knocked and came in.

"Tessa, you look beautiful. I thought that dress would suit you, and it does. It brings out the colour in your lovely eyes. Since you've been so good, I'm going to let you come down to have tea and toast with me. A little reward. Follow me."

There were hideous fluffy pink slippers by the bed. I pushed my naked feet into them, and he supported me down the stairs and into a large kitchen, Shaker-style in white, with blue accents. A very pretty kitchen for a single man. I assumed he lived on his own. Surely no wife or partner would have allowed him to abduct me. There was no natural light, as the window was again covered by white internal shutters.

"Sit down at the table, dear, and I'll make you something to eat."

I suddenly realised that I was ravenously hungry. Trembling a little, but holding it together, I sat on the wooden chair he indicated. Watched him bustling around the kitchen.

"Tea or coffee, Tessa?"

It was such a strangely domestic scene. Like a weird dream, with everything looking normal, but oddly out of place. My head seemed to be floating some way above my body.

"Tea, please." More rehydrating. I felt the need of that.

Soon the food and drink were in front of me. I could smell the toast and was itching to eat.

"Go ahead, Tessa. I ate earlier."

I peered searchingly at him. Had he drugged them? I would have to take the risk. I began to eat, and it was all I could do to slow myself down to a reasonable level of decorum. I gulped the tea down thirstily and he poured me another cup, from the flower decorated porcelain teapot he had used. He seemed to have an obsession with floral patterns.

When I had finished, he took the crockery to the sink.

"I have a dishwasher, but I don't like to use it. I don't think they wash as thoroughly, do you? Would you mind washing up for me, dear?"

I gaped at him. He really expected me to wash up for him? Do his chores?

He nodded, a severe look in his eye. I rose obediently, wobbled a little, and then went over to the sink.

"Use the washing-up bowl and dishcloth, and run the water nice and hot, please, Tessa. Dry them all up carefully, too. I don't like to see things standing on the draining board. We want it all nice and tidy, don't we? Mother always kept our house spotless. We have to keep up our standards. I'll show you where to put them when you've finished. Take your time, and tell me if you're too dizzy. I'll allow you a short break if you need it."

He watched my every move, making me repeat anything that was not completed to his exacting requirements. Smiled approvingly.

"Good girl. You're learning. You deserve another reward. Let's go and sit in the living room for our little talk. Come with me."

This was like something out of the Stepford Wives. I was puzzled, confused, uncertain. The food had done me good, but there was an inner tremble, which I could not quell.

The living room, once again enclosed behind anonymous white shutters, and lit by a rather pretentious crystal chandelier in the centre of the ceiling, was chintzy and old-fashioned. Dresden shepherdesses on the mantelpiece and porcelain angels and cherubs in an illuminated display unit in the corner. I shivered. There was something spooky about all this.

He made me sit on the sofa next to him. I would have preferred to be further away. He noticed my shrinking and the quiver.

"Don't be afraid of me, Tessa, my dear. You mustn't be scared. If you continue to behave well, you have nothing to fear. I can give you all kinds of treats and rewards for good behaviour. Yes, there are punishments available, and I'll show them to you before we go back upstairs. But I don't want to have to use them. It's entirely up to you. If you're compliant and cooperative, I'll be very kind."

He took my hand, feeling it shake.

"You're really frightened, aren't you? Please don't be. I promise, I won't hurt you if you're good."

I tried to draw my hand away, but he held onto it, possessively. As if it belonged to him rather than me. Even in my weakened state, it was a struggle to control my rebellion.

"Well, then, Tessa, what would you like to know?"

I could not speak for a moment. Then found the strength to open my mouth. Ask what was on my heart.

"Why did you kill Harriet? Why did you kidnap me?"

"Oh, Tessa, don't be so melodramatic. I haven't kidnapped you. I'm just looking after you here for a while, to make sure you don't cause me any more trouble. Keeping you safe here with me. And enjoying your scintillating company!"

He laughed at his own sarcasm.

I sniffed dismissively. But was a little afraid of his response, all the same.

He released my hand, rose to his feet and began to walk around the stuffy room, declaiming, his arms waving to emphasise his points. Like a stage actor. Telling a story. Entirely from his point of view, of course.

"As for Harriet, I believed that she was destined to be my soulmate. It was fate. We met, quite by chance, in the library, did you know that? Drawn to the same comforting spot at precisely the right moment. Fate."

He paused for a moment, a reminiscent smile on his bland face.

"She liked the same type of novels that I did. Warm, escapist, romantic fantasies. A homely dreamworld, so far from the horrid reality of modern life. That's what we talked about at first. We clicked instantly. An immediate bond, complete mental, physical, even spiritual chemistry. Love at first sight, you might say."

Poor Harriet. She had so much sadness to escape from. No wonder she had been easily swayed by a man who appeared to share her every taste.

"We met a number of times there, over several weeks, seeking out corners and hidden areas. But we couldn't really talk in depth in the library. There was no privacy, and that's very important to me. To her, too, after her former husband's dreadful behaviour. She was also extremely conscientious. Always made sure she did her job properly, insisted on giving it priority over our time together."

There was disapproval in his voice.

"And I didn't want to be seen with her. I had it in mind to bring her here and share my life with her, even at that early stage."

That explained all the efforts to disguise her identity. He had always intended to hold her here. That was a frightening thought.

"I asked her to keep our romance a secret and she did," he went on. "She was afraid that her ex-husband might find out. I was worried someone might notice us together, pry into our relationship, ask who I was. But I think the secrecy made it even more exciting for her. She so wanted a special romantic relationship. She needed some magic in her humdrum life."

I was moved with compassion for her once more. She did not ask for much.

"She asked me to have a celebration lunch with her in the city centre when we had been seeing each other carefully at the library for six weeks, but I was concerned about us being observed. By that husband, who kept following her, if no one else. So, I invited her for a walk around Caldecotte Lake instead. Explained that we needed to keep our love secret from everyone, especially that man."

That must have been when she was seen walking with him.

"I picked her up in my van by the library," he continued. "I worried, afterwards, that I might have been spotted. That's why I instructed her to get a taxi next time. From a different pick-up point. I told her to telephone for it, give a false name, and pay with cash. For security, I said. It kept things private, intimate, between the two of us. No one else needed to know. She understood the need for secrecy."

I nodded slightly. That chimed with what she had said and done. He droned on, unstoppable, enjoying his reminiscences.

"Our walk together was delightful, a genuine pleasure, and she seemed to enjoy it very much. I had never seen her so happy, so full of light. She revelled in my company and in the natural surroundings. However, the paths were all quite busy, and we couldn't really talk properly about our future. So I invited her to come down again the following week. You brought her. On time, thank you."

He smiled his approbation.

"I met her on the path and brought her here. You'll have gathered that my house is not far from the lake. We chatted and ate cake, drank prosecco, had a marvellous time, dreaming of our life together, sharing our love for one another."

His voice softened.

"She was perfect. She adored me, worshipped me, I could see it in her face. We kissed properly, for the first time, and it was heavenly. Blissful. We eventually went upstairs and made love. It was marvellous, for both of us. She said she had never been with such a gentle, caring, and considerate man, had never experienced such pleasure. I was over the moon. Full of such happiness and contentment."

There was a dreamy look in his eye. Then it changed as he caught sight of my face, and his voice hardened.

"Even that, you managed to spoil for me. I wanted to stay in bed with her, luxuriate in our mutual love, but she started to worry about you coming to fetch her at five o'clock. She didn't want to let you down, she said. Not after you'd been so kind. I persuaded her to let me cancel the return trip. I'd hidden her phone downstairs, when she was in the toilet. I told her there was no signal for me indoors, but I would pop down to make the call for her. Of course, I never did ring."

He looked at me with a fresh touch of hostility.

"I don't know why she was so concerned about you. You're just a taxi driver, after all. She must have really taken to you, for some strange reason."

There had been a genuine bond. I was glad that she had felt it, too.

"Anyway," he said, "once I'd sorted that concern out, she agreed to stay overnight with me. We ate our meal and had one perfect night together. I've never been so contented, satisfied in every way. She seemed full of joy, too. She said it was like paradise, being together like that."

"So what went wrong?"

He paused. His nostrils tightened.

"I'd got toiletries and clothes for her, everything she needed to stay here in comfort. I knew she wouldn't have any luggage with her. She was surprised at that. A little wary, I thought. She said that she preferred to choose her own clothes. She had her own style and was proud of it. We had breakfast next morning, and she washed up, just as you did, but without even being asked. She was perfect company. I was looking forward to spending the day with her. Then she started talking about going into work."

His face darkened.

"She wouldn't take 'no' for an answer. I didn't want to lose her. I wanted her here with me, all the time, available whenever I needed her. In the end, she agreed to remain with me, on the understanding that she would attend work on the following day. She felt terribly guilty for missing her shift. I'd already destroyed her phone so that it couldn't be traced, but she thought it was simply lost. I don't have a landline. I offered to ring the library for her. She accepted, but I could see in her face that she did not totally believe that I would do it. She was moving away from me. Withdrawing. She asked to go for a walk again, but, of course, that wasn't possible. We might have been seen."

"What's the problem with that? She'd agreed to stay with you that day, hadn't she?"

He looked sternly at me.

"You don't understand at all, Tessa. She was my princess. My special one. I couldn't have other people looking at her, distracting her from her true purpose. Contaminating her. I needed her here, all the time, under my eye. Safe and clean and happy. Set apart. All mine."

I could see why Harriet would not like that. Not after her ex-husband. Asking to go for a walk was probably, even then, a prelude to an escape attempt. He spoke increasingly quickly.

"She – she became quite distressed, upset. Said I was trying to control her. Of course, I was, but only for her own good. She – we could have been so very happy."

"She needed her freedom."

There was anger in his eyes now.

"She said that, too. She loved me, but she wanted to be free. I couldn't have that. I calmed her down, appeared to agree to her demands, to concede that she was right, then gave her drugged tea. I thought that would make her more compliant."

He sighed, deeply.

"It did, for a while, but when I tried to make love to her again, she fought against me, resisted me. Something had changed, deep inside her, something more powerful than the drug. But I – I wouldn't force her. I'm not a rapist, as I told you. I showed her how hurt I was, that she didn't want me any longer. She relented and calmed down, but still would not allow me to touch her. Not even to kiss her. She looked at me as if I were a stranger. As if she'd never seen me before."

At least she had not been violated against her will.

"I knew it was all ruined. Spoiled. Our relationship would never be the same again. The trust was gone. For both of us. I was glad that I had drugged her quite heavily. When she fell fast asleep next to me, looking so angelic, so innocent and precious, I knew I wanted to keep her that way. Prevent her from changing. I put the pillow gently over her face and pressed down hard. I don't think she ever knew I had ended it for her. It was quite peaceful, you know. She barely moved at all, just one convulsive shudder."

There was a strange icy tone in his voice. He had killed her, quite deliberately, but seemed to feel no remorse. No human emotion at all. The rage and sadness had completely melted away.

"I left her on the bed for a while. She looked so calm and contented. It was pleasant to sit and watch her. Like keeping vigil, I suppose. I have a portable air-conditioning unit, and I put it in there to keep her cool. I was going to dispose of her quietly, respectfully, in the lake near here."

The cold voice lost its detachment.

"But you, you got the police involved. It made everything much more difficult. I planted the phone, by the road bridge, and hoped that they would just think she'd fallen in or killed herself. That they might give up and go away."

"They wouldn't do that."

"Oh, I think, without your interventions, they might well have done. Then, there was your reconstruction. That's how I knew who you were. I managed to shift their activity over to the other side of the lake, out of my way, by dropping the purse there, but nothing seemed to get rid of them. They kept their base at the car park and I could not risk them seeing me. You appeared to be able to keep them focused on her, keep her in the news. I became very cross with you then, Tessa."

A sharp jag of fear shot through me. Angering a killer was dangerous.

"I decided I had to see you, meet you. Booked your taxi. Even then, although I was very cautious about what I said, I think you were a little suspicious of me. I made sure you didn't see where I lived, or even which direction I walked off in. I didn't trust you at all. But I have to admit that you were more attractive in person, much nicer-looking than you appeared on television. I saw that you were acting, not out of malice or an attempt to hurt me, but out of care for Harriet. You were rather appealing. You have a delicate charm of your own."

Thanks, I thought. *You're not my type at all.*

"Was Harriet lying in the bedroom all that time?"

He smiled patronisingly.

"Of course not, Tessa. What a silly idea! I couldn't keep the bedroom cool enough. I brought her down to the garage, where it was much colder – it's linked to the house, so it was easy. Put the air-conditioning on in there. But I knew I would need to get rid of the body soon. It was beginning to decompose and the smell was becoming offensive. No longer my precious Harriet. Just a corpse. You'd made the south lake impossible, so I decided on Simpson. The river would be easier than the lake, and the current would bear her away."

As if it were my fault.

"As long as I went long after dark, I knew that there would be no cameras, no witnesses. Although there are streetlights nearby, there are none in the car park. It was easy to get from the van to the river. I moved her in a large and very strong Christmas tree bag, with some bungees tied around it to hold her limbs together. It was perfect. She wasn't too heavy. Easy for me to move around. No mess. Her body was a little soft and squishy by then. Fluids had begun to leach out. But she was much easier to deal with, after the rigor had gone. I slid her gently out of the bag into the water. In her lovely dress. Quite respectfully. Like a burial at sea. I even said a few words of farewell. I thought she would be washed much further downstream, and not found or identified for a long while. That was disappointing."

I felt intensely nauseous.

"Did you – did you move me in the same bag?"

"Yes, of course. It worked so well. Practical, watertight, and discreet."

That was where the foul smell of corruption had come from. Harriet's decomposing body. Horror filled me to overflowing.

"I'm going to be sick – where's the toilet?"

With commendable promptness, he pulled me after him to a small downstairs lavatory and lifted the toilet lid. I lost all the tea and toast. Painful heaves. Mingled with desperate sobs.

"I'm so sorry, my dear. I didn't think of how that might upset you. You're quite a delicate little thing, aren't you? Over-sensitive. Never mind. Come and sit in the kitchen again. I'll make you a hot drink. Perhaps a dry biscuit. That might settle your stomach."

How could he sound so reasonable when he had done such awful things? He must be mad.

It percolated deeper into my brain. Yes, he was disturbed. Not sane. I would need to be very careful. He might appear rational, but, in fact, he was completely unbalanced. The fear grew, then. And a corresponding determination to survive, escape, tell Harriet's story. And my own. I knew I would have to deceive him, persuade him that I was positively cooperating, if I was to have any chance of escaping. It would be difficult but it had to be done.

Back in the kitchen, my courage grew once more.

"So why did you kidnap me?"

He looked sadly at me.

"Please don't use that word again, Tessa. It's very crude. I haven't kidnapped you. You're here simply to prevent you from causing further damage. And, in addition, because, now that I'm getting to know you, I think we could develop a genuine personal relationship. You could replace Harriet at my side."

I tried to hide the deep shudder at that prospect.

"What had I done that was so wrong?"

"Oh, Tessa, you know what you did. Beginning with reporting Harriet missing. If you hadn't done that, the police would never have taken her disappearance seriously, and would not have had any idea where to search for her. If anyone had been suspected of involvement, it would have been her ex-husband. She had told me how unpleasant his behaviour had been. Then, when her body was discovered, by accident, I believe, you were the one to give them a swift identification. Enabling them to move much more quickly."

I was starting to feel proud. Perhaps I had honestly done something which made a difference.

"Worst of all, you were suspicious enough to tell the police about me. You gave them a description, helped them to make an identifiable portrait of me. I had to clipper and dye my hair and my eyebrows. Tint my lashes. It was a major undertaking. Of course, I couldn't go to a barber for it."

He sounded peevishly annoyed.

"I don't speak to my neighbours, here, and none of them really know me, since I usually only leave the house in the van, but I couldn't take the risk. Someone might have spotted me at the supermarket. Mostly I use online shopping, but I like to go and buy key essentials personally. Mother always recommended that. But even a delivery driver might have recognised me."

I was lifted by a spark of hope. It seemed that he might go out at some point. Or someone might come to the door of the house. If I persuaded him I was cooperating, I might yet have a chance to escape, or at least attract attention.

"I – I'm sorry."

He stared at me. Weighing me in the balance. Finding me wanting.

"Are you really, Tessa? I can't be sure, yet. You should be. Your intervention is the reason you are here. You are responsible for your own situation, your own fate. I knew I couldn't leave you free any longer. I did consider simply killing you immediately, but I could not force myself to carry out such a ruthless act. Not without giving you a chance. An alternative option. I had to have you under my personal control, though. Ensure that you didn't cause me any more trouble."

An uncontrollable quiver ran down my spine. Under his control.

"I tried to take you once, before, and it was a different driver who arrived. Disappointing, but a useful dress rehearsal. I called myself Jones, that time. Disguised my voice, of course, so that your receptionist would not recognise it. Used a different phone. I have quite a stock of them. And then, this time, I lured the right person. You. And you performed exactly as expected. So predictable, so easy to trick. You hurried to help the poor old Scottish man with his bag. Bent to pick it up, as soon as you saw it. Made it so very easy for me. As if you were destined to be mine. To be in my power."

I burned with shame. How could I have been so naïve and stupid?

"It was not all that straightforward to get you into the bag once you were unconscious. Fortunately, the blow to your head was harder than I'd planned, so you were completely out of it throughout. No struggling. But you're taller than Harriet and a little heavier. I was very worried, despite the darkness, that someone might come along and catch me at it. It wasn't late. But once you were safely in and the bungees were tightened securely, I was back in control, and could relax. After all, what was there to see? A man moving a large heavy bag. Nothing to worry about."

He laughed lightly, proud of his cleverness.

"I left your keys in the car. Placed your phone on the seat. With gloves, of course. No traces or fingerprints to find. Then I destroyed the new burner phone and sim I had used to call your company. Heaved you into the back of the van (as gently as I could) and left. No witnesses. No trace. You've just vanished. Into thin air."

There was smug satisfaction in his voice. Enjoyment of his own ingenuity.

They would be looking, then. Rob and the police. It would be obvious that I had been taken. My sister would not let them rest. I just had to make it possible for them to discover where I was.

"I'm sure you're hoping to be rescued, my dear. It won't happen. I've thought of everything, you see. You're quite secure, here."

I glared at him. I could not help it. He saw the anger.

"You need to learn to accept your situation, Tessa, my darling. I'm becoming more and more reconciled to the new status quo, I can tell you. You're very attractive and I think we will fit together very well. You're prettier than Harriet, and much younger. That has advantages."

Really? I don't think so. I hoped he could not read minds.

"I would love to have children, you know. It's quite possible, here. All secure, safe, secret. I would look after you during your pregnancy and help you to deliver safely. I know I can develop all the skills needed. I'm a very fast learner. Then we could have our own perfect, private, little family. Self-contained. Quite out of reach of all the nastiness of modern society. You're a very private person, yourself, just like me. Wouldn't you like that?"

My bones turned to jelly. Of course, I wanted children. But certainly not his children. I did indeed value my privacy, but not in this extreme, perverted way. I was not like him. Not at all.

I felt so vulnerable. Frightened. Shaky, but dulled by a numbness creeping into my bones. He saw it in my face.

"Don't worry, Tessa. There's time enough for us to settle and have a family. You're not ready yet. Are you starting to feel sleepy, now? I put more drugs in your tea, I'm afraid, to calm you down, and allow you to get the rest you need. You still need to recover from your concussion."

I looked at him and my vision slipped sideways. Began to spin. I tried to speak. Could not make a sound.

"Come on upstairs, my dear. You'll feel much better after a good relaxing snooze."

He pulled me up onto my deadened and useless feet, and supported me up the steep straight stairway. I could not prevent my heavy head from slipping sideways onto his shoulder. Inside, I was revolted, but I was completely incapable of pulling my neck up. I heard myself moan, quietly.

His hand came up and stroked my head.

"It's so nice to sense your reliance on my strength, Tessa. Just let yourself go. I'll keep you quite safe. You're my precious charge, now. And I'll hear at once if you are in distress. I have a baby listener in your room. It's very sensitive. So don't worry. You're quite safe here with me."

My mind was screaming inside my uncooperative body. I could not control it at all. He seemed to feel that all was not well.

"I think I'd better help you to the toilet before putting you to bed. We don't want another incontinence issue, do we?"

I could not resist even in the slightest way. He took me to the small shower room. Lifted the dress. Pulled down my underwear and put me on the toilet, supporting me to stay upright by leaning on him. His body so offensively close to mine. Watching me.

I wept with impotent frustration, tears rolling silently down my cheeks, as I passed water on command. Utter humiliation. He wiped me and pulled up my pants again. I had no control over my body at all. I wanted to scream, kick him, run away. Nothing was possible.

Back in the bedroom, he undressed me, holding me upright, sitting or laying me down, as he wished. He pulled a frilly pink nylon nightdress over my flopping head. There was nothing overtly sexual in his touches, but I felt profoundly violated by his ability to use me as he liked. He seemed to me to take longest about the most intimate areas.

There was a detached part of me, up above my useless body, which watched and railed at my pathetic inability to resist him. It was as if I were a doll, a plaything to be moved as he wanted, at his whim.

He laid me down on the bed. Tied both of my ankles to the lower bedposts, my right arm to the bars at the head, covered me with the clean quilt. Stroked my hair away and kissed me on the forehead.

I retained enough control to turn my head away very slightly, a few millimetres, that was all. After a moment filled with the burning acid of shame, oblivion overcame me. I welcomed the inner darkness to cover my vulnerability, my utter exposure to his will.

CHAPTER SIXTEEN

Consequences

I held myself very still and quiet when I regained consciousness, taking stock of my physical position and the overall situation. I now knew he had a microphone connected and would hear any sounds I made. I hoped he did not have a camera, too, but could not be sure, so I remained as motionless as possible.

Opening my eyes, I was aware that the light level was exactly the same as before. There were no clocks in the room and, indeed, I had not seen any in the house. My watch and phone had been removed. I had absolutely no idea what time it was or how long I had been his captive. I sensed that it was deliberate. A technique to confuse me and make me even more dependent.

I was hungry. Having vomited again, there was an acid taste in my mouth and my stomach felt bruised. I was reluctant to eat and drink what was on offer, since he was clearly drugging me, but I needed more strength if I was to take advantage of any chance to escape. I resolved to focus on food and avoid more than a few sips of drink.

My body was very stiff. Being bound for so long was already having an impact, and my limbs felt weak, as if the muscles were beginning to waste away. How long had I been there? I had no real idea. My head felt less painful, but the wound was sore and itchy. It was healing. That might mean that I had been lying here for much longer than I realised. If I was allowed any freedom of movement at all, I must use some of it to exercise, or at least to stretch.

It suddenly struck me, with a powerful flood of warmth, that, while I was alone in here, at the mercy of a madman, there were many people outside who would be searching for me. Out in the world, where real life was going on. The world I felt completely cut off from. But I was not Harriet, isolated and lonely. I had family and friends who would leave no stone unturned. My heart lurched as I thought of the pain they would be suffering, the consuming anxiety.

My personal privacy would be lost. My photograph would be all over the news and the police would be searching through most aspects of my life, trying to find out where I could be, any clues to my abductor and why he had taken me. I knew that, whatever misleading indications he might have left behind, none of them would imagine for a minute that I had run away or killed myself. So they would be hunting for me. Urgently. After the discovery of Harriet's body, they would know that I was in mortal danger. I simply needed to find a way to reach them and I would be safe.

It was a small comfort. I sighed as I pictured Rob and the inspector, working hard on any clues, Naomi urging them on, perhaps John even writing an article about me. I preferred a private life, yet in these circumstances publicity had to be my friend. Even with the changed hairstyle, I hoped that a neighbour might recognise Brown. I still did not know his real name.

At that moment, he entered the room. I felt my insides contract with instinctive revulsion and fear. Knew he had heard the sigh. Even slight noises were audible on his system. I was under constant surveillance. It was a very unpleasant feeling.

"I'm glad you're awake, Tessa, dear. Time to have some food, I think. You must be very hungry."

Remember to keep on the right side of him. Show him your

cooperation. I cleared my throat.

"I am. I'm sorry. I don't know your name."

He smiled encouragingly.

"That's better. Yes, we need to get to know each other properly. My name is Joshua McNaughtie. Of patrilineal Scottish descent, as you'll gather. But I've always lived in England. I feel English. My beloved mother was English, although she kept my inadequate father's name, out of respect for tradition. You may call me Joshua."

I nodded. That was how he had been able to imitate a Scottish accent so convincingly.

"You're right, Joshua. I am very hungry."

"It's nice to hear my name on your tongue. Your accent is very attractive."

I controlled my reaction of repulsion at the compliment.

"Thank you."

"Well, since you're being so polite and so good today, I'll release you, and let you go to the bathroom and get dressed. I'll go down and prepare some food for you. Remember that I can hear every move you make, and I'll inform you, now, that there is a camera on the landing."

"I understand."

So there probably was no camera in the bedroom. Or bathroom, hopefully. If I could trust him.

Even that tiny burst of freedom would help. I kept as still as possible while he undid my bonds, but I looked carefully at what he had used on my ankles to tie me. Not rope or duct tape. Some kind of black bands. Not excessively tight, but unpleasantly abrasive if I struggled and quite impossible to shift.

"There, you're free, my dear. I'm going to trust you to continue your good behaviour. I'll see you downstairs soon. Come to the kitchen. If you need clean underwear, it's in the top drawer."

I did my best not to shudder noticeably at the mention of intimate garments. I was still horrified at the thought that he had put me on the toilet the previous evening. The loss of autonomy was even worse than wetting myself. I had to make a deliberate effort not to think of it, to erase it from my mind. Otherwise the inner cringing would paralyse me.

He did not close the door behind him, but I heard his steps on the stairs and breathed again. Followed my plan and stretched carefully on the bed, then stood and did some slow toe touches. Did not risk anything more, but it felt good to move. My head seemed to cope with it better now. No more flashes or dizziness, just a dull ache.

I checked not only the top drawer but the other three. Only clothes. Nothing useful. No socks, interestingly.

I took a shower. I wanted to wash off all traces of his touch, even though it had not been sexual. He did not have my permission. It was my body. Not his to use as he pleased.

I dressed slowly. Noticed that there was untouched make-up, in fresh packaging, on the dressing table and applied some. It felt a bit like putting on my personal armour. I took a very deep breath, put on the oversized pink mules, which were the only footwear available, and went down to the kitchen.

I hesitated in the doorway. He looked up and smiled broadly.

"You're so very pretty, in those clothes, Tessa. You should always dress like that. And your subtle make-up really enhances your appearance. So feminine."

Despite his comment, the make-up gave me more confidence in myself, for some reason.

"I prefer trousers."

He shook his head.

"Oh, no, they don't suit you at all. You have a lovely figure and a dress shows that off so much better. You'll always wear dresses and skirts here with me."

Always. A dreadful word to hear. He seemed to notice that his words had pained me.

"Come and eat, my dear. You must be starving. So unfortunate that you were sick last time. I've made you scrambled eggs on toast. Easy to digest. I'm afraid I'm not a very creative cook. You'll be able to prepare us both some more interesting meals once you've settled in properly, when I can trust you with cooking equipment."

I put the ominous words to one side and focused on the food. It was bland and the texture was oddly gloopy, but it tasted unpolluted. I hoped the drugs were in the drink. He had made coffee. I only took a few sips. I was very thirsty, dehydrated probably, but resisted the temptation to gulp it down.

"You need to drink more, Tessa," he prompted. "Don't you like my coffee?"

How could I respond without offending him?

"It's fine. I just feel like a glass of water, that's all."

"You should have asked. Of course, you may have water."

He turned away and filled a glass. I did not think he had a chance to drug it, but how could I be sure? I could not risk dehydration, however. I took several long swallows. It tasted like normal Milton Keynes water, rather chlorinated but pleasant enough when cold.

Once again, he asked me to wash up and put things away. The knife I had used to cut the toast with was extremely blunt with a rounded end, no doubt deliberately. No use at all as a weapon, even if I had been confident that I could use it quickly enough. The fact that the thought crossed my mind, however, indicated that I was beginning to recover some strength.

He took me into the sitting room once I had finished. Allowed me to sit in an armchair this time, opposite him. I could feel his gaze on me constantly. It was subtly intimidating. Like being under surveillance. I looked around the room, as if curious about it. Anything to avoid catching his eye.

No clocks or calendars. The same muted lighting. The twee knick-knacks everywhere. No newspapers or magazines. There was a television in the corner, however. He saw me notice it.

"I'm afraid I don't have an aerial or any other connection, Tessa. I only use it for watching my favourite DVDs. Perhaps we can watch one together, later. A nice romantic love story. It'll put you in the right mood."

For what? I tried hard to look enthusiastic.

"Well, Tessa, what are we going to do now? We could play a board game or do a jigsaw together. Would you like that?"

I shook my head. Forgot that it was not a genuine question.

"I hate board games and puzzles are boring. Can't we go out for a walk?"

A quiver of anger shot across his smooth, bland features.

"That's not very polite of you, when I'm suggesting doing something I enjoy. I will give you a straight choice. Puzzle or board game. That's it."

His need for control was absolute. Even a mild expression of dissent was too much for him.

"I would prefer to do a jigsaw, please, Joshua."

His expression lightened.

"That's much better. Good girl. Let's go and choose one together."

He took my arm, as we left the living room. I controlled the shudder at the touch of his flesh. There was another door in the hall, which I had not previously been through, and it led to a dining room. Old-fashioned and formal, with dark, imitation

Georgian furniture. More kitsch bric-a-brac in a display cupboard. Mainly china cats. And row upon row of board games and puzzles.

"Landscape or animals, which would you like better?"

"I don't really care," I responded, without thinking.

His arm tightened. I had made him angry again. I had to be perfectly attuned to his desires. He turned me to face him.

"Your manners are not good, Tessa. I will need to train you. Rewards for good behaviour. And punishment for rudeness. Come with me."

He pulled me roughly out of the room, through an outside door into the garage, switching on the glaring white strip light. It was cold and dank. Repellent. I could not avoid recalling my last experience there and also that Harriet's body had been stored there. Was it my imagination, or was there a lingering smell of decomposition? I could not see the dreadful bag, but knew it would be in there, somewhere.

The space was double width and there was plenty of room for storage, as well as his small silver van. There seemed to be an automatic garage door. Presumably a remote control, too, but my eyes were drawn to a lit button at the side of it. I ensured that I did not turn my head in that direction. I did not want him to know what I had spotted. He dragged me to a dark corner at the back.

"Do you see this dog kennel, here? It's quite small and rather old and dirty, I'm afraid. Look inside."

He actually pushed me forward. Forced my head down and inside with a strong hand on my neck. His voice was cold and implacable.

"On all fours, please, dear. I want you to go inside."

With intense reluctance, I dropped to hands and knees. Crawled forwards slowly and hesitantly.

"Oh, come on, Tessa. You can do better than that."

He pushed my backside with his foot.

"Keep your nice dress clean, won't you? Use bare knees so that you don't stain it."

I obeyed, seething inside with ineffective hatred.

"Can you see the new metal chains with wrist and ankle bindings, attached to the floor? I bought them in advance, especially for you. It's amazing what you can find on the internet. I knew I might need a punishment place and this kennel has seen some similar use in its time. And proved very effective as a training tool."

I began to shake. Fear was twisting my bowels. Who or what had been held here before?

"And the leather strap is to hold the thick cloth gag in place, going right round the back of your head – or should I call it a muzzle? Perhaps I should get another one to act as a dog collar. This is where you will be left to reflect on your misdemeanours, if you misbehave. Excluded from the comforts of my home. Quite literally in the doghouse!"

He laughed, gaily, as if he had made a wonderful joke. I was increasingly sure that he was quite unbalanced.

"Don't you think that's funny, Tessa? I do hope you share my sense of humour."

I did not dare not to force out a short laugh.

"Good, that's good. Spare the rod, spoil the child, that's my motto. My mother always said that and she was, of course, right. Such a wise woman. She raised me so well. We must have a stick available as well as a carrot, you know. But you'll no doubt be glad to know that I'm far too kind and gentle to beat you, as they did in the old days. I just have my own version of the naughty step: the doghouse."

I joined him in laughing, mirthlessly.

"Excellent. You've recognised already how effective it can be. What a powerful deterrent it is. You may come out again, now. And stand up."

The space was so constricted that I had to reverse back out. I sat back on my heels, brushed my hands together to remove the dirt and managed to stand up straight again. My muscles and sore knees had already been protesting at the painful grit on the hard floor and the unaccustomed position.

"Now that you've seen the consequences if you do wrong or lapse into rudeness again, would you like to come back into the warm, wash your hands, and choose a nice puzzle for us to do?"

"Yes, please, Joshua. I would love to do that."

He patted my head in a patronising way. I cringed inside, hating his touch and disgusted by my own craven behaviour. I would avoid the crippling chains if I could, but it was torture to repress my reactions like this.

I chose a beautiful landscape, blue sky and mountains, which made me think yearningly of freedom and fresh air. He set out the pieces on the table. Insisted on sitting by me, guiding me on which pieces to choose, where to put them. Taking the opportunity to touch my hand and shoulder whenever it arose. Testing my reactions. Looking for small signs of resistance. He praised me when I finished the outside border. As if I were a small child, and it was an amazing achievement.

"Time for a nice cup of tea, I think, don't you, Tessa? No, don't worry. I'll fetch it. You carry on with the puzzle. You're doing so well with it. You'll soon be a dab hand at jigsaws. You just need a lot more practice. I won't be long."

The sense of relief when he left the room was overwhelming. It was as if a thick heaviness in the air had cleared and I could suddenly breathe freely. Blindly, I put my head in my hands. How was I ever to escape? His constant presence and obsessive observation were stifling.

"Are you unwell, Tessa?" he asked, on his return, concern in his voice.

"I have a headache, Joshua, and I'm very tired. Looking at the detail in these tiny pieces strained my eyes."

He stroked my shoulder. I managed not to flinch, but it was an effort.

"Poor Tessa. You haven't quite recovered from your head injury yet, have you? Never mind. You'll soon get over it. Let's have a nice cup of tea and a cake."

"May I use the toilet, first, please?"

He smiled.

"Of course. I see you've learnt from your little accident. And thank you for asking so nicely. I hate it when people say 'can' instead of 'may', don't you agree? Do you remember where it was?"

I nodded.

"I think so."

"Off you go, then. Don't be too long."

I escaped into the downstairs toilet, which had been thoroughly cleaned since my last visit. It smelt of bleach. It was slightly less warm in there and the light, which came on automatically, had a greyish tinge. A pleasant change. I tried to open the shutter, but it was locked. Frustration threatened to overwhelm me, but I held it down. Escape would take time, a cool head, planning.

Returning to the dining room, I did not dare to avoid drinking the tea he had made. I ate the cake, too. It was delicious, and I said so, earning myself more praise. I offered to wash up, but he suggested I continue with the puzzle, since I was making such good progress. Quite soon the picture began to blur and my eyelids to droop.

"Time for a rest, Tessa. Come on upstairs."

With support, I made it to the bed and fell face down onto it. I barely noticed him rolling me over and binding me.

CHAPTER SEVENTEEN

Resistance is futile

When I next awoke, he was there in the room, watching me, a faraway smile on his face. I shivered. For a very private person, this constant scrutiny was oppressive. I felt like a lab rat.

"Hello again. I've been waiting for you to return from your sweet dreams. You know, it's lovely to have some quiet feminine company. I think we will enjoy our peaceful life here together, don't you?"

I blinked at him. Too afraid to voice my profound disagreement, yet unwilling to concur, I found refuge in feigning sleepiness. One arm and one leg were free and I was able to rub my eyes.

"I can see you're not quite awake yet. Never mind. I'm afraid I do have to go out to the shop. I won't be long, don't worry. But I will therefore need to tie you more securely and gag you, just in case you become distressed or decide to behave badly. I could, of course, choose to confine you safely in the kennel, but you were so good doing your puzzle that I would prefer to leave you up here in the warm. You deserve the comfort. It's a special reward for you."

He obviously expected me to appreciate his kindness.

"Thank you."

I managed to force the words out and he smiled his approbation.

Surges of emotion shook me, quite literally. Hope, that he was going out. At least I would have a break from his oppressive surveillance. Might it provide an escape opportunity? Trepidation at the thought of the gag. What if I could not breathe properly? Relief. Not the doghouse. Not this time.

He only saw the fear.

"Don't be afraid, Tessa. I really don't want to hurt or upset you. You're going to be my life partner, after all, once I've trained you properly. My other half. Her indoors, as they used to say. So nice and traditional."

He laughed again at his own witticism, if you could call it that. I managed to squeeze out a faint smile.

"I just have to make sure that you're safe and secure, while I'm out of the house. We don't want any nasty accidents, do we? You know you're not very steady on your feet yet."

He stood and looked down at me. Revelling in his power. A rather manic gleam in his eye, this time. I must try not to provoke him. He looked different, dangerous.

"Do you need to use the toilet? I haven't brought you a drink, because I don't want to put too much pressure on your unreliable bladder. We don't want you wetting the bed again, do we? Such a childish and embarrassing thing to do. So, do you have to go now or are you capable of waiting until my return?"

I shook my head.

"I don't need to go now, thank you, Joshua," I mumbled. I was dehydrated if anything. And I could not be sure, in his present mood, that he would not insist on watching me. I could not bear the thought of him observing my private bodily functions.

Smiling, with what appeared to be genuine amusement, he took my other wrist and tied it behind my head. Dragged the other ankle away and bound it, tightly. I felt like a piece of meat. Did not dare to struggle, but could not make myself cooperate either. Turned my head away in despair as he approached with the gag.

Fortunately, he did not seem to be angered by my mute and minor resistance. Perhaps it perversely pleased him in his current mood. Gave him an excuse for cruelty. He turned my head, quite gently but with steely strength. I could not open my mouth for him. Would not. He pressed on the edges of my jaw hard, but I still kept my teeth clenched.

He sighed in a longsuffering way, like an adult with a recalcitrant child, and pinched my nose tightly, so that I could not breathe. As soon as I was forced to open my mouth and gasp for air, he thrust in the scrunched up cloth, making me retch impotently, and covered my mouth tightly with silver duct tape. He smiled in satisfaction down into my wild, terrified eyes.

Now that he had his way, he became affectionate once more. Wiped away the single tear which fell from my left eye. Kissed my forehead.

"I'm so sorry, Tessa. I can see you don't like this and are very frightened. Poor little thing. Such a scared baby. It's quite pathetic, really. You don't have much strength of character or bravery, do you? We'll have to see if we can remedy that. Teach you some resilience."

His contempt hurt. I could feel the blood rushing into my cheeks.

"Never mind, dear. I'll be as quick as I possibly can and hurry to release you. I would have preferred to have gagged you while you were drugged and sleeping, but I was worried that you might choke if you were unconscious. I do care about you, you see."

He smiled down at me, indulgently.

"I can't say it was love at first sight, as with Harriet, although there was an immediate frisson of attraction, I have to admit, at our first encounter. But I feel increasingly close to you, responsible for you, and my deep care is swiftly turning to love, profound protective love. You can be my precious new princess.

You certainly need someone to look after you, take care of you. You're not really strong enough to cope on your own."

He stroked my cheek. Chose to take the strangled sound I made as an affectionate goodbye.

"See you soon, my sweetheart."

He was gone. Trying to breathe evenly, to avoid panic, I closed my eyes. What could I do? I tried, gently, to loosen the bonds on my wrists and ankles, but they only seemed to tighten, and became sore and painful. I tried to rub my cheek against my arm and pull some of the tape off my mouth. It did not move much, if at all. I was trussed up and helpless, like a chicken ready for the oven. Completely powerless.

Despair rose up in me like an oily engulfing wave. I would never escape. They would never find me. Either he would end up killing me and throwing me in the lake, or I would be trapped here, forever, at the beck and call of that foul man. I tried not to cry, knowing it would make my predicament worse, but the tears still fell.

Suddenly, I was dragged from my despondency, when I heard the doorbell ring. The first sound from outside of which I had been fully aware since arriving here. There were times when I had almost forgotten that there was an outside world. Even that one sound made me feel a little less isolated, brought back some of the courage and resilience he thought I did not possess.

There was no one to answer it. It rang again and there was a loud knocking at the door. I tried to make some noise, anything, but the muffled moaning sound was pitifully thin. Tried heaving myself on the bed, to make it hit the wall. Hurt my arms and legs trying, but to no avail. It was impossible.

I knew I had not been heard, and that they had left. *Abandoned me to my fate.* I knew that thought was unjust, but it flashed through my head, nevertheless. Self-pity poured into the vacuum of my mind.

Time passed. So slowly. I had nothing to measure it by. Not even the ticking of a clock. I tried to count my laboured breaths, but it seemed to make the effort of taking in air even more difficult. I almost wished for death. Only just about held on to hope, by the tips of my fingernails.

I prayed. Over and over. Wordlessly poured out my desperate plea. And a sense of calm began to illuminate the darkness of my soul. The place he could not invade. My essence. Someone more powerful was with me and would keep that part of me safe. Whatever happened to my body.

Eventually, he returned. With newly sharpened hearing, I was aware of the hum of the electronic garage door opening and closing. I hated the thought of him being back, but desperately needed the removal of the additional bonds.

I heard him leap up the steps, as if he could not wait to see me. Like an eager lover.

"I'm back! See? I wasn't too long, after all. Let me take that unpleasant gag out."

I winced with pain as he tore off the tape, then retched uncontrollably as he removed the revoltingly moist cloth. The edges of my mouth were sore and raw and my tongue was so desiccated that I could barely move it.

"You've been struggling against it, trying to rub it off, haven't you? Silly girl. You've hurt your poor mouth. I'll put some cream on it."

"Please, let me do it myself," I whispered. He would have to release a hand if he did.

He shook his head.

"No, no, I must take care of you. I'm responsible for you, my poor child."

He bounded out, fetched some antiseptic cream and stroked it over the sore patches. It stung bitterly, like salt in a wound. I hated the feel of his fingers on my face. I would have loved to bite them. Resisted the almost overwhelming temptation.

"I can see you've been crying, too. Your nose is running. Not very attractive. Here, blow into this tissue."

"Please, let me do it myself," I whispered again, swallowing hard to try to moisten my mouth.

"Just do as you're told, Tessa, my child. I'll clean you up. Don't you worry."

I gave a feeble blow into the tissue and felt him wiping away the snot. I was infantilised, helpless, spread out and pinned down, like a butterfly in a lepidopterist's collection. The tears began again, followed by sobs.

"This is ridiculous. Stop crying. Nothing bad has happened. You're quite safe. I'm taking care of you. Stop at once."

I tried. I could not. Hysteria was building. I wanted to shout at him that I hated him. I must not let it out. He might kill me.

He slapped my cheek, hard. There was genuine anger in the blow. It sent my head crashing back against the iron bars at the head of the bed. He spoke with clipped authority and a hint of contempt. Demanding my attention. My submission.

"I'm sorry, Tessa, but you needed that. You were becoming hysterical. I did not realise that you were so fragile, that you lost control so very easily. It's a little pathetic, for a woman of your age. I'll need to take better care of you in future. And I must teach you better self-discipline. Now, I'll untie one hand, if you can manage to calm yourself."

I told myself to breathe evenly, slowly. Closed my eyes so that I could not see his hated face. Went back into my internal safe space. He did not touch me, and I regained control.

"Good. That's better. There, I've released your left hand. Open your eyes and look at me."

I obeyed, with deep reluctance.

"You mustn't allow yourself to get into that state again. It's not acceptable for a grown woman. You've damaged your pretty face and ruined this pillowcase. And all for nothing. I can see you've been struggling as well. Look at your wrist. You did that to yourself. It's self-harm. No more of that, please, or I will have to chastise you. You know what that means."

I did. And nodded, fearfully. There was satisfaction in his acknowledgement of my compliance.

"You must learn to manage your emotions better. You're an adult, not a toddler. My mother would have been so cross with you for that kind of over-emotional reaction. She would never have tolerated it. I have to say that I expected better of you. Are you going to be good now? You do understand what the alternative is, don't you?"

I nodded, biting my sore lips to hold back the flood of tears which threatened to overwhelm me again.

"I'm going to put the shopping away and then come back to fetch you. You will remain calm and be ready for me when I return. I'm very disappointed in you."

My lips quivered. I actually felt ashamed of myself, sorry that I had let him down. Had I really become so dependent on him, lost all sense of self, of reality? I had to hold onto something.

When he had gone, images of Rob and Naomi floated into my head. I knew they were thinking of me. I felt suddenly surrounded with their love and care. John and my other friends, too. They would be thinking of and praying for me, I knew that. Hold onto that, said a voice in my head. Eyes closed, I pictured each loved face. They were real. This was a terrible dream.

Renewed strength enabled me to respond as he wished when Joshua returned. He was pleased and rewarded me with a trip downstairs, food, and drink.

I did my best to mollify him. To please him. But I was very cautious with the drink. Consciousness was more important than hydration at that moment. This time, I offered eagerly to wash up. I made an effort to please him, to do everything precisely as he liked, to speak politely, to ask permission. Pretended to be interested in his lengthy anecdote about his mother. Forced myself to join in his laughter at his own bad jokes. Ignored the voice in my head raging at my craven collaboration with the enemy.

He told me it was time to get ready for bed. I feigned sleepiness, staggering a little as if my balance had gone, to satisfy him that his drug had worked. Went upstairs with him, was permitted to use the bathroom and put on the repellent nightdress in privacy, and meekly allowed him to tie me for the night. One wrist and one ankle, opposite sides this time. I closed my eyes and consciously breathed more deeply, allowing my head to roll to one side and my mouth to open slightly. He seemed convinced and left me alone.

I was, by this time, pretty sure that he did not have a camera as well as a microphone in the bedroom, so I felt able to exercise and stretch my free arm and leg, once he had gone downstairs. The movement seemed to send more oxygen to my brain and I began to think more clearly. Where or when would I try to escape? How could I exploit an opportunity?

Weaving plans, unrealistic but encouraging, even exciting, I drifted into a light doze, quite unlike the heavy drugged sleep to which I was, by now, accustomed.

CHAPTER EIGHTEEN

Opportunity

I was brought abruptly to the surface by another ring at the doorbell. Of course, Joshua would not be aware that there had been an earlier caller. He would assume that I was in a drug-induced stupor. There was insistent banging on the door, too. They had come back. Whoever they were. Possibly a delivery?

Would he answer? Even if he didn't, could I draw their attention? I was not gagged. I could try to shout. If it did not work, I would face the most severe punishment yet. He might even kill me, but it was my first, and possibly my only opportunity. Someone was by the front door. They just might hear me. I steeled myself to yell, as loudly as I could.

"Help! Help! Please help me!"

The volume increased with each word and I repeated it, screaming with every ounce of power in my lungs. It was liberating to shout. I banged my free hand painfully against the hard bars on the bedhead. It did not make much noise, but it might help. There was another ring and knock at the door. Had I been heard? I continued to make as much noise as possible, desperately hoping for rescue.

I heard him start up the stairs to silence me and screamed even more loudly, giving voice to all the depths of my desperation. The door was hammered upon, this time, with a shout from outside, and I could hear him going back downstairs. Unlocking and opening up. I yelled with all my might and struggled to try to free my other arm, kicking out against the bedframe with my unbound leg.

I heard him speak, loudly, projecting his voice, trying to cover my cries.

"What is it? Why are you banging on my door like that?"

"We're from the police, sir. We came round earlier to speak to you and you seemed to be out. What is all that screaming and noise? May we come in and take a look?"

I yelled again, using every ounce of breath. Praying that they would hear me.

"Please, please help me. He's got me shut up in the bedroom."

His dismissive voice.

"I'm sorry officers. Can I see some ID? I'm afraid the noise is just my DVD player upstairs. I'm watching rather an exciting film. That's why I was slow to answer the door. I'd love to get back to it, if I may."

My most piercing scream yet clearly made them all jump.

"Very realistic, I must say, sir. Quite scary. Might disturb the neighbours. Could you please turn the volume down? I think everyone would appreciate that."

"Of course, of course. No problem. I'll go and do it now."

"We'll just wait here, if you don't mind, sir. We've got a few questions for everyone in the street."

"Please don't go! I need your help!"

But despair was creeping into my heart. *Why won't they come in?* I could hear his hated feet thudding up the stairs.

He opened the door, uncontrolled rage convulsing his plain features. He dared not shout at me. He would be heard by the officers down below. But I cowered in the face of his incandescent fury. I managed to utter one last scream, rather a pitiful moan. He charged across the room and grabbed my throat. I tried to beat his hands away with my left arm, but it was not strong enough. Blackness began to rise up and take me, my desperate struggles were weakening.

"Everything OK, sir?"

A questioning voice floated up the stairs.

"No problem, officer. I'll be right down."

He released me suddenly so that my head fell back and hit the iron bedframe.

"I'll deal with you later," he hissed in my ear, his mouth so close that I was sprayed with venomous spittle.

I could no longer shout. Only croak feebly. I knew that I was in very deep trouble. The voices from downstairs droned on politely, asking Joshua if he'd seen or knew Mr Brown, if he recognised the artist's impression, if he had seen Harriet Beckinsale or Tessa Fordham, showing him our pictures.

I knew how convincing he could be. How sweetly reasonable he would seem. He would hide his rage until he was alone again. I had only made things worse. A dark bubble of bitter resentment burgeoned in my chest. How could they ignore my appeals for help?

After a short while, they left. Abandoned me to his mercy. Disappointment made me angry. I had made a lot of noise. Surely they should investigate further, given they were searching for a missing woman. How could they simply go and leave me here?

He did not come up immediately. Waiting to be sure that they had gone, perhaps. My stomach was in spasm, the terror at what was to come finding a physical expression. My hands were clenched and teeth gritted.

After a while, I heard him on the stairs. Not running, this time.

Slow, steady, measured. More frightening, somehow. I closed my eyes and breathed a prayer for strength.

Pulling myself up as far as I could by my bound arm, I steeled myself for his fury. I would not face it lying down.

He entered calmly, as if nothing dramatic had happened. Smiling in self-satisfaction.

"There you are, Tessa. You are a silly little girl, aren't you? What a racket you made! And it still didn't help you. Never mind, my poor sweet. You're quite safe with me. You always will be."

He shook his head sorrowfully.

"Now I have to punish you. Poor dear. I'm afraid it's going to be rather unpleasant. I'm sorry, but you knew the consequences of bad behaviour. I have to enforce it, otherwise you'll never learn good manners. Always follow through with your sanctions, even when they beg for mercy. Mother insisted on that. Don't be afraid, though. I won't hurt you. Not personally. Not by my hand. But you have to spend some painful hours alone in the doghouse. A little suffering to atone for what you tried to do. Hardly a punishment at all, really."

He laughed lightly. Smiled down at me, smirking at my obvious terror. But the intense killing rage of the strangler had completely evaporated, as if it had never been. I was not certain that he even remembered doing it.

"It's such a shame I can't trust you. We could have had a lovely time later on. I was going to let you watch a film with me after our meal. A nice relaxing romcom. Never mind. I'll watch it on my own while you're in the doghouse. We can share that pleasure another time. When you've really learnt your lesson and know how to respect me."

His eyes glinted.

"I'm becoming quite passionate about you, you know. There's something very endearing about your vain attempts to resist me, to resist your physical attraction to me. I really can't overcome my desire for you."

He was certain that I was paralysed with fear. Completely under his spell. He patted my head, leant down, and untied my ankle first. I pumped my foot up and down to restore the blood flow. I had to be ready for any opportunity. It might be the only chance I ever got.

To my utter disgust, he bent his head and kissed me, full on the lips. Forcefully. With what he would no doubt call passion, hand hard behind my neck, pushing my head powerfully back so that I could not keep my mouth closed, as hard as I tried. I closed my eyes in horror. Wanted to kick at him, hit him, punish him. But there was no point until I was free of all my bonds. I held my breath and suffered it, demeaning as it was.

Eventually it stopped.

"Oh, Tessa, that was such a pleasure. Thank you for treating me to that. For not fighting me. I'm sorry I didn't ask first. I was just overcome by your beauty, your wild spirit."

I narrowed my eyes in revulsion.

"You don't believe me, but it's true. You drive me mad with desire. But I still won't force you. I'm not like that."

"Huh," I croaked. He was not above taking advantage of my vulnerability. His manner became schoolmasterly.

"But I'm still so disappointed in you. Trying to attract their attention like that. Such a foolish, futile, and vain attempt. I was prepared to trust you, in fact, before you let me down so badly. Ready to calm your fears, to soothe your hysterical anxiety. Still, after your punishment time you should be more malleable. More friendly. Grateful to me for releasing you from your merited detention. Happy to respond fully to my demonstrations of affection."

Some hope. Never. The simmering anger in me was giving me strength. I kept the rebellion well hidden inside, though. He shook his head, sadly.

"Oh, well, let's get it over with. You'll have to go through it, in order to be purified. Cleansed. Pay your debt. Do your penance. Like mother said. I'll untie you and we'll go downstairs."

In the flimsy nightdress?

"May I get dressed?" I whispered. It was all I could manage.

"No, I'm sorry, it would ruin your nice clothes to wear them in the doghouse. I can't have that. Such a waste. Just the nightdress. I'll let you put the pretty slippers on, though."

I was already trembling at the thought of imprisonment in that cold dark kennel with little or no clothing on, nothing to protect me. He could feel it as he began to take me downstairs, grasping both wrists tightly, pulling me after him, so that I stumbled and fell against him. Coupled with my lack of physical resistance to his unwanted embrace, it appeared to him to indicate that I was completely cowed. I could see satisfaction on his strangely transparent features.

As we arrived downstairs, I forced myself to plead with him. To confirm his sense of victory.

"Please, Joshua, don't do this." My weak voice, damaged by the throttling, broke and he took it for emotion.

"Now, dear, you know that you brought it on yourself. It's entirely your fault. You made your choice. I never wanted to chastise you. I'm a kind and generous man. I want to spend happy times with you. Share my best life with you. But you have to learn that I mean what I say. If I impose a sanction, I will go through with it. I won't be disobeyed in my own house."

He spoke patronisingly, as if he were explaining something eminently reasonable to a person lacking in basic intelligence. And he could see the consuming fire of utter terror in my eyes. He pinched my chin.

"It won't be so bad. Just a few difficult hours in the doghouse, and then you can come back into the warm. I'll make you a special meal. It would be kinder, I suppose, to drug you first, but

I need you to experience it fully, so that you never risk it again. A truly powerful deterrent. No pain, no gain, as they say."

He laughed again. Enjoying the power he had over me.

I had to try to take advantage of this moment, of not being bound or gagged. It might be my very last chance of freedom. I nerved myself to try to fight him. Knowing full well that he might kill me, with the knife concealed in his pocket. And that, if I failed, my punishment would be terrible.

"Can I have a glass of water?" I asked, pitifully, hanging my head.

"Of course, dear. Although you may regret it later when you wet yourself uncontrollably again, in the cold. Not very nice. It's impossible to hold on when your body has to let go. Still, you can't say I don't give you what you want. Even though you forgot to say 'may'."

"Thank you," I murmured. Trying to sound genuinely grateful.

I hoped he might leave me while he went to fetch the water, but he gripped my arm tightly, and insisted I go with him. There was no opportunity for flight.

He handed me the cold water.

"Drink up quickly, Tessa. I want to get this over with. I'm so looking forward to having you back, ready to cooperate fully. We can have such a pleasant time together."

My arms shaking, I held the glass with both hands, as if struggling weakly to get a grip, then transferred it to my right. That was much stronger. It was now or never.

I threw the water straight into his face and hit him on the nose with the glass, then followed it up with a powerful punch from my left hand into his eye. At least, I intended it to be powerful. I was disappointed in my lack of strength. It was a pathetic blow.

It had an immediate effect, however. His hands flew to his face. I kicked sharply at his shins with my softly slippered feet and turned as swiftly as I could. I knew that he had relocked the front door, so I ran, as fast as I could, into the garage. His place of punishment. My only chance.

He followed me, slowly, confidently. No doubt there. No concern. He had not even bothered to pull out the knife. So sure of his own superior strength.

"You silly child, Tessa. I wanted you in here, anyway. You know that. Now you'll be confined to the doghouse for twice as long. More unnecessary pain and suffering. You've brought it on yourself. I never wanted this. It's entirely your own responsibility."

Wildly, I looked around for any kind of tool I could use as a weapon. Picked up a thin rake, the best thing I could find to keep him at bay with. He laughed, a genuine note of amusement in his voice. Wiped a trickle of blood from the bridge of his nose. The glass had not even hurt him.

"That'll never work. You know it. Hopeless. Give up now, and take your medicine, like a good girl. It'll be easier in the long run."

I knew where I was going, however. I made it to the garage door and pressed the illuminated button. Kept my hand on it.

His voice sharpened.

"Now, come away from there. Right now. You know I'll catch you straight away if you get out. And I'll have to punish you severely. You won't be able to run far in those pathetic slippers."

The door was rising. As soon as it reached hip height, I ducked under it and scraped myself out, still carrying the useless rake. He was close behind but taller than me and had to wait for the door to rise. I turned and ran.

CHAPTER NINETEEN

Escape

He was right. The slippers were worse than useless. I let them slip off and ran barefoot, hardly noticing the pain from the grazing grit. I was out. I was completely unable to shout for help, but surely there must be someone around. Or a door I could knock on. I was still waving the rake, which suddenly felt very heavy in my weakened arms.

It was dark. I had no idea what time it was. And very cold; the vapour in my breath was condensing in front of my face. I glanced behind, and he was out and after me. So fast. Too powerful. Despair lent me a final burst of energy and I stumbled forwards. Anywhere away from him.

Suddenly, I found myself wrapped up by strong arms, from behind. I tried my best to struggle against them. They forced me to drop the rake, my only protection. I moaned in distress, completely confused by a new attack from a different direction.

"Don't, Tessa. You're safe now."

Such a blessedly familiar voice in my ear. My Rob.

I would have fallen without his support, the relief was so intense. My legs simply gave way. Car and van headlights suddenly illuminated the scene like a stage. There was a cacophony of noise all around me. Loud, aggressive, masculine shouting, people surrounding Joshua, yelling in his face, pushing him to the ground, handcuffing him behind his back, despite his insistent protests that he had done nothing wrong. His sweetly reasonable tone.

"That poor girl has gone crazy. I've been caring for her, but she's lost all sense of reality and tried to run away. She's mentally disturbed, you know. No one in their right mind would be running around in the cold in a nightdress. I'm afraid she lives in a fantasy world."

I felt rather than heard the growl of hostility in Rob's chest. I turned in towards him, away from that man, away from the nightmare I had fled. Another officer handed him a hypothermia blanket and he held me steady, while he wrapped it tightly around me, but then hugged me to him safely again. He did not want to let me go. And I did not want to be released. The shivering was intense, head to toe, more like shock than chill, although the air felt bitterly cold to my mainly unclothed limbs and bare feet.

Turning away from the scene on the driveway, Rob looked down at my face, searchingly. Kissed my forehead, so gently. Then he picked me up, wrapped in my foil blanket, as if I weighed no more than a duvet, and carried me, very carefully, over to the police van, which was parked up a hundred yards away. He cleared his throat, tried to speak, but couldn't. I saw tears streaking down his face, shining in the streetlights.

He set me down on the front seat, with such care, as if I were made of eggshell porcelain, keeping me fully covered, no longer exposed. Protected from curious eyes as well as the cold. I was profoundly grateful. I tried to smile, but it crumpled immediately, and I could not keep a dry, hoarse sob inside. He held me tight again and I could feel that he, too, was crying.

"For so long we thought you must be dead, Tessa. But I – we couldn't give up on you. We had to keep on looking. Keep hoping. I can't believe I've got you back."

He sobbed it out into my hair. I understood. It must have been a traumatic time for all of them. I pulled out a hand to stroke his heaving back. It made me feel stronger to give him comfort.

Someone appeared behind him, shadowy in front of the blazing lights. After a moment, I realised it was the inspector. She touched Rob's shoulder, gently. He raised his ravaged face and tried to put on an official, impersonal mask. She shook her head.

"No, it's absolutely fine, sergeant. We're all feeling pretty emotional, just now, and we don't have the personal connection you have. I just wanted to let you know that the ambulance is here. We're sending her to hospital to be checked over. Just to make sure she's all right after such a lengthy ordeal. And to check on and document any injuries. You may go with her, if you like. In fact, I would prefer you to, if Miss Fordham agrees."

I nodded silently. Rob thanked her, lifted me gently again and walked swiftly over to the waiting ambulance. Insisted on carrying me inside. Sat beside me and held my hand tightly. Soon I was whisked away and driven, at high speed, to the hospital. The urgency was not really necessary, but it felt like an express journey out of hell and into safety. With every second I was further away from that house, that man, that hideous captivity.

As ever, Accident and Emergency was busy and rather chaotic, but I was seen surprisingly quickly, in a curtained bay. I appreciated the discretion, the concern for my privacy. My lost dignity. Things I would once have taken for granted.

Rob was ushered out, almost immediately, and a businesslike female doctor came to check me over. She was a tall, imposing, and composed figure. A little intimidating, in my pathetically feeble state. I was gently assisted to remove the repellent pink nightdress, and it was bagged and put outside as evidence. I wanted to cover myself up, hide away, but understood that this was necessary. She began to examine me carefully.

The bruising on my neck was becoming increasingly obvious and my throat was too swollen to allow me to speak clearly. The doctor asked her accompanying nurse to make notes about any and all injuries and asked permission to take photographs for evidence.

I nodded. Anything to put that man away.

I was asked if I had been sexually assaulted.

"No," I whispered. "He forced me to kiss him earlier, that's all."

She took swabs from my mouth and noted some bruising on the lips, which felt acutely sensitive to the touch.

"Where did the raw patches all around your mouth come from?"

I tried to explain, in my very weak voice, about the gag. The tape. For one moment, her composure slipped, and she looked revolted.

"And the deep abrasions on wrists and ankles?"

"He – he used to tie me to the bed." Just saying it brought back the intense sensation of vulnerability, stretched out, legs apart, gagged. I began to shake again. She took photographs to document the injuries and then covered me with several blankets.

"I'm sorry that we're doing this and not looking after you. It's important that we don't lose any evidence. I hope you understand."

I nodded, my teeth chattering.

"Have you been fed? Given enough to drink?"

I tried, in my weak and feeble voice, to explain about the drugs he had used, and the very occasional times I had been given food.

"I'll take some blood. There will be drug residue. You won't be totally free of its effects for a while, I'm afraid, from what you say. It also means that I'm reluctant to prescribe you any strong pain medication, especially any opiates. I don't know what you've been given and it would be too risky."

After she drew blood, I was given liquid paracetamol. She put in a fluid drip, because I was so dehydrated that she had struggled to find a vein.

I realised that I had forgotten to mention the head injury. Managed to explain.

"Did you actually lose consciousness?"

"Oh, yes. I was completely out. I don't know how long for. And fainted again when he carried me upstairs."

"Did you vomit at all?"

I explained about being sick in the bag because of the terrible smell. And again, when I realised what had caused it.

"I think your head injury may have had something to do with that. May I check the back of your head?"

She held me up and examined the wound carefully, causing me some discomfort, asked the nurse to take a photo, and then laid me back down with great care.

"There's a contusion here, half healed, but quite deep. It looks as if he struck you with an object which had a jagged or sharp edge. There's some infection in the wound. You'll need antibiotics. I don't think there's a skull fracture, but I will order an X-ray to make sure. We need to check for any further damage to the brain as well, which may mean a scan."

I nodded. I knew that I had not been thinking clearly, but could not be sure whether it was the drugs or the head wound which had caused it. The idea of brain damage terrified me.

"I'd like to admit you for at least one night. You're in shock, that's why you're shaking so much, and we need to keep you under observation. Your blood pressure is very low and there are some concerning variations in your pulse rate. Probably due to the remnants of the drugs in your system. Nothing serious, I'm sure."

She saw my fear and tried to comfort me.

"I'm afraid we won't be able to move you up to the ward for

several hours, but we'll make sure you're taken care of here. And that you have some privacy. I – I imagine that might be what you need more than anything."

Her voice deepened a little in the last sentence. I nodded, feeling the tears come at her tacit understanding.

"Thank you," I whispered.

"Do you want to be alone now, or may the police sergeant come back in? He seems to be very anxious about you."

I smiled.

"He can come in. He's my friend. I can trust him. I don't want to be on my own. It's too frightening, just now."

It was difficult to make myself understood, but she nodded and seemed to comprehend what I was trying to say. She took the notes from the nurse and gave her some brief instructions on how to make me more comfortable, before taking her leave.

The first thing the nurse brought over was a hospital gown. Not smart, but something to cover my nakedness. I was profoundly grateful. She urged me to lie down, and wrapped me in plenty of blankets. Asked me to take regular sips of water.

"I'll see if I can get you some soup, or at least a sweet hot drink. Your sergeant friend can sit with you, while I go. You won't be alone. Don't try to talk. It'll just irritate the throat even more."

She called Rob in. His beloved face, each feature so well-known to me, looked terrible, as if he had not slept for days. As if he had been through hell. He sat beside me and held my hand, his own trembling slightly. He raised it to his lips.

"I'm so glad you're safe. They told me not to make you talk, so I won't. I don't think you're up to listening either. We'll just sit together. I've told them to let Naomi in as soon as she gets here."

I nodded. Closed my eyes. Tried to grasp the fact that I was safe. Attempted to relax tight muscles, stop the shaking. Without much success. The paracetamol did begin to soothe my throat, however.

Obediently, I sipped the water. Drank the sweet tea the nurse brought. Breathed deeply. The antiseptic smell of the hospital was, for once, comforting. So different. Clean and fresh. Somehow bright.

Naomi burst in like a firework, full of nervous energy, and overflowing with relief.

"Tessa! You're here. I'm so glad. I – I thought I might never see you again."

Rob tried to calm her.

"Not now, Naomi. She's not up to it. Just give her a hug."

She swallowed down the words which were trying to flood out of her, nodded and gave me a tender and gentle hug. Held my other hand. And began to weep, silently, tears pouring down her cheeks and onto my hand, as she bowed her head over it in her distress. She never cried. Not even when she had a miscarriage. Not when she left her husband. Not even at our parents' funeral. Never.

I wanted to comfort her and squeezed her hand. It was all I could manage. I closed my eyes, with difficulty, and let go. The shivering gradually eased, with both hands clasped safely, and I fell asleep, warmth transferring slowly up my arms. Since our parents died, in a car accident four years previously, the people I loved most in the world were here with me. I was no longer on my own. No one could take me.

I woke to the feeling of Rob shaking me gently.

"You were having a very bad dream," he whispered. "Making terrible noises. I thought I'd better wake you."

"Thank you." I looked down. Naomi was fast asleep, her head on my hand.

"She's been brilliant, but she's exhausted."

He sounded affectionate, which surprised me. They had never

been close.

Shortly afterwards, they came to move me up to the ward. Or rather a side room. With its own toilet. I was so grateful for that small token of privacy and humanity. Rob and Naomi insisted on remaining with me all night. I did not fight them. I was too glad of their presence, which enabled me to sink into a much needed sleep.

CHAPTER TWENTY

Found, safe and well

For the whole of the following day, I remained wrapped in my hospital cocoon, focused on recuperation, rest, and recovery. Everyone was kind, attentive. I wanted to go home, but the blood test showed strong traces of opiates and, surprisingly to me, other powerful drugs, apparently used to make me more compliant. My blood pressure was still fluctuating. I could not talk properly, yet. If anything, my neck and throat were more swollen and painful than before.

Naomi was able to spend most of the day with me, taking over some of the tasks from my nurses. They allowed her the space to help me. Professional courtesy. It was good to be cared for by a loved one, after suffering Joshua's invasive ministrations. The ward sister came and spoke to her. Gave her instructions, which she obeyed to the letter. She insisted that I must not try to talk, despite the burning curiosity in her eyes.

"You'll have to go over it all for the police, tomorrow I think, and I'll try to be there then. I don't want you to have to relive the trauma more than once. Rest now, and give yourself a chance to recover."

So I did. I switched off the painful repeats flickering tormentingly through my brain, as far as I could. My dreams were horrible, but Naomi said that was partly the drugs, and would wear off over time. Hopefully. I let things happen around me, allowed myself to be wholly passive, while I tried to recover my own personality, my own sense of vitality and purpose.

The following morning, the medical consensus was that I was well enough to go home, as long as I had someone there to take care of me, until the drugs fully dissipated. There could be difficult withdrawal symptoms to deal with. Not to mention the emotional consequences of incarceration.

At this point, Rob returned, looking much more his normal self. Sleep really does knit up the ravelled sleeve of care. There was some brightness back in his eye and the dark, sunken patches underneath had already faded a little.

He smiled tentatively at me.

"Hello, Tessa. How are you feeling?"

"Much better, thank you," I whispered. I was trying not to do any more damage to the throat, knowing that I had a lot of talking in front of me.

"That's great," he said, in an artificially hearty tone. I knew he was hiding something.

"Come on, Rob. Out with it. What's wrong?"

He smiled ruefully.

"You always did know when I wasn't being straight with you. I'm afraid you have a bit of an ordeal to come, when you leave the hospital. The press and paparazzi are camped outside here, waiting for you to appear. They all want photos and a comment if possible."

I had not expected that. I was found, safe and well, as far as they were concerned. Why would they need photographs? I did not want my weak and damaged state publicly documented. But Rob had an explanation.

"If you can make some kind of comment, we'll do our best to try to ensure that they leave you alone for a while. Naomi can read it out for you, I can hear that your voice isn't up to it. They just want something for their front pages. It's a good news story for once. You can understand it. There's been so much concern for you. Everyone's delighted that you're alive."

I nodded, humbled. How often had I wished that good news received as much publicity as bad? It was not being done to make life harder for me. Just an experience to live through.

I asked Naomi to tidy me up, make me look as normal as possible, cover the injuries up with make-up. She had brought a sponge bag for me alongside my own clothes to wear. The bruises on my neck stood out, black and purple, and there was a dark red mark on my cheek where he had slapped me so hard. The other wounds, thank goodness, were invisible.

Rob and Naomi pushed me, in a heavy hospital wheelchair, to the main entrance. He was right. There was an enormous crowd of reporters, mostly male and very voluble, awaiting my appearance. My body was shaken for a moment by a desperate urge to hide away. My hands went to my face of their own volition. But I knew I had to face this. After several deep breaths, I lowered my hands, raised my chin and painted on a smile.

I looked up at Rob, whispering to him: "The hospital must be desperate for me to leave. My presence seems to be disrupting their whole operation."

He nodded, squeezing my hand.

I blinked at the flashguns popping and tried to look cool and in control. Unphased. Not how I felt, at all. Rob spoke first. I was impressed with his calm and official manner, and the control he maintained over his voice.

"We are delighted that Tessa Fordham has been found, alive and well. Impressively, she managed not only to alert us to her presence, but to escape her captor before we were ready to storm the building. Fortunately, we were already outside the house, and were able to protect her from his vengeful attacks."

There were murmurs and a few claps in the waiting crowd.

Unperturbed, he carried on.

"As you know, the man called Joshua NcNaughtie, also known as Brown, and Johnson, is in custody, and under arrest on charges of kidnapping and false imprisonment, to begin with. We believe that he was also responsible for the murder of Harriet Beckinsale. We are indebted to everyone who assisted with our inquiries, and particularly to Tessa, here, who contributed so much to our investigation from the start, and has brought the case to a satisfactory resolution, by her own brave actions. We'll obviously be taking a detailed statement from her, as soon as she is well enough. I won't take questions right now, but we will be making a further statement at the police station at five o'clock this evening. Thank you."

There was a buzz of reaction to his speech. I knew I was flushed and bright-eyed. I had not expected such public praise. Then people started to call for me to speak. Naomi took over.

"I'm Tessa's sister, and I'm speaking on her behalf, because her throat was severely damaged by her attacker, during her captivity, just before she escaped. She would like to thank everyone who worked so hard to find her, especially the local police, and all those who prayed for her safe return. She is very moved by everyone's good wishes and support. She would like to ask for some privacy now, so that she can recover from the mental and physical injuries inflicted."

I tried to smile calmly, but knew my mouth was trembling a little and that my eyes were full of tears. Naomi had added a few words at the end which I had not written, but it was what I would have wanted to say.

Many more photos were taken. Suddenly a few people began to clap and, all at once, there was a full round of applause. It was overwhelming. I raised my hand and mouthed the words 'thank you'.

Then came blessed relief, as a police car pulled up, and I was carefully loaded in. Uniformed officers kept the press at bay.

I was breathing hard. That had been emotional and, for someone so totally unused to the spotlight, quite demanding, if less embarrassing than I had expected. It had been nice to spot smiles on the faces of the reporters, once I recovered from the shock of seeing so many of them. Especially the local television newsreader. I recognised her face, and it was obvious that she was intensely pleased with the way it had turned out.

Naomi grasped my hand.

"Well done, sis. That was tough and you held it together brilliantly."

"You spoke very well. So did Rob. I was proud of you both."

Whispered praise, but no less heartfelt for that.

"You'll hardly recognise the house, Tessa. It's full of cards and flowers from well-wishers. You have no idea how many people were thinking of you and praying for your safety. I believe there are flowers in Simpson car park, as well as candles. For Harriet, as well as for you. And in the church nearby. They kept it open so that people could go in and pray for you. There's been a constant stream of people, apparently." Naomi's emotion was evident in the fast flow of words.

"That's lovely. And I'm so glad that Harriet is being properly remembered and mourned now."

The police driver had taken several detours to ensure that no one followed us, and our address had not been made public, so my return home was only watched by neighbours, who had come out of their houses to wave and clap. The tears fell again at the kindness of strangers and acquaintances.

"I won't come in, for now, Tessa," said Rob, a little to my disappointment. I had wanted to thank him properly and give him a hug. He smiled reassuringly.

"I'll be back with the inspector after lunch. Will one o'clock be suitable? We know you need a rest first. Take the time to settle in at home."

Naomi took charge and agreed arrangements. I had shot my bolt for now and definitely needed a break before the ordeal of the interview, which loomed large in my near future.

CHAPTER TWENTY-ONE

Debrief

I could not yet face the stairs, so I slept soundly on the sofa for several hours. Exhaustion conquered anxiety, and there were still sedatives and other medications in my system. He had evidently used quite a cocktail of drugs, some of which were slow-acting and longer-lasting. I wondered how he had got hold of them. As he had said, it was surprising what you could find on the internet, if you knew where to look.

After a strong coffee and managing to stomach a sustaining lunch, I felt ready to face them. Naomi insisted that she would be present throughout, and would make them give me a break if I needed one. I did not really want her to hear all the embarrassing details of my weakness and subjugation, but I supposed that she would find out in the end. I could not hide it. It would be easier to confess it just once.

The room was redolent with the peppery and aromatic scents of lilies and freesias. Naomi had not been joking when she spoke of flowers and cards. They were perched everywhere, many still in their wrappings, since she had run out of vases. Piles of cards and letters littered all the surfaces and some of the most attractive ones decorated the mantelpiece.

The inspector and Rob, with a stolid female uniformed officer, who sat silently in the background, tried their best to make it easy for me, to make it seem informal and unpressured. I knew, however, how important my evidence would be in convicting Harriet's killer and could not hide my tension. I was also afraid of what their reactions would be to my story of weakness and cowardice.

To ensure nothing was missed, they used two separate voice recorders, and the additional officer made hand-written notes, since my voice was so unclear and fragile. The inspector began with a reassurance.

"We understand that you've been through a terrible ordeal, Miss Fordham. Tessa, if I may now call you that. And that you may not always find it easy to describe what happened or to keep it in chronological order. Don't worry about being precise. We can tidy things up later. For now, we need as full an account of what happened to you as you can manage, and, in particular, anything which can help us in the investigation into Harriet's murder."

I nodded gratefully. I knew that my mind was not at its sharpest. According to the doctors, there was no obvious brain damage, but the fog still floated around my skull, preventing me from clearly organising my thoughts. I would need all the support I could have. I tried to speak as clearly as possible, given the state of my throat.

"There is some physical evidence of Harriet's murder at the house. Shall I tell you, now, where to look for it?"

The inspector and Rob exchanged significant glances. She was keen to agree.

"Yes, please, Tessa. If you could begin with that, it would be enormously helpful. Then I can immediately call forensics and guide them to the key areas. As you can imagine, searching a whole large house, van, and garden is a time-consuming and often frustrating business, especially when you don't know exactly what you're looking for."

I drew in a deep breath and tried to speak as distinctly as possible.

"First of all, there is the bag in which her body was moved. It's a large green bag, like a Christmas tree storage bag, in the garage somewhere. It – It's full of my vomit, I'm afraid, but – I was sick because of the smell. The hideous stench of a dead and decomposing body. He told me later that he had moved her in it, when he dumped her in the river, by Simpson."

Naomi gripped my shoulder from behind and I could hear her gulping.

"Did he transport you in it, too, then?" asked the inspector, gently.

I nodded, nausea rising in me again. Breathing deeply, I swallowed it down with more water. A dark memory I might never be free of.

"Yes. All bent up and held tightly with bungees. It'll have my DNA in it, as well as hers. I'm so sorry I was sick in it. I couldn't help it."

"Don't worry at all. It's enormously helpful to know what's there. We already have a DNA sample from you, so we'll be able to distinguish them easily. There won't be many traces in the van, if you were both enclosed in a bag, then."

"Possibly none at all. But he apparently kept her body on the bed they had slept in for some time, too. Used air conditioning to keep it relatively cool. I – I don't know, and definitely don't want to know, if it was the same bed he kept me on. He mentioned a plastic sheet. Anyway, there are bound to be some traces to find, I think. And on whichever pillow he smothered her with."

"Right. I'm going to stop you there, and go and ring the team at the house. It's incredibly useful information. Thank you, Tessa. We'll start again in five minutes."

The inspector bustled out, well satisfied.

Rob looked emotional.

"If that's just for starters, this is going to be pretty tough to hear, Tess." He reached forward and touched my hand. I was almost undone by his kindness. I took a deep breath and focused on what I needed to tell him, personally.

"I wanted to thank you, properly, Rob, for the other night when you caught me, when I ran at you from that hideous house. You were so kind, so thoughtful. Protected me. Kept me covered, hid me away. It was so important at that moment. You made things so much better. Can I please have a hug?"

"Of course," he said, in a rather stifled voice.

We both stood for a moment and hugged, tightly, until Inspector Chilwell came back in. Naomi moved from where she had been standing, behind me, and sat next to me on the sofa, holding my hand. As much for her own comfort as for mine, I think. Her face was already stained with tears and I could feel her trembling.

The recordings were set up again and the interrogation began. Not hostile, but probing. There was nowhere to hide the things I was ashamed of. My guilty secrets. I knew I had to allow it to pour out. Drain the festering wounds.

We started with my abduction. The easy deception, my foolishness, and then the blow to the head. Waking up in that dreadful bag, constricted, crushed. The terrible smell and suffocating vomit. I could not look at them. I knew I had reddened.

"What is it, Tessa? Why are you so embarrassed?"

"I know I should have been much more wary, more careful, not have allowed myself to be abducted. After all, I knew there was a killer out there. Ralph had threatened me that very day, told me he would be waiting for me around some corner. So I should have expected something. Joshua told me I made it very easy for him. That I was pathetically predictable, far too easy to trick."

"Not at all," Rob jumped in. "You were brave enough not to allow your anxiety to prevent you from doing your job properly. You care about people and were trying to help. He simply turned your good qualities against you."

He was trying to make me feel better. It did not help much. Shame rose up again.

"But the main thing is, after being sick in the bag, I was so very scared. Terrified. Shaking with fear. I – I thought it was Ralph at the time. I thought that he was going to drown me in the bag, dump me into the water somewhere. I was so petrified. Absolutely paralysed by fear. So cowardly. He said I had no courage, and I'm afraid he was right."

Naomi's arm came around my shoulders and gave them a convulsive squeeze. I could hear her sniffing. The inspector spoke up.

"You have nothing to be ashamed of. Anyone would have been frozen with fear. It was justified. You knew what had happened to Harriet. Of course you were scared. I would have been. I'm positive that the sergeant would have been, too."

She showed unsuspected depths of empathy. I was grateful for her understanding. She went further.

"And you were right to be frightened. I'm afraid my assessment of the situation, all along, was that he would have killed you and dumped the body. I couldn't see a reason why he would keep you alive."

She looked down at her hands.

"I didn't share my fears with the sergeant, here, although I know he probably thought the same, in his darker moments. He was so keen to keep us all positive. To hold onto hope."

Rob flushed and tried to bring the conversation back on track.

"OK, Tess, can you go on? He had you in the bag in the van. What happened next?"

I explained how disorientated I had been by his almost kindly manner. How confused I had felt. That I had cooperated. Collaborated, as it seemed to me now. Cowardice in the face of the enemy. The inspector responded.

"That was definitely the right thing to do. Any hint of opposition, and he could have killed you, straight away. Almost certainly would have. There was every incentive for him to put an end to such a risky situation."

It made me feel a little less bad. When I had to admit to wetting the bed while unconscious, however, I could not bear to raise my eyes from the floor, see the pity, and probably contempt in their faces. They might even laugh at me. So childish, as Joshua had said.

"Tessa. Look at me." Rob was insistent. His voice was slightly shaky. "That's not your fault. You were drugged. Unconscious. It's entirely his responsibility."

He leant forward and took my hands. I peeped up at him and saw nothing but care and compassion.

I gulped and went on. Explained the whole strange surreal experience, the rewards and threats of punishment. The vulnerability. The terrible feeling of being tied up and unable to move, especially when gagged as well. The deep humiliation of him putting me on the toilet, undressing me. My face was burning with shame. I should have been able to stop him. So hopelessly helpless.

Naomi sobbed, suddenly, and put her head into my shoulder.

"I don't know how you coped, how you survived it. How absolutely dreadful."

The inspector concurred.

"Such controlling behaviour: the threats, the binding, the constant observation, the drugs, the total vulnerability. Terrible. Horribly oppressive."

I told them everything he had said about Harriet's murder. How it had caused me to vomit again, when I realised that I had been transported in the same bag, that the smell was her bodily fluids fermenting and decomposing.

The desperation of being trapped, spreadeagled on that bed while he went out. The suffocating gag. The hysteria and the hard slap. His anger about my poor behaviour and manners. My apologetic, submissive response. All a little confused and mixed up, but I had to get it all out. All my shame and guilt.

Rob intervened, suddenly.

"You do understand that you have absolutely nothing to be ashamed about, don't you, Tessa? It was all his fault, his manipulative behaviour. You did exactly the right things. I'm amazed you kept so much inner strength, despite the drugs and the conditioning."

Rob sounded desperate for me to believe it. I tried hard to accept what he said. Still felt the acid bitterness of guilt burning away inside me.

The unexpected hope when the police came to the door and he was forced to answer. Deciding to risk the punishment, even if he chose to kill me for it. The desperate screaming and yelling. Hoping for rescue. How he throttled me to shut me up. The moment of absolute blackness when I thought my opportunity had gone. Thought I had been abandoned, left at his mercy.

The inspector had blanched and her mouth was tense.

"I just want to assure you, Tessa, that my officers were not deceived. They heard you and knew it needed investigation. But they did not know your situation within the house and felt they could not risk your safety."

Her voice deepened and she frowned.

"I'm so sorry that they made the mistake of asking for the volume to be turned down on his supposed DVD. They were pretending to accept his story, in order to get him to drop his guard. But they realised they had put you in immediate danger while he was upstairs and tried to call him back. It was too late. The officer who said it was distraught, afterwards. Terrified that he might have caused your death. Right then, while they were standing uselessly outside."

She shook her head, as if to take away the guilt.

"They called it in straight away, as soon as they left the house, and we came down, ready to rescue you, as soon as we had decided on the safest way to do it. That's procedure in a hostage situation."

"So I could have waited for you?"

"I suppose you might have done. But your escape was much more effective. And who knows what he might have done to you in the meantime? He might even have killed you. He seems to have been frighteningly unpredictable."

I confessed that I had not fought him when he forced me to kiss him. Dripped out the poisonous truth about my craven obedience. Could not look at Rob as I said it. Shame squeezed out reluctant tears.

"Don't, Tessa. Please. There was nothing else you could have done."

His voice showed no anger, only compassion. Heaping coals of fire on my guilty head with his generosity.

I explained about his planned punishment. Insisting on me not getting dressed, just that hideous nylon nightdress and the pathetic fluffy slippers. How he would have chained me in the kennel and used a foul cloth and leather belt as a muzzle, and then left me there in the cold for hours. How he laughed, giving me water, saying that I might urinate uncontrollably again. All so that I would never resist him again. To completely cow me, have me totally in his power.

Rob's face was red with anger.

"That evil man! I'm so glad you got away, yourself, before that happened. If I'd come in and found you imprisoned like that – I don't know if I could have controlled my rage."

The inspector agreed.

"It would have been even worse than what actually happened. As it was, it was very difficult for my officers not to overreact or use excessive force. You were incredibly brave, Tessa. You should be proud of yourself."

I did not feel proud. The humiliating vulnerability, the forced cooperation, the bodily shame had left their mark, and I could not shake off the feeling that I was the one who had done wrong. Naomi saw it in my eyes, and stroked my forehead, smiling into my shrinking face.

"I'm so proud of you, Tess. You were amazing. I understand that you don't feel that, right now, but hopefully it will gradually sink in. It was a dreadful experience, but it's over now."

I nodded jerkily. All done with. Maybe.

"What happened out here, in the real world, when you knew I had gone?"

"Of course, you have no idea, do you?"

I shook my head.

"I don't even know how long I've been away. There were no clocks, I was completely disorientated. No natural light, so I never knew what time of day it was. No idea how long I slept when he drugged me. No news or television. No idea of what was happening."

Rob drew in a deep breath.

"That's a form of torture, too, you know – keeping you unaware of time passing. The sort of thing cults use, I believe. You – you were missing for well over a week. It's been – difficult, to keep hoping that you were still alive, especially after what happened to Harriet."

No wonder I had lost so much strength. I had been given so little food for that stretch of time. I must have been unconscious or sleeping for days.

I could see the imprint of that prolonged anxiety on his and Naomi's faces. Traumatic for them both.

"I'm so sorry you had to go through all that worry."

"Will you stop apologising for things that aren't your fault? Please." Naomi sounded quite cross. But she put her arms tightly around me and hugged me.

The inspector began to tell me what had happened. Sally had tried to contact me within half an hour of my arrival at the car park, with no success. She immediately called the police. No delays. She said she sensed that something was wrong, especially as it was a phone booking from a man, but would have done it anyway. Procedure. A wise precaution, even if it was not entirely successful this time.

They had found my car straight away. Key still in the ignition and phone on the front seat. Only my prints. No sign of me, or of violence. No indications in the car. They searched the whole area, carefully, but discovered no clues. Dragged the river, hoping to find nothing, but fearing they might.

"I was frantic with worry," said Naomi. Her voice still carried the panic.

"Me, too," agreed Rob. "I knew if we didn't find you quickly, the chances were that we might never find you. It was horrible. After a while, we knew, we had to accept that you were probably dead. Like Harriet. It was torture."

The inspector nodded.

"I felt responsible, guilty that I had allowed you such a close involvement, and that you had been so publicly identified with the case."

I shook my head.

"Not your fault. I wanted to be involved, you know that. Wanted desperately to find Harriet. Joshua – that man – did say that I had caused him a lot of problems, though. Been troublesome. I should be pleased about that, I guess, even if it did put me in danger."

"Mm. I think you were lucky, even if it doesn't feel like that right now. If he hadn't liked you enough to want to hold onto you, to make you his long-term captive, he would have just killed you, then and there, or on the following day. I'm afraid it's what I expected, as I said earlier. Feared. Tried not to talk about, especially to Naomi and the sergeant. So it was very important that you did cooperate with him to an extent. Without that, you almost certainly wouldn't be here today."

I dropped my head into my hands, down on my lap. The air was knocked out of me. I should not feel ashamed. If I had not made him like me, I would be dead and he would have got away with murder. Two murders.

"What is it, Tessa? What's wrong?" Rob's voice was anxious.

"You just convinced me – that maybe I did the right thing, not fighting him all the way. Cooperating. Finally made me believe it. I don't need to feel ashamed of myself. Don't need to feel like a collaborator. It – it's overwhelming."

I could hear Naomi crying, as she rubbed my back.

"Of course you did the right thing. Without your courage, your ability to keep your rebellion inside and put up with his controlling behaviour and awful treatment of you, we wouldn't have you back here with us, now. We wouldn't have caught that man. And he might well have gone on to kidnap and kill again."

Sounding rather gruff, the inspector continued, talking about all the steps they had taken to find me. The public appeals, televised reconstruction, speaking to the press, searching, searching, searching. Continuing to publicise the artist's impression. Going house to house throughout Caldecotte and

Walton Park.

They had ruled out Harriet's ex-husband, Ralph, quite quickly. He had not been in custody when I was taken, but was arrested within a few hours. Given the imminent danger and his previous threats to me, they were granted permission to search his house, take his DNA. There was a room filled with a concerning collection of secretly taken photos of Harriet, and items belonging to her, which he seemed to have stolen or collected, almost like a sick shrine. But no sign that she had ever been there in person and, more importantly, no indication that he had taken me.

They had spoken to Sylvia, the lady who was so kind in the shopping centre. She had given clear evidence and agreed to go to court if necessary. And had expressed great concern for my safety. Organised a group to distribute leaflets and photos around the city to try to find me. I decided that I would get in touch with her to thank her. Her behaviour represented the better side of human nature.

"We have charged Ralph with threatening behaviour," said Inspector Chilwell, with satisfaction. "He's been released on bail and seems somewhat chastened. He'll either go to court or possibly be given a caution, if he accepts what he has done. Let's hope he changes his ways."

"Mm," responded Rob, sceptically. "Stalkers don't often stop."

The information that I had uncovered at the library had made Brown an even more likely suspect, and they had focused most of their efforts on finding him. An assistant had contacted them from a local supermarket, sure they had recognised him, but he had paid in cash, and not used a loyalty card, so even though they had a poor quality image on CCTV, it led nowhere. It was less useful than the picture they already had.

John had written multiple articles about me and my disappearance, helping to keep the case in the national consciousness. He had used the fact that he had met me more than once to make the appeals more personal.

"He's not bad, for a journalist," Rob admitted. "He really did his best to help. Kept in close touch and did as we asked."

I smiled. I had felt the same about him. I must try to give him an exclusive. It was only fair. Naomi joined in.

"It felt as if the whole city was in an uproar, looking for you. As I said, flowers and messages were laid where you disappeared, tributes to Harriet, too. Groups of people did impromptu searches in their areas, churches prayed for your deliverance. There was even a vigil at the Cornerstone church. We really came together. That's why everyone was so overjoyed when you were found. Alive."

I was humbled. So many people caring what became of me. And it was even worse for those who knew me.

"I'll never forget how it felt, that awful moment when we knew you were missing." Rob's voice had dropped an octave and he bit his lip. "I felt so helpless. And guilty. I'd told you that I would keep you safe. The anger and frustration were almost physically painful. I had to go to the gym later, and hit a punch bag for an hour or so. Just so that I could do my job properly."

Naomi nodded. "I remember that time, too. Such terribly powerful emotions. And it went on for so long. I tried to hang on to hope. I know how strong you are. Right down in your core. What you've already survived. But, in the end, even I started to believe you might be dead. That we would find your body, like Harriet's. Even though there was something, deep inside, that insisted you were still alive and we must keep looking."

Rob laughed.

"You hid it well, that sense of despair. You were the one who kept geeing us up, telling us it would end well."

Naomi flushed slightly. "I know. I had to. Someone had to."

Rob smiled affectionately at her and continued.

"All your drivers had pictures of you in their cabs, as well as the artist's impression. Soon, all the cab companies followed suit, and then the buses. Your face was all over the city centre. In shops, cafés. There are even posters on some of the footbridges near the centre. Some local businesses clubbed together to offer a big reward."

"Oh dear, there goes my anonymity, I suppose. I'll be recognised now."

Rob laughed.

"Afraid so. Your face is better known than anyone else's in MK, right now. But in a good way. Everyone will be pleased to see you."

"I might have to hide away until people have forgotten."

Naomi snorted.

"No way! You'll just have to put up with it, sis. They'll want to see you. You're famous now. Even I'm famous, just for being related to you. I made several appeals on the local news. It wasn't easy, keeping control of my emotions, but I had to try."

We all laughed. Suddenly, a tide of happiness swelled through me, but it manifested itself in tears not laughter. They seemed to sense that I had absorbed all I could. The inspector shook my hand and said how happy she was about the positive resolution to the case. She was confident that the murder charge would stick, too. She went out, taking the constable with her.

Rob hugged me and I felt him trembling. I understood that it had been hard on him, this case. Knowing the victim. Aware that I was probably dead. I lifted my face to him and allowed him to kiss me gently on the cheek. I could not speak, but it was not necessary. We understood each other. He squeezed my hand tightly and then followed his colleagues.

Naomi put me to bed and brought me food and drink upstairs. I was anxious about sleeping alone up there. It was very different from that dreadful place, but still brought back memories.

"Look, Tess, I'm in the next room. We won't shut the door. Ever, if you prefer. I'm not going back to work until you're fully recovered. You're not alone. That man is behind bars. You are safe. And free."

I nodded, swallowing hard and trying to smile.

"I know. I'm home."

The best thing of all was being able to switch off the lamp. Blessed relief to sleep in darkness and wake up to the light.

CHAPTER TWENTY-TWO

Press

In the morning, Naomi had a message from John, asking if he could come and see me. I was still without my phone, although Rob had promised to return it soon, since it was not needed for evidence. I took a moment to consider, but then agreed. He had obviously done his best for me while I was kidnapped.

The word still struck fear into me. I had never felt so much like a victim before. Not even as a teenager, when the bullies had it in for me. Then I had my own space to retreat to, my family to support me.

This time, it was different. The mixed guilt feelings, and the sense of inadequacy and shame, after being so much at the mercy of someone else, still took me by surprise and overwhelmed me, at times. I did not know how to deal with them. My head recognised that they were illogical. My body could not resist the waves of them.

While I waited, I opened my laptop. Was rather horrified to see clickbait about my case. I decided to check on the BBC website and see what the papers had included.

Every national paper had a photo of me on the front page.

Looking weak and exhausted, dark shadows around my eyes, not well hidden by the make-up Naomi had applied. You could even see the bruising around my neck, as well as the dark patch on the cheek and the damaged mouth. I was so embarrassed. It was humiliating to have it out there, for all to see.

Tears started in my eyes. Not all the papers had me in the headlines, thank goodness, but some of those were deeply embarrassing. *'Brave Tessa thanks supporters.'* *'Tessa escapes captor before rescue.'* *'Tessa's ordeal over at last.'* John's was a little different. *'Safe and well, but not unscathed.'* A little less personal, and I was grateful for that small mercy.

None of them had pictures of Joshua, but some carried the artist's impression which I had helped to construct. I shuddered at the sight of it. His bland features, which could express such anger and dominance at times, still had the power to horrify, and jumped into my mind at unexpected moments. Especially when I closed my eyes. I was not yet wholly free of him. It was as if he was continuing to observe me, watching my every move.

Trembling and tearful was not how I would have wanted John to see me first, but Naomi brought him in at that point. He looked painfully anxious, the frowning eyebrows locked together over the bridge of his nose, eyes shadowed. He was carrying a large box of chocolates.

"Tessa! Lovely to see you," he said, quietly. "I know you have masses of flowers, but hoped that chocolate would be acceptable."

"Always," I said, with a sniff and a smile. I tried to tidy myself up with a tissue.

"What's up, sis? Why are you upset?" Naomi came over and sat down beside me, putting her arm around me in comfort.

"Oh, I don't know. It's silly, I suppose. I'm so embarrassed by the horrible pictures of me in the paper, embarrassed by being on all the front pages, humiliated that everyone can see what happened to me. And I can't get that detestable man out of my head. It's as if he's still controlling me."

My weakened voice broke, as I betrayed what I felt deep down.

Naomi hugged me tight.

"Oh, Tessa, my darling, don't. You've been through a terrible time. It's going to take a while before you feel normal again. I think you're likely to need some counselling. Anyone would. Being trapped, at someone's mercy, like that – the consequences won't go away immediately. But don't be embarrassed about the photos in the paper. You look fine. It's only you who sees them as horrible, isn't it, John?"

He cleared his throat.

"Absolutely. Everyone is simply delighted that you're free, and amazed at your courage, your iron will, daring to get away, managing to escape. We admire you. Please, don't feel embarrassed or humiliated."

There was deep emotion in his voice.

I tried to nod.

"Thank you both. I know you're probably right. It's just that it doesn't feel like that to me. I'm still so full of mixed feelings, horror and shame at what I allowed to happen. Definitely not someone to admire. But I'll try not to let it upset me so much."

Naomi released me and stood up, briskly.

"Right, I'm going to make you both a hot drink, and you're going to eat some biscuits, Tessa, while you talk. You need to build up your strength. You've hardly eaten over the last ten days. John won't overtire you, I'm sure."

There was a warning gleam in her eye as she looked at him.

"Of course not, Naomi. Black coffee for me, please."

He sat down opposite me, placing the luxurious box of chocolates on the coffee table. I thanked him.

"But you didn't need to bring me anything, John. I'm very grateful to you. Rob and Naomi said you worked hard to keep my case in the news during the search."

"I did my best. It was deeply frustrating not to be able to do more. I – I was terribly worried about you. It's quite different when you know the person who is missing, kidnapped. The anxiety was terrible. I couldn't get you out of my head."

"I'm so sorry."

He looked surprised.

"What on earth for? It's not your fault. It's just the first time I've had a personal connection to this kind of case. I'll be more understanding of the trauma that family and friends go through, in the future, I can tell you."

I smiled. One positive result.

"I would like us to be friends, Tessa. Is that possible?" he asked, hesitantly.

"Definitely. I'd like that too."

We shared a slightly shy smile. Then Naomi came in with the coffee.

"You look a bit better, Tess. Try to relax and eat your biscuits. I'll leave you two together for a while."

I nodded meekly. After all, I was in the habit of obedience now. The thought jagged through my brain like an electric shock. John noticed something in my face.

"What is it, Tessa? What did you suddenly think of?"

I tried to explain.

"He conditioned me to obey him. Like training a dog, I suppose. I'm afraid the habit is ingrained now. Even after such a short time. I don't feel as if I have any autonomy left."

He stood up and came to sit beside me. Took my hand.

"I'm sure it will return. You still had enough autonomy, courage, and determination to risk shouting to the police, and then to take your chance to escape. It's there underneath. Don't worry. You're still you."

I sniffed, grateful for his understanding. I hoped he was correct.

"Right, then, John. What do you want to ask me? I presume you'd like an exclusive."

He laughed, then realised I was serious.

"Honestly? You'd do that? I – I didn't expect it, you know. I came today as a friend and supporter, not a reporter."

"I know. But you helped to save me, worked hard to help the others to find me. You deserve a reward."

Again the phrase triggered an uncomfortable jerk in my stomach. Joshua had said that to me on a number of occasions. I tried to ignore it, but it was an important warning. I refused to conform to his conditioning.

"I'm sorry, John. I shouldn't have said that. It's not a reward. He framed everything as punishment or reward, and I won't – I will not do the same. I refuse to let him do that to me. But I do feel that I owe you, and your editor, something, after all you did for Harriet, and then for me."

He shook his head.

"You don't owe us a thing. Of course, I would be delighted to interview you and write up an article you would be happy with. It might keep the rest of the press off your neck. But you absolutely don't have to do it. And you could be well paid for the same thing, if you went to one of the tabloids. They'd be over the moon to have your personal story."

"Perhaps they would. I wouldn't. I've seen your writing. I can trust you. I know you can make it less unpleasantly revealing and personal. But I think I should make sure that people know what Harriet went through, at least. I owe her that much."

"I see what you mean. Well, if you're sure, we can give it a try."

"I'm sure."

There was a long pause, while I tried to collect my scattered thoughts.

"I think Harriet was a rather special person, and I wish I had known her. After escaping from an abusive and controlling marriage, instead of growing bitter, she still dreamt of something better, a happy future, a fulfilling romance. That's a powerful thing. Hope and positivity. It's so sad that the person she encountered was Joshua McNaughtie. Another manipulative and ultra-possessive man."

John nodded. He was recording me, but also taking a few notes.

"He abused her trust from the beginning," I told him. "She found the idea of a secret romance exciting. And knew she needed to keep it from her unpleasant ex-husband, who was stalking her. But Johua told me that, even at the start of their relationship, he was already planning to keep her at home, for his private pleasure."

"Had he really made that plan, so early in their romance?"

"I'm afraid so. I don't know what made him like this, what twisted him, but he seemed to want some kind of literal stay-at-home wife who would housekeep, look after him, and keep him company. Never leave the home. Be his private possession. He couldn't bear the thought of others even seeing her, once she was his. As if that would defile her."

He shivered. "Horrible."

"I know. He managed to get her to his house, quite willingly, on the day I dropped her off. And at first, it must have seemed romantic and enjoyable to her. But she soon saw through his pretence, to the profoundly controlling behaviour underneath. I think she recognised it so quickly largely because she was sensitised to the signs, by her previous experience. She fought against him, withdrew from him. Even under the influence of his strong medication, she would not fully cooperate. Unfortunately, that's why he killed her. He knew their relationship would never again be as he wanted, so he destroyed her instead. He drugged her and smothered her in her sleep. He said she didn't struggle, and I really hope it's true that she didn't suffer."

I gulped. I clung on to that hope. Poor Harriet. She deserved so much better.

"At least it means all the indignities she suffered were after death. When she was beyond feeling them. That's a comfort, to me."

"That's a very wise way of looking at it, Tessa."

"Not really. One of my elderly passengers helped me to see it that way, when she was missing. It helped."

"How do you feel about talking over what happened to you? I totally understand if you aren't ready to do that."

"No, now I've started, I should be able to tell you some of it. I think. It might help me to process it."

I took a moment. What did I need to say? Something which he would be able to use, but which would not add to my sense of exposure and invaded privacy.

"I felt deeply ashamed of having been so easily tricked, when he caught me. He told me I made it simple for him, but he exploited my desire to care for my passengers, and I'm not going to stop trying to help them. We're going to get CCTV in our cabs, though."

He nodded, remembering the call I had received when he was interviewing me, in the same fateful car park.

"One of the worst things," I went on, "was waking up in that dreadful bag, all trussed up, in the back of the van. I fully expected be dumped in the lake or river, like Harriet. At the time, I thought it was her former husband who had taken me. He'd threatened me earlier that day, in the shopping centre. So I knew he was aggressive and very angry with me personally."

"The others didn't tell me you'd had a frightening confrontation with him that day. I suppose it wasn't relevant, once they knew he wasn't the guilty one."

"I honestly thought I was going to drown in the darkness, all alone. And I found out later that he had used the same bag for moving her body."

It still nauseated me. The stench was still in my brain, if not in my nostrils. He shuddered.

"Ugh. How disgusting."

"I know. The smell made me throw up. I couldn't stop it. Please don't mention that."

"I won't."

"The doctor thinks it's partly because of the head injury. He knocked me out, you know, when he captured me. I don't know, but she could be right. I certainly suffered from a great deal of dizziness and nausea during my time there."

The scans had not shown any brain damage, thankfully, but the hospital had stressed that I was still suffering from concussion and needed to take care. Not to risk any further blows to the head.

"I think he's mentally unfit. His behaviour was very odd. He would switch from appearing to be kindly and considerate to ruthless implacability in an instant. He was very sensitive to any sign, however minuscule, of non-compliance, and always reacted by threatening punishment, immediately."

"What kind of punishment? Can you tell me?"

I saw the doghouse in my mind's eye.

"I can, but you may not want to use it. He - he laughed about it. Called it his version of the naughty step. The doghouse. I was to be chained up in a small dirty kennel in the freezing cold garage, gagged with a foul leather belt. To muzzle me, as he put it. The time he was going to enforce it, when I had alerted the police to my presence, he insisted on me only wearing a tiny nightie."

I shivered again. I could not look at him. The humiliation still stung.

"That's when I managed to escape. I asked for a glass of water. I threw it at him and hit him on the nose with the glass. Anyway, I got away briefly and ran into the garage. He followed me, taunting me. Sure of himself and his ability to catch me. I'd spotted the automatic door previously and managed to get to the switch. Made it through. Just about. He was right behind me. Luckily, Rob and the police were there. If he'd caught me again – I don't know what he would have done. Probably killed me."

John's arm came round me.

"You've been so brave. I'm so glad the police were there for you."

I nodded.

"I couldn't shout for help, because he'd strangled me, to shut me up, when the police were at the door. At that moment, I think he really wanted to kill me. Fortunately they called him back, and he had to stop, but the damage was done. That's why my voice is still so strange."

He squeezed my shoulders.

"You've really been through the mill, poor Tessa. No wonder your head isn't right at the moment. I'm amazed you're as *compos mentis* as you are."

"The very worst thing about it all, and I don't know if you can write this, was the sense of being under his control. Totally. The interminable moments of being tied to that bed. The terror when he stuffed a cloth in my mouth and taped it. I thought I might suffocate, die like that, all alone. And the time he took me to the toilet and then undressed me, because I was so drugged I could not manage on my own."

My voice was a whisper by the last sentence. I could still feel the violation, the humiliation, the powerlessness. It scrunched me up inside, made me want to curl up and hide, in a way I had not been able to when it happened.

I heard emotion in his voice.

"I won't use that, Tessa. It's too personal. I'm so very sorry. He may be insane, as you say, but he was also profoundly cruel in a subtle way. Deliberately so, it seems to me. He knew exactly how to undermine your confidence in yourself and destroy your personal dignity."

"Mm. And I lost all sense of time. No natural light. Those white shutter things that are so fashionable, closed day and night, and soft lamps keeping a steady level of brightness. It was so disorientating. I had no idea how long I was there. I would wake up or regain consciousness and have no idea at all how long I had been out for. I completely lost track of hours and days."

"That's a brainwashing technique, I think. Do you believe it was done on purpose?"

I nodded.

"He never mentioned morning or night, today or tomorrow. There were no clocks, anywhere."

"I think he was trying to dissociate you from everything familiar, everything you could hold onto. Put you totally in his power, make you rely on him for everything, so that he could mould you into what he wanted."

I remembered how thinking of family and friends had tethered me to the real world. Without them, I would truly have been at his mercy.

"Is that enough? Can you write something from that?"

"Definitely. More than enough. I think I know the style you will prefer. I'll get it done this afternoon."

I was tired and he could see it.

"Can I come and visit again tomorrow?"

I was puzzled.

"Won't that be a lot of travelling?"

He shook his head.

"I'm staying at The Caldecotte. Have been ever since you went missing. I had to be here. Wanted to discover some clue, myself, you know. I walked right around the lake every day, hoping I could find you or some indication of your whereabouts."

"You're a good friend. Thank you. I appreciate it."

He picked up his equipment, and the notebook in which he had hardly written. He had truly listened. That was a special gift.

CHAPTER TWENTY-THREE

Background

I was about to say goodbye, when Naomi came in, accompanied by Rob, who smiled approvingly.

"Hello, John. Good to see you. I wanted to thank you again for all your help."

I had not even realised that they knew each other personally.

"No problem, Sergeant."

He looked down at me.

"We got to know each other while you were gone. Helped one another out a bit. We were both desperate to find you before – well, you know. Before the worst happened."

I smiled. It was nice to see the people I cared about becoming friends. Like a supporting network. A web of love.

"Sit down for a bit, John," said Naomi. "Rob's got some news for us, I think."

We all sat back. I felt less exhausted. It was easier not being the focus of attention. I had never liked that.

"Well, I've got Tessa's phone for her. It's in one piece, you'll be glad to know, although you'll probably want to change your PIN.

Just to be on the safe side."

I nodded.

"I'm so glad he never had it. It feels clean of his polluting presence. Thanks, Rob."

Having my phone gave me back more sense of being in control again. Less reliant on others. It was surprisingly comforting.

"What's happened with – with Joshua? Have you been able to charge him with Harriet's murder?"

Rob looked down at his hands for a moment.

"Well, your tips on where to look for forensic evidence were enormously helpful. We've got plenty of physical and DNA traces from the bag, the pillow he used, and the bed. You were right about all of it. We have more than enough to charge him, convict him. And that's without your damning testimony."

That was something. Why did he look shifty, then? His mouth twisted as he spoke.

"We haven't done a formal interview yet, though. He – his behaviour has been so very strange. So contradictory. He's had a couple of meltdowns, total rages about being held in custody. Literally hurling himself hard enough at the door to injure himself. And then, all of a sudden, he smiles, and it's as if nothing has happened. The inspector felt we should get a psychiatrist to see him first. I don't know if he's even fit to plead."

There was silence. I could feel tension in the room. They were worried about how I would react.

"I understand. I – I realised, when I was still under his control, that he was completely unbalanced. It was partly why I was so scared, all the time. He would change at the flick of a switch. Totally unpredictably."

I could not suppress a shudder.

"And he seems to have genuinely loved Harriet, as far as he is capable of love. Yet he talked quite happily about killing her and disposing of her body. So I could never be sure what he would do. Even if I made him like me, he might still murder me, on a whim. And feel no regret or remorse. I knew there was something seriously wrong with him. I – I think he might end up in a secure mental hospital rather than a prison."

"Do you mind about that? Wouldn't you rather see him punished?"

I closed my eyes for a moment.

"No, I don't think so. It'll be a punishment for him, being away from his precious house, anyway. I can't imagine those hospitals are exactly pleasant places, either. And I would much prefer not to have to give evidence in open court about what he did to me. It would be almost like living through it again. I wonder what made him like that."

There was a collective sigh from the others.

"I don't know if I could have been so forgiving, so understanding, Tessa," said Naomi, and John shook his head.

"Me neither."

Rob continued, his expression much less tense.

"We've found out a fair bit about him, now that we know his real name. No criminal record, of course. He's had no direct contact with the law until now. He does have a job, you might be surprised to know."

I was astonished. When did he have the chance to go to work? He had appeared to be spending all his time watching me, keeping me under surveillance.

"There was a whole study set up in one of the larger bedrooms upstairs. Well away from where you were kept. Computers, office equipment, everything he needed. Very fast wi-fi. And, of course, his CCTV system and the audio he was monitoring from the bedroom. He worked remotely, running websites for small companies. Was very good at it, apparently. But he was only rarely available for phone calls or online meetings. And no one saw his real face. He always used an avatar and a disguised background."

"Is that why he drugged me so much, then? Why I never knew what time of day it was? So that he could work without me noticing?"

Rob shrugged.

"Could be part of it, I suppose. I believe he's been working as usual all the time Harriet was missing and then when you were in his house. I spoke to a customer, who was absolutely flabbergasted at the news that he was the one we were looking for. Of course, no one he worked with could identify him from the artist's impression, because they didn't know what he looked like. As it was his own business, he never had to prove his identity for a personnel department."

"Weird."

"Yes. He wasn't especially highly paid, but obviously liked the independence. The control over his own time."

I nodded. He certainly wanted control. Absolute control.

"We think he inherited money, and the house, when his mother died," Rob added.

I had not even stopped to wonder how he could afford such a large place on his own. Or whether he worked. It had not been my place to question him. I was a subordinate. I felt that I should have been more curious. Perhaps even asked questions. The police had found some of the answers.

"We also uncovered some information about his childhood. Social services were briefly involved. His mother was extremely over-protective, after his father left them, and kept him home from school frequently, for very minor reasons. In the end, she chose to home-school him, and that was that, as far as the authorities were concerned. A social worker visited, once, to check up on him, and found him apparently healthy, enjoying life, able to read and write, well-nourished. He said he was happier at home than at school and loved learning. Nothing obvious to worry about, so he was taken off their books. But he must have been extremely isolated. The library seems to have been the only place he was allowed to go to as a child."

I breathed deeply.

"It tallies. He mentioned his mother a number of times. Talking about manners, expectations, behaviour, 'spare the rod and spoil the child'. Punishment. I wonder if she abused him in some way, psychologically at least. Used on him the techniques he tried on me. Perhaps even the kennel."

It somehow made the ordeal less horrific. He was a rather sad case. Not an all-powerful kidnapper, but an unbalanced man, who had been programmed by a possessive mother to behave in an abnormal way. I could feel pity for him, and that gave me back my power, my agency.

"I don't suppose I can use any of this, can I, Sergeant?" asked John, plaintively.

"Call me Rob, John. I'm not at work right now. No, sorry. I only spoke about it, because I know I can trust you not to use it. It'll probably come out when the case comes to court, but for now it's absolutely confidential. I just felt that Tessa had a right to know. Normally victims are kept out of the loop. I couldn't let that happen this time, and the inspector agreed. But it must stay between the four of us."

I smiled at him.

"I'm so grateful to you, Rob. It's actually been a big help to me, for now. I don't feel so powerless. I can begin to understand why it all happened and that's a positive."

"I'm glad. It's not much, but it's better than nothing, I hope. We – we're still so sorry that he was able to hurt you again, when the police were on the doorstep. And that the officers left without trying to see you. At the time, it seemed like the right, the orthodox decision, but now we're regretting it bitterly. He could have killed you, then or straight afterwards. We can't let that happen again. We're reviewing our procedures, and risk assessment process. If you'd died then, it would have been our fault."

I remembered the terror, when he bounded up the stairs to shut me up, and the bitter despair, when I had heard the police leave.

"You're right, it did put me in added danger. He almost murdered me while they were waiting downstairs. It was a close run thing. Afterwards – well, he could have stabbed me then and there. Or finished his strangulation. I – I fully expected him to."

Those moments, hearing him coming slowly back up the stairs, were among the most painful to revisit. The fear had been so visceral.

"When he came back, after the police left, he had undergone one of those weird mood changes, and chose to punish rather than kill. He thought he'd won. Was happy about it. He might have finished me off right then, I suppose. But you weren't to know, and you did what you thought was the right thing at the time."

Rob looked down at his hands.

"I don't know how we would have lived with it, if that had been the case. Especially the officer who sent him up to 'turn the volume down'. He's having nightmares about it, I know. I hope we've learnt our lesson."

"Right, that's enough of that for now," stated Naomi firmly. "Time for Tessa to rest and you two to leave. I can see she's shattered."

I smiled.

"You're right, Naomi. But I'm not going to let you boss me around, from now on. I know you're the oldest, but I have to get my own way sometimes."

"Yes, Tessa," she said, obediently, and we all laughed. Cleansing laughter between equals. No one in control.

CHAPTER TWENTY-FOUR

Memorial

Several weeks later, the four of us embarked on a special pilgrimage to Caldecotte Lake. In memory of Harriet. In the sparkling spring sunshine, with clouds of white blossom frothing on the trees, it was almost impossible to believe that dark and terrifying events had happened here.

The river had regained its normal gentle flow, meandering peaceably between the spiky reedbeds. The intense blue of the sky was mirrored in the calm surface of the lake, now an expanse of surpassing beauty. Just being there was balm to the soul.

Joshua had, as expected, been committed to a secure mental hospital. The diagnosis was complex, and it was unlikely that he would be released for a long time, if ever. I wondered how he would handle the experience of being under control and scrutiny himself. Perhaps he would revert to his childhood coping mechanisms. Compassion and better understanding had enabled me to forgive him, despite the lingering trauma and disturbing dreams. Counselling was helping, but I knew the psychological wounds were deep and would not be quick to heal.

Harriet's family had arranged for a small funeral at the Crematorium. There was no wake, and the service itself felt perfunctory and impersonal. The minister had never known her, of course, and there was no eulogy or tribute from her relatives. I was not surprised that she had not turned to them for support after her divorce. There seemed to be no compassion or forgiveness in them. No care for her as a person.

A number of local people had attended, including several of her colleagues from the library. Imogen was wearing black and shed a few tears, despite the coldness of the surrounding environment. She gave me a big hug while we were waiting for admittance. Others had come in support of me, and a few out of curiosity. A reporter from a local paper, who looked very disappointed at the lack of emotion on display. Sally was there from my firm. She had told me that she still felt illogically responsible for what happened.

Rob and the inspector were there representing the police. The only flowers were from the library staff, my sister and me, and the police. While the service itself was not moving, I found it an intensely sad occasion, emphasising Harriet's isolation and loneliness. I broke down in tears once we were out of the crematorium. I knew I had to give her a better send-off than that.

After discussion with my friends, I decided to have a memorial bench installed by the lake. We chose a spot on the north lake, with an uplifting view of the area. It was an elevated position, from which, in a few months, we would be able to watch the troops of yellow goslings, nibbling contentedly among the daisies, under the watchful eye of the adults, and the velvety grey cygnets risking their first swim. There was the wreck of an old boat nearby, which herons and cormorants used regularly as a perching platform.

I drove. I had decided to park in the Simpson car park, facing up to my lurking fears. I could not let my experience limit my life going forward. As I expected, there was not much free space, because of the inviting weather. It looked very different in the bright daylight. Not at all traumatic. All the bushes had been cut back in preparation for the growing season. His hiding place had gone.

I breathed deeply as I stopped and turned to the others. Relief made me slightly giddy and I could not help grinning at them.

"Here we are. Let's go and pay our respects, shall we?"

The anxiety in their faces lessened somewhat. They had all been concerned that this might be too much for me, that it was too soon. I hoped to prove them wrong. It had been difficult to arrange our shifts so that all four of us were free, and I wanted to share this special moment of tribute with them.

We walked slowly together up the path next to the river. A little egret, pure white, and so delicate, was disturbed, and took flight from the reeds. We stood and watched in silence, until it disappeared. Felt blessed by the sighting.

Up at the top of the hill, we turned left and had our first sight of Harriet's bench, pale new wood gleaming in the sunshine. There was a clean brass plaque. *In memory of Harriet Beckinsale, a courageous woman who fought for her freedom.* It had been difficult to compose. I had wanted to avoid the ubiquitous 'Rest in Peace', although I did wish that for her.

It was solid, and long enough for three of us to sit side by side. John insisted on standing in front and taking a photograph. Not for his paper, just for us. A memory to share. Rob fumbled in his rucksack and pulled out a bottle of non-alcoholic prosecco and four champagne flutes.

"I thought we should drink a toast to Harriet."

I nodded, too emotional to speak, for a moment. He poured out the wine, which was fizzing even more than usual after its jolting journey on his back.

We raised our glasses. I knew that I had to find some suitable words. Unprepared and inarticulate, but heartfelt.

"To Harriet. I wish we could have been friends. I feel a bond to you, even now. I wish that you had found the joy you deserved in this life, and pray that you will be at peace in the next. Our lives will never be the same because of you. You brought us all together in friendship, and for that we thank you."

"To Harriet," they chorused, and we drank a toast to the quiet mystery woman, whose disappearance had made such a mark on us all.

The End

THE MK MURDERS

A series of murder mysteries set in the new city of Milton Keynes.

Tessa, a local taxi-driver, becomes involved in solving major crimes in the area she loves, with her police officer ex-boyfriend.

Rage On The Redways

Coming soon!

Love them or hate them, E-scooters are an increasingly common sight on the cycle path network of Milton Keynes. But when their riders become the targets of increasingly violent attacks, Tessa is drawn into the case by chance, and must use her local knowledge and logical brain to help to solve the crimes.

BOOKS BY THIS AUTHOR

Sam Elsdon Mysteries - Coffin Morning

What could be nicer than a quiet post-Covid coffee morning with friends? You don't expect it to lead to murder and deadly danger for your precious baby. Sam's exciting first case.

Slaybells Ring

Christmas is coming. But the festivities are on hold until Sam can solve another crime and there are so many suspects …

Jubilee Jeopardy

The Platinum Jubilee celebrations. Exciting times. Until a friend disappears and the police don't seem to care. A thrilling Sam Elsdon mystery.

Deputy Dead

Just one day a week at the local primary school. Surely that should be easy for Sam. But the new deputy head has other ideas. With fatal consequences.

Cold Cold Heart

All you need is love, right? So why should it bring only secrets, conflict, and murder? Sam's toughest case yet calls for all her inner strength.

Long Division

A new renewable energy project deepens divisions and leads to conflicting protests, violence and death. Can Sam help solve the crime and restore the peace?